Dark Ages Nosferatu

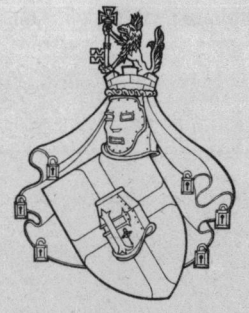

Dark Ages and Vampire Fiction from White Wolf

The Grails Covenant Trilogy
To Sift Through Bitter Ashes by David Niall Wilson
To Speak in Lifeless Tongues by David Niall Wilson
To Dream of Dreamers Lost by David Niall Wilson

Other Dark Ages Fiction
Dark Tyrants by Justin Achilli & Robert Hatch (editors)
The Erciyes Fragments by C. S. Friedman

The Clan Novel Series
Clan Novel: Toreador by Stewart Wieck
Clan Novel: Tzimisce by Eric Griffin
Clan Novel: Gangrel by Gherbod Fleming
Clan Novel: Setite by Kathleen Ryan
Clan Novel: Ventrue by Gherbod Fleming
Clan Novel: Lasombra by Richard E. Dansky
Clan Novel: Assamite by Gherbod Fleming
Clan Novel: Ravnos by Kathleen Ryan
Clan Novel: Malkavian by Stewart Wieck
Clan Novel: Giovanni by Justin Achilli
Clan Novel: Brujah by Gherbod Fleming
Clan Novel: Tremere by Eric Griffin
Clan Novel: Nosferatu by Gherbod Fleming

For all these titles and more, visit **www.white-wolf.com/fiction**

Gherbod Fleming

AD 1204
First of the Dark Ages Clan Novels

Author: Gherbod Fleming
Cover Artist: John Bolton
Cartography: Conan Venus
Series Editor: Philippe Boulle
Copyeditor: Anna Branscome
Graphic Designer: Aaron Voss
Art Director: Richard Thomas

© 2002 White Wolf, Inc. All rights reserved.

No part of this book may be reproduced or transmitted in any form or by any means, electronic or mechanical—including photocopy, recording, Internet posting, electronic bulletin board—or any other information storage and retrieval system, except for the purpose of reviews, without permission from the publisher.

White Wolf is committed to reducing waste in publishing. For this reason, we do not permit our covers to be "stripped" for returns, but instead require that the whole book be returned, allowing us to resell it.

All persons, places, and organizations in this book—except those clearly in the public domain—are fictitious, and any resemblance that may seem to exist to actual persons, places, or organizations living, dead, or defunct is purely coincidental. The mention of or reference to any companies or products in these pages is not a challenge to the trademarks or copyrights concerned. Dark Ages Vampire, Dark Ages Nosferatu and Dark Ages Assamite are trademarks of White Wolf, Inc. All rights reserved.

White Wolf, is a registered trademark.
ISBN 1-58846-817-8
First Edition: July 2002
Printed in Canada

White Wolf Publishing
1554 Litton Drive
Stone Mountain, GA 30083
www.white-wolf.com/fiction

Part One: The Lycus Vale
9
Part Two: Constantinople
13
Part Three: Anatolia
187

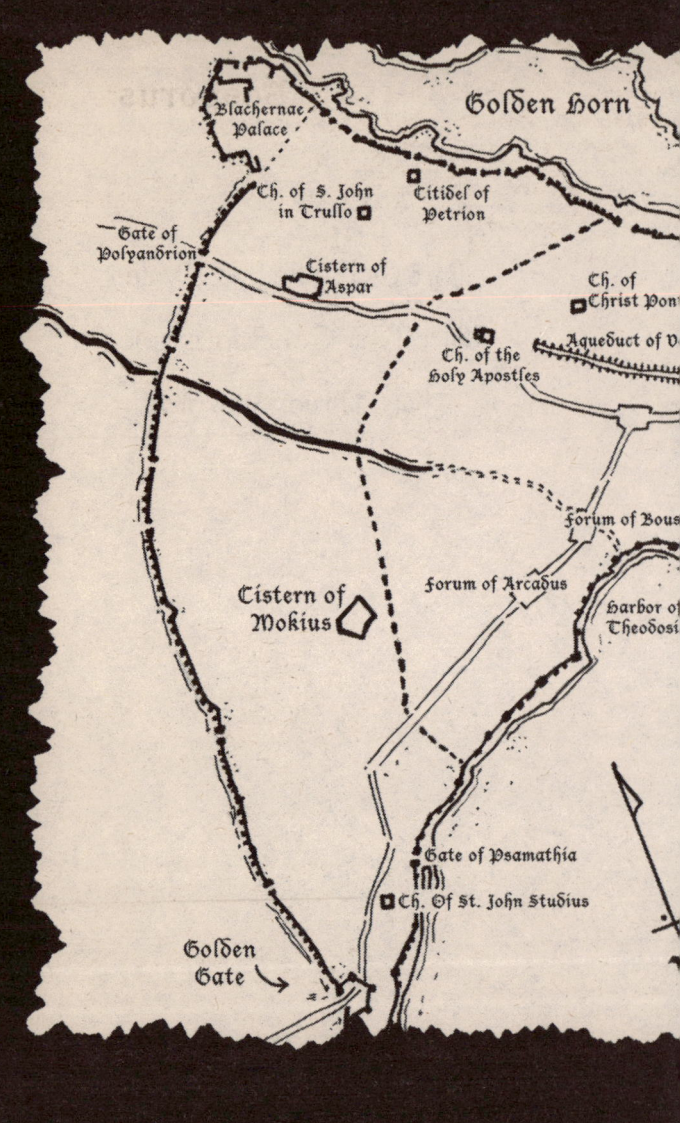

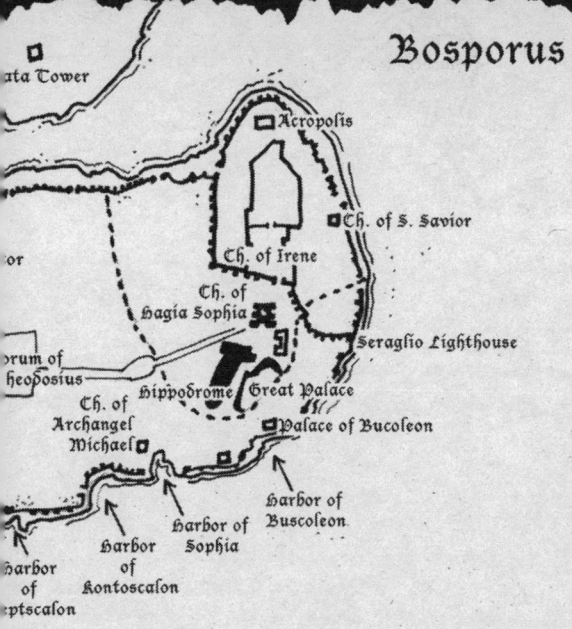

Part One:

The Lycus Vale

Chapter One

The cries of the dying beckoned him like a gilded promise of immortality—a lie, just as the gilded domes of the city, now collapsed, burning, were lies, broken promises, fleeting visions of eternity unattainable. Though he was not yet within the outer walls, smoke and fine ash covered his traveler's robes and the frail, limp body he cradled against his breast. The deep hood which shielded his face from mortal sight protected him as well from the mocking fumes of Constantinople aflame. Yet tears of blood drew their tracks down his face's dead, cracked skin. He could not deny the tears, could not hold them at bay, much as the once impenetrable defenses of the city had been unable to hold back the barbarous Latins: Franks and Venetians, prostituting themselves to Mammon. Inconceivable as it was, the city of Heaven on Earth had fallen, not to heathens, but to Christians.

He was the weeping Madonna, mourning; he was the crucified Lord, struck down by his own.

"It is dying," the boy in his arms said with a voice so weak as barely to be heard over the crackling of flames. "The Dream... it is dying."

"Do not say such things," Malachite whispered, attempting to comfort the boy but feeling no comfort himself. *It is already dead*, he thought, at once recoiling at the sacrilege, pushing it down—deep into the darkness where he kept imprisoned his fears, his weakness, his hunger.

"I feel nothing," said the boy. "I see nothing."

If only I could be so afflicted... Malachite thought.

Battlements, like jagged teeth of an overturned skull, loomed to the fore atop the Walls of Theodosius II. Fires licked heavenward from several of the towers, lending thick billows of smoke and a hellish red haze to the night. In puddles along the flagstone road, moonlight created shimmering pools of supernal illusion, streets paved with silver and gold, but the image was vanquished by Malachite's sandal, leaving only rippling confusion, cracked and decaying stone submerged beneath dank water. Pungent odors clung to this part of the city beyond the walls—tanneries, butchers' pens—but Malachite barely noticed them. They hardly compared to the pent-up stench of enclosed sewers, which circumstance had forced him, on occasion, to traverse. The bodies scattered along the road and ditches had not yet begun to rot, so that odor was not yet added to the mélange. Some of the dead displayed obvious signs of violence; others appeared almost peaceful, as if the victim had simply grown weary and laid down to rest.

The living were not unaccounted for among the destruction. Glassy-eyed mortals staggered from the city, forming a swelling and ebbing tide against which Malachite made his way. They were all the same now: merchants and peasants and nobles, stripped of all but what they could carry, and even that might be seized by the roving bands of crusaders, men who had taken the cross so that they might pillage with God's blessing. Wives and daughters were subject to seizure as well. Except for the oldest and most wrinkled of crones, the fleeing women wore veils or concealing hoods, lest they attract unwanted attention. Most of the Latins were within the city proper, though. The riches of palaces and basilicas held greater allure than the smuggled possessions of refugees. Still the emigrant peoples of

Constantinople cast their curses in low voices, fear and dismay muting hatred, resentment. Then the clatter of horses' hooves spread waves of silence along the length of the throng—and suddenly the road was empty—

Until the armored knights passed by. *Clop-clop clop-clop clop-clop.* Clipped echoes of hooves filled the silence. Towering steel giants atop the mounts, the crusaders gleamed red in the night, swords drawn. Malachite allowed the horses a wide berth, lest their keen senses give him away. The urge was strong to chase down the warriors, to pull them from their mounts and open their veins, these despoilers of his city and home, of the Dream. He held himself back. His purpose was best served by remaining concealed from the eyes of mortals. There was the boy in his arms to consider as well, and beleaguered citizens who would undoubtedly be caught up in open combat. Why should they suffer further, why should more of them die, merely to sate his thirst for vengeance? Gradually the sharp *clop-clop clop-clop* of horses receded into the distance.

—Hesitantly, a few at a time, the people emerged from their hiding places, returned to the road, to their journey west, north, away. They shuffled along like ghosts, eyes downcast, the mortals did. Malachite moved unseen among them. He shared their disbelief, their shock, but unlike them, he could not turn from the walls and the burning city.

What of our sins could be so great that God would punish us so? he wondered. With each step, he scoured his own soul for unworthy deeds left unconfessed, for thoughts tainted by pride or avarice. For centuries he had been diligent in admitting his trespasses so that God might afford him redemption—and the penitent's confessor none other than the Patriarch himself, Michael, namesake of the foremost archangel of

Heaven, first among Cainites, architect, creator of the Dream.

How could they have allowed this to happen? Malachite thought, casting his net wide to discern who was at fault: Michael, Caius, Gesu. And then despair reached out a black hand and took hold of Malachite's heart. Where was Michael now? God was surely in His Heaven, but what of the Patriarch? Could his weariness with the world have grown so great that he slumbered beneath the Church of Hagia Sophia even now? For surely not even the creeping madness in his soul could stay his hand were he to witness the plight of his city. *He does not know*, Malachite decided. *I must find him.*

No crusader would dare stand before the gleaming brilliance of the Patriarch, the light of a thousand suns reflected through the stained hues of living glass. His wrath brought down upon the enemies of Constantinople would prove as overpowering as his benevolence toward the faithful.

I must find Michael. He will set things right.

But Malachite's conviction was less real than the wasted body he held in his arms, and his rage at the invaders was tempered by guilt that he had not been here to face them, to perish in the fires if need be, when there had remained something of worth that his sacrifice might have saved.

"I feel nothing," the boy said. "I see nothing."

"Quiet, then," Malachite scolded gently. "When your strength has returned, you will see." *Or perhaps you will be spared seeing this*, he thought, again denying the darker notions as soon as they took shape.

He continued weaving his way against the mortal tide, returning to that which they fled. They made way for him, not realizing that they did so. He was hidden from their eyes, but their suffering filled his vision, person after person, hundreds of them, perhaps thousands. Where would they go now that their homes were destroyed, their city sacked? Perhaps east, for those able to secure passage over the water, toward Nicaea, as had two of their recent emperors preceding them in flight, Alexius III and Alexius V Murzuphlus. Perhaps west, like Alexius IV, who had ruled, albeit briefly, between the other two. How was it that the deadly game of thrones among the mortal rulers of the empire and of the greatest of cities upon the Earth had grown so twisted and vile, and yet, as always, it was the people who suffered?

It is we who are to blame, Malachite thought. *Mortals and Cainites are merely two faces of the same coin, peering at the world from opposite sides of death, inseparable until God tires of His Creation and forges it anew.* Every general, every royal cousin born to the purple, whether he knew so or not, courted the favor of undead patrons, each vying for prominence and influence, each twisting, corrupting. *And what part of the Dream is this?* A diseased part, eating away at the heart, spawning cruelty among those mortals who should be most noble.

And we who have the opportunity to gather the wisdom of eternity, Malachite thought, *we are no better than they are, setting one against another*. He felt shame for his race. Surely the blame lay with the major families of the Triumvirate: Michael, his glory matched only by his madness and his increasing detachment from his city; Caius, playing his games of generals and emperors as if they were toys carved from ivory; Gesu, obsessed by the internal life of the Divine, blind to any external threats.

But they will unite now that the greatest danger is obvious. Michael will rise up and lead them, Malachite decided, much as he had thought months ago that

Michael would step to the fore against the Latins, when they had first arrived as supposed allies to the *Romaioi*, the citizenry of the New Rome. His expectation had not proven true then, but now... now that the flames were burning, now that the stately buildings of the city were crumbling to rubble...

"The Dream is dying," whispered the boy.

"Quiet, boy." Malachite shuddered. The boy was gadfly to his conscience. *But I have done all that I might*, he thought. It was those like himself of the lesser families who had recognized the threats facing the Dream, who had entered into secret covenant so that they might preserve it.

We were too late. The crackling flames exclaimed as much.

The cries of anguish that drew Malachite were closer now, though in truth they had never been far, riding the wind, penetrating his heart. He had followed the sound while watching the looming walls of the city and the tattered procession of humanity spilling forth like blood from an open wound. Sight and sound were one, the wails those of the city itself, crying out against its violation.

He turned from the main road, the Egnatian Way, and darted more quickly among what structures still stood. The fires here had by now mostly burned themselves out. He was thankful enough for that. Screams and moans were the only inhabitants remaining to this desolate quarter, formerly a bustling maze of industry and labor, now a haphazard collection of ruined stone walls, smoldering beams, and deserted workshops. When the boy groaned at being jostled, Malachite slowed his pace. There was no hurry. The sun would not rise for several hours still, and death and suffering had settled in for a long stay.

The cries were coming from a compound of buildings, a lumber yard emptied of wood by the crusaders, who had commandeered it and used it to construct their siege engines. A different harvest now filled the buildings and the yard: bodies, the injured and the dying. The strongest of them, Malachite presumed, those with less serious injuries or who were simply too exhausted to continue onward, crowded in the open with only a wall to their backs or canvas sheets tied to poles as shelter from the early spring chill. Mothers held crying babes to breast. Old men and women slept, and children also, their grimy faces angelic in repose. Malachite skirted the yard. Too many mortals in one place. It was unlikely they would take note of him at all, another dispossessed soul carrying a stricken loved one. Yet if someone did take notice, mistook him for a leper, perhaps… Mortals were unpredictable in their passions, and not to be trifled with in large numbers. At times like these, the world was little more than a tangle of parched kindling, and the tiniest spark of panic could ignite a conflagration to consume the dead flesh of a Cainite.

So he slipped through a side door into the main building—and found himself among the tortured penitents of Hell. The cries, echoes of which he had heard from without, reverberated from every wall, every rafter. They soaked into the grain of wood, seeped through skin. Mangled and broken bodies were stretched across every available surface: the floor, work tables, benches. And the stark aroma of blood—

Malachite stepped back, pressed his shoulder against the door frame as he ground his own desiccated flesh between his teeth. Before him, a physician leaned heavily into the stroke of a fine-toothed saw beneath the constricting band of a tourniquet, grating into bone.

Two other men held the patient down. His cough-wracked screams wrenched the soul, yet the doctor drew back the saw through the cut, leaned into the next stroke. A woman. The doctor was a woman, Malachite realized as he tried to concentrate on the bend of her back, her dark hair—not on the droplets of blood splattered on her face, the patches splashed across her hands and wrists and smock, dried beneath her fingernails….

Father have mercy!

Urgently he brushed past the surgery, out of the room. The next room was little better. The wounded lay or were propped upright in tight confines. The smell and taste of blood permeated everything. The cries, now that he had found them, carried an unbearable immediacy—not the collective entreaty of the city as he had thought, but the voices raised in pain of individual mortals, each with a life and a story, each suffering injury unto himself, each bleeding, spilling life-giving, life-sustaining blood.

Malachite staggered onward. *The boy… look to the welfare of the boy!* he reminded himself. Steps, a narrow stairwell to his left. He clambered up. The infirm and injured filled the second floor as well, but Malachite sensed no fresh, flowing blood like below. Most of these people likely had climbed the stairs of their own power. The staff of this makeshift hospital were few enough that they would not have carried the worst cases any farther than necessary. Most of the patients were asleep, senses numbed, oblivious to the continual cries of suffering. Seeing the shocked stare of a caregiver, however, Malachite realized his own mortal mask had dissolved with his lapsing concentration, so great had been his agitation. He stood revealed. Quickly but awkwardly, with the boy still in his arms, he shifted his hood to better hide his skeletal head, jagged fangs, and knife-sharp nose, the deeply sunken eyes and tight, brittle skin, which cracked and sloughed away with his every movement. His hands were little better: a collection of bulging veins and paper-thin skin barely concealing bone. He shielded, too, the boy's gruesome features with a turn of shoulder.

"Malachite?" whispered the caregiver, his shock underscored by something approaching awe.

Malachite recognized the man now, a monk, newly of the family, not Cainite but nourished by the blood. Curtly Malachite flashed a hand signal that would be understood by any of his people, its meaning unequivocal: *Bring blood. Now.* With a quick glance to make sure that no one else had recognized him—for *what if not who* he was—he stalked out of the room. His mortal façade restored, he found another, smaller room, this one with a ladder to the roof. A woman and an old man, along with three small children, were sprawled asleep on the floor. Malachite calmed himself and woke the woman gently.

"Forgive me, sister," he said when she opened groggy eyes. "The physician told me we should use this room. The boy is ill and should not be near others. Keep your children at a distance." Even in shadow, the boy in his arms did look ill, emaciated and deathly pale. The woman drew back. "There is room across the hall, if you wish," Malachite added kindly.

She took heed of his advice, gathering her children to her skirt and herding them as well as her ailing father out of the room. Malachite laid the boy on the floor, propping a sack under his head for a pillow. A moment later, the monk joined them and closed the door. He carried in his arms a different withered, old man, whom he handed to Malachite.

"He will not be missed?" Malachite asked.

The monk shook his head. "This one grows weaker with every hour. He will not live to see the morning light." He made the sign of the cross. "May God have mercy on his soul."

"May He have mercy on ours," Malachite said. He laid the old man on the floor beside the boy, hopeful that the blood, even weak, would call to him.

But the boy did not stir. He did not take hold of the failing body, did not feed.

Malachite felt the eyes of the monk, watching. "I do not know what is wrong with him," Malachite admitted, answering the unvoiced question, which would have remained unvoiced, for the monk would not have spoken until spoken to—not in the presence of Malachite, patron of the city's Nosferatu and favored of Michael. "We were returning to the city," Malachite said. "I had... left." *I had been sent away*, he thought, pained by the fact. "We knew that the Latins had breached the walls and entered the city during the day. He and I were discussing whether Emperor Murzuphlus would continue the resistance in the streets, house to house, when... the boy swooned. It was as if all his strength deserted him." *And his vision*, Malachite thought. *He who has been my distant eyes. I've grown dependent upon him.*

"I have seen others like him over the past days," the monk said, his voice weary and burdened by the horrors he had witnessed. "Mortals, I mean... but that have given up hope."

"There is hope!" Malachite snarled, suddenly enraged, striking with the force of lightning, pinning the monk to the wall by the neck. The Cainite's fangs began to slide down farther, moving through flesh as fissured as the sun-baked desert. After a moment, the monk's futile gasping brought Malachite back to himself. He pushed the Beast back down, retreated to the other side of the room, kept his face to the wall. "Forgive me," he said, shaking. "The blood… downstairs. It…"

The monk continued gasping. He struggled to speak through spasms of coughing. "Do you require more?"

"No." Malachite said. He had no true need to feed. He was accustomed to denying the call—not so much as the Obertus monks who followed the teachings of ascetic Gesu, but neither was he a slavering Latin vampire, used to the blood feasts of Bishop Alfonzo.

"Murzuphlus has fled the city," the monk offered, still hesitant.

"Has he, now?" Malachite said, anxious to turn his thoughts to other matters. So Alexius V Murzuphlus was gone, usurper of an usurper of an usurper, chased from his golden throne. And whose play toy had that one been? Alfonzo's, perhaps, so that the city was sure to fall to his Venetian brethren; or maybe Caius's, or one of his multitude of warring underlings? Malachite preferred the sewers to the stink of politics and king-making. If more Cainites had felt the same, perhaps the golden city would not lie prostrate to the ravaging of false Christians.

"The boy will not feed," he said, disgusted, wanting to distract himself from the fate of the city but unable even in this small thing to be of any use. "Watch him," he told the monk, and then turned to climb the ladder to the roof. At the trap door he paused and looked back to the monk, this servant weaned on Cainite blood. "You are one of Fra' Raymond's people." The monk nodded. "Is he…?"

"He survived the initial attack," the monk said deferentially. "Many did not. He sent us out with the instructions to help the suffering where we could."

For the first time this night, Malachite knew the faintest trace of hope. His friend and protégé, Fra' Raymond, was not destroyed. He remained at the head of the Order of St. Ladre. Still the leper knights strove to aid the victims of circumstance, though in this time of cataclysm surely the victims outnumbered the victors hundredfold. *It is a duty I should have been fulfilling*, Malachite chastised himself. But he'd had no choice. Michael had commanded him away from the city. How could he have found the strength to refuse the wishes of the Patriarch? Malachite's thoughts as he perched on the ladder seized again upon Michael's possible whereabouts. *I must find him, and quickly*. Much time had passed since Malachite had been forced to think in terms of nights and weeks rather than years, but mortals had seized the initiative now, and they could be such hasty creatures.

He turned away from the monk, pushed open the trap door, and climbed onto the flat roof. Doing so, he traded the scent of blood, such a temptation to his body, for the sight of smoke rising from beyond the city walls, a considerable trial to his soul. He tried to plan his strategy for the nights to come, but the shrouded vista before him was a damning condemnation of his past failures. He had failed to penetrate Michael's deepening malaise and to warn him how many Cainites had lost sight of the Dream. They cared nothing about a city of infinite beauty, a reflection of divine pleasure, a tribute to God destined to last throughout the ages.

Even among the most favored families of the Triumvirate, recklessness and disregard had become the rule. Of Michael's own Toreador, only dutiful Petronius had refused to bury his head in the sand and ignore the raging factionalism within the city, the Turks pressing from the east, the Slavs and Franks from the north and west. But Petronius was over-burdened by the mantle of leadership in Michael's stead and had turned to the slippery Magnus for aid and comfort—as if ever a trustworthy soul had stirred among Clan Lasombra. Malachite well knew there had not.

Gesu and his Obertus Tzimisce, meanwhile, could not be bothered to step beyond the walls of the Monastery of St. John Studius. In fact, Gesu had closed the gates to all outsiders, turning his back on the city as well as his responsibilities as leader of a Trinity family. His brood, Symeon and Myca Vykos, while not consumed by the monastic mysteries and more accessible, had been unable to sway Gesu from his isolation.

The Antonian Ventrue were worse yet. Caius pretended—or perhaps actually thought—that he ruled the family with an iron hand, yet squabbling and petty maneuvering among the prefects was rampant. And as for matters imperial and military, ostensibly the purview of the family, the proof was damning: Four emperors had sat atop the throne over the course of the past year alone, and invaders had breached the walls and even now looted the city.

None of this had to happen, Malachite thought. Yet he had seen it beginning to happen for decades: the political disarray among the mortals, barbarians claiming more and more of the empire's distant and then not-so-distant holdings each year, the local economy suffering under the privileges granted to the damnable Venetians, the imperial coffers ringing hollow. Malachite and a very few others had recognized the peril. They had formed their own secret Trinity, hoping to ward off disaster, but disaster had come so soon.

And now the city burns.

He gazed eastward at the massive defensive works, at the smoke rising from atop and behind them. Never in more than three and a half centuries had he been forced to see those walls and wonder what yet remained on the other side, what remained of his city, of the Dream.

From below, voices drew his attention back to the improvised hospital. Voices… the boy and the monk? Had the boy then fed and recovered some of his strength? No. Malachite did recognize the voice of the soft-spoken monk, but the other words were not spoken by the boy.

"Of course I won't stay away from them," came a woman's gruff and impatient tones. "Step aside then, if you can't be of any help."

Malachite at once was at the ladder, descending into the room with the extraordinary furtiveness of the blood—neither the monk nor the woman kneeling beside the boy and old man saw him.

"They're both dead," she said, but she was staring at the boy, her brow furrowed. She held his hand in hers, feeling for a nonexistent pulse. "Except this one doesn't seem to know it yet." The boy's eyes were open, moving slightly as he watched her.

"Away from him!" Malachite barked, stepping forward to the defense of his childe.

The monk jumped back, obeying without question. The woman, too, started, but she gave no ground—nor did she express but the briefest shock at Malachite's sudden appearance, his inhuman visage.

"I doubt there is any harm I could do him," she said, rising to her feet. She was not young for a mortal.

She had lived perhaps a decade for each of Malachite's centuries. Her features were Jewish, and Malachite recognized her as the physician he had seen downstairs. Wisps of gray streaked her dark hair, pulled back severely. Wrinkles were etched deep in her face, at the corners of her eyes and mouth, on her forehead. She had washed her hands, but blood still speckled her sleeves.

"This cannot be a safe place for a woman," Malachite said, "especially a daughter of Sarah." He stepped between her and the boy, knelt beside the two bodies on the floor. The old man was indeed dead, but the boy had not fed, was just as weak as before.

"Where would you rather I be?" she asked. "I was in Acre when Richard the Lion Heart took that city," she said with a shrug. "When the Christians claim what they believe is their rightful prize, the Jewish Quarter is not exactly the safest refuge."

Malachite regarded her intently, impressed both by the steel of her voice and the manner with which she met, unflinching, his gaze. He did not spare her the skeletal features, the mouth cramped with misaligned fangs. "Close the door," he said to the monk, and it was done.

"They are no true Christians," Malachite said, "who would pillage the greatest place of worship to God there is on Earth." His tone dared her to contradict him.

The woman was noncommittal in return. "The masters of the city may change their robes, but the life of my people will continue much the same."

Malachite heard the truth in her words. Though the Jews might be misguided in refusing to recognize the Christ as their Messiah, Malachite afforded them the respect due the branch from which the shoot of

David had sprung. Many Cainites were less generous; many mortals as well.

"What is your name?" he asked.

"I am Miriam of Damascus."

"A physician."

"Yes."

Malachite noticed the blood again. The drying, tacky stains on her smock were more than enough to attract his attention, if not, now that he had collected himself, to cause him undue discomfort. "You do not fear me," he said.

"Death wears many faces," Miriam said.

"Some easier to behold than others."

"The result, in the end, is the same. I have seen death closely enough, cheated it enough times on behalf of others, that when it comes for me…" She shrugged again, not flippant but resigned.

"So you embrace it," Malachite probed.

"No. That is not the same thing at all." She glanced at the monk, wondering perhaps what connection he had to this creature of death before her.

"There is more," Malachite said. A mortal was not so difficult for him to read.

Miriam nodded, resigned to the telling as seemingly she was to eventual death. "I know of your kind," she said. "I have met one of you. I have learned much of death, and of life, at her side."

"What is her name?"

The woman hesitated, weighed her options. "That I will not say."

Malachite smiled, though truly the woman might not have recognized the twisted expression for what it was. *She is bound by blood oath*, he thought. *She will not betray her master, cannot betray her.* He did not push for more of an answer. In truth, he already suspected who her patron likely was, and his guess filled him with foreboding. Lady Alexia Theusa, the solitary member of the Cappadocian scion family, had served as physician to emperors, directly or indirectly, for many years. Such an elder Cainite—far older than Malachite—when she did seek the company of mortals, often tended to seek out those who shared qualities or skills similar to those she possessed. Miriam, too, was a physician. She was headstrong, perhaps a loner, as far as Malachite could tell. All of these things might bring her to the notice of the Lady Alexia, whose inscrutable machinations would no doubt ensnare and eventually consume the mortal, body and soul.

Before he could comment on any of this, however, he cocked his head, suddenly aware of something besides smoke and the sounds of human suffering carried on the breeze. For a second time, he climbed the ladder to the roof and paused to listen to the night....

There. Horses' hooves clattering against the cobbles, drawing closer.

Miriam and Fra' Raymond's ghouled monk were close behind Malachite. After a moment, they too heard the noise. Not long after, the armored knights rode into view.

"There are no riches for them to plunder here," said the monk.

"Better if there were." Miriam's concern was obvious upon her face. "They could take what they like and then leave."

Malachite did not wish to meet any crusader, whether brigand opportunistically bearing the mantle of the cross, or pious warrior fueled by holy zeal.

"They are of the blood," said a voice from behind. The three roof-top observers whirled to see the boy. Somehow he had climbed the ladder and crawled onto the roof. His eyes fluttered with the fading vestiges of consciousness. "They are of the blood, and they wish to destroy us."

Chapter Two

Among the refugees sheltering in the open of the lumber yard, a handful caught sight of the approaching knights shortly after Malachite did. A muttering buzz of apprehension began to spread through the crowd of mortals. Riders wearing the cross of the Latin crusaders might conceivably bear no ill will, but certainly they brought no welcome tidings. Those mortals who were able, who could still walk and were near a gate, began to slip away from the makeshift hospital and fade into the night.

Malachite took all this in distractedly, his attention devoted to the boy lying on the roof—his childe, one of three brothers. *They are of the blood*, the boy had said of the knights before he collapsed, *and they wish to destroy us*. Malachite knew better than to dismiss the boy's pronouncements, least of all in a time of urgency, but while the words rang like distant alarm bells in the elder Cainite's mind, the sight of the boy's eyes rolled up in his head held Malachite frozen. Was this the last gasp of unlife for the boy so mysteriously stricken? There was no labored breathing or erratic pulse of which to keep track, as Miriam had discovered.

She and the monk, having seen the crusaders' approach, had climbed down the ladder. They were making their way quickly from room to room and issuing brusque warnings, attempting to alert the patients without creating a panic. "There are Franks coming. Take your family and go. No, don't gather your things, just *go*."

Malachite heard their voices emanating from below, as well as the shuffling of feet and bodies, mothers shushing their children, mortals roused from sleep and exhorted to action in the middle of an already hellish night—yet on the roof above the confusion, all was quiet and still as the grave. His childe was an unmoving corpse, devoid of any spark.

"'And God breathed into man's nostrils the breath of life, and man became alive,'" Malachite recited. "I am not God that I have the breath of life to offer," he said, "but what is mine I give freely." Scooping the boy into his arms, Malachite tore with his fangs into his own wrist. To this ragged wound he willed blood to flow, and from the wound blood ran into the slack mouth of the boy.

"They are entering the yard," said the monk from the trap door. "We must go."

But Malachite was directing each drop of blood into the boy's mouth, watching with relief as the boy swallowed, if weakly. *He lives*, Malachite thought. *As much as any Cainite can be said to live*.

The clomping of horses was much closer now, and harsh words: arrogant threats in French and guttural German; curses and entreaties in a mishmash of tongues more common to the city, Greek, Italian, Armenian, Aramaic.

"I will do what I can to delay them," the monk said when Malachite did not respond, and then the trap door was again empty.

The flow of Malachite's blood had slowed to a trickle. He did not force it to continue. The boy showed no more signs of life, but he had fed. He had responded to the blood. For now that would have to be enough: knowing that the boy had not yet left him, had not crumbled to dust in his arms. Malachite rose to his feet, still cradling the childe.

Miriam was scrambling up the ladder now, her cheeks ruddy, flushed with exertion. Her chest rose and fell rapidly with her breathing. Malachite noticed such markers of vitality—markers that he and the boy lacked.

"Why are you still here?" she asked him.

Malachite drew closer to the edge of the roof. Below, able-bodied patients and refugees helped some of the more seriously injured away from the lumber yard—except that the knights, now, were blocking the way, barring exits with their horses, which stamped and snorted and terrified the mortals. The steeds carried an air of the grave, towering above the mortals like fuming demons born from a fiery cauldron and breathing out the choking mists of Hell.

Ghouled beasts, Malachite knew, *grown strong and terrible on Cainite blood.*

The monk was among the swirling chaos, forcing his way toward one of the mounted knights and calling as loudly as he could: "There are only poor, sick souls here! They shelter under protection of the Church!"

"Which church would that be, you eastern heretic?" snarled the knight.

"The Church of our one God, and His son, our Lord the Christ!"

"Out of my way, heathen!"

"This hospital, like yourself, wears the armor of the cross!"

The knight sneered. "Hospital? Are you heretics so foolish that you have carpenters for doctors, or so blasphemous that you worship in their wooden stalls?"

"Was our Christ not a carpenter?"

"I'll hear no more blasphemy!" And the knight raised his sword and struck.

Malachite watched the arc of the blow from above, unable to reach out and stop it—and in the speed and force of the blow, he recognized the inhuman strength of the wielder.

The heavy blade sliced cleanly through the arm the monk raised for protection and struck fiercely into his brain pan. The monk's body, wracked by spasms, tried to crumple, but steel lodged in bone held it aloft. Not until the knight kicked at the monk's face did the body jar loose and fall twitching to the ground.

"God of my fathers... no," Miriam said, hand covering her mouth, gaze ensnared by the bloodshed below.

Had she not been standing beside Malachite, he would not have heard her, because with the fall of the sword, true panic seized the crowd. Screams. A press of bodies, but in conflicting directions. Some of the fleeing dropped or knocked the injured to the ground. A few foolhardy souls flung themselves at the knights but were quickly struck down or trampled under hoof.

"There is a cellar," Miriam said. "We can hide."

Malachite shook his head as he saw the knights, several with torches, converging on the wooden building. "No." Perhaps they had wished at first to search the compound, but now their blood was up, and they were determined to cleanse the world with flame. And there were Cainites among them. The boy had said it, and Malachite had seen as much now with his own eyes. But these Cainites were of the West, or recently returned from the Levant, perhaps. They cared nothing for Malachite's authority under Michael, nor for Constantinople. To them the Dream was nothing more than a vision of gold to fill their coffers.

But they will stay back, Malachite thought, *back from the flames*. His nose twitched at the scent of smoke—not from within the city walls or the smoldering ash of the surrounding neighborhood this time, but from flames licking fresh timber at the base of the building. *There are mortals among them as well*, he suspected. To handle fire so brazenly, they would likely be mortals. He hoped as much, for it would increase his chances of escape—his, and the boy's, and…

"They're setting the building on fire!" Miriam realized, her mortal senses lagging behind Malachite's.

He grabbed her by the sleeve and dragged her stumbling to the far side of the roof. "Climb onto my back," he told her. "Hurry."

"But they're setting fire to the building!" she told him, as if somehow he did not understand that. "There are still people downstairs—some of them can't walk!"

Malachite understood that as well. "You can do nothing more."

"They can't walk! They can't get out!"

"Thousands are perishing in this city. Go down there, and you will be one of them. Are you so ready for death?"

She hesitated, unable to argue with his blunt assessment.

"Climb onto my back and hold tight. Now."

She did so, but Malachite could feel the weight of her guilt at saving herself while those she had cared for would die. He gave her no time to reconsider but jumped at once. The ground rushed to meet him. His bones and stringy muscles absorbed the jolt, aided by the strength and resilience of the blood. Miriam coughed and sputtered, the breath knocked from her.

"Hurry!" Malachite said, jerking her to her feet when she staggered. She had bitten her lip, and blood ran down her chin. "Can you carry the boy?" he asked, seeing that she could walk. "He is not heavy." She was confused for a moment but then nodded. Malachite handed her the frail body.

Taking her by the sleeve, Malachite began leading her away from the building. This was no orderly siege but rather an impulsive slaughter. The crusaders had formed no organized perimeter. Still, to remain near the building was to court disaster. Already the flames were whipping high on the other side.

Screams filled the night: terrified, pained, silenced by sword, tortured by fire.

Alone, Malachite could have melted into the darkness and escaped with relative ease, but he had the boy and the woman. Malachite ran—in this city where he had been among the undead lords, he now was hunted. He ran, as fast as he could without causing the woman to stumble as he pulled her. He shied from the open spaces, angling instead for a clump of smaller buildings that were not yet aflame. But then mortals fleeing in panic from among those buildings warned him away. Horse and rider emerged suddenly from the darkness into the firelight, armor and raised sword gleaming red and gold. Malachite let go of the woman. She was buffeted, slowed and then stopped by the people rushing past her in the other direction. Now she stared helplessly at the huge warhorse bearing down on her—

Malachite leapt. He struck the rider from the flank with the force of a catapulted boulder. They crashed to the ground, but Malachite was not hurt, not surprised. With bestial claws, he tore off the knight's helmet, ripped apart mail hauberk—and was met with the rewarding gush of mortal blood. Malachite slashed at the exposed throat three times—for the boy, for himself, for Michael the Patriarch. Driven on by the blood, by the carnage and upheaval of the night, Malachite thrust his face into the churned meat, shredding with his fangs, drinking in the warm blood of the violator.

Vengeance!

He would have lost himself, then, if not for the need of the moment: the need to be away from that place, to escape the mortal warriors and whatever Cainites lurked. He could feel, too—among the swirling, screaming chaos—eyes. Watching him. Miriam. The woman cradling his childe against her breast. Malachite looked up at her, bloody sinew caught and dangling from his fangs. She stood in the same spot where she had cowered from the horseman—except now she stared at him with the same terror-filled eyes.

Malachite spat in the dust. He fought down the urge to give himself over to the blood. There was no time. Other knights remained, other swords, other Cainites. He was at Miriam's side in the blink of an eye, leading her again by the sleeve. He could feel her watching him, though. Glancing at him with fear in her heart—though he had saved her, though he was not one of these Latin monsters who were burning the city and killing untold thousands!

"Surely you have seen Lady Alexia feed," he snapped, grabbing her more roughly. "Or perhaps she is more dainty at the trough."

Miriam looked away from him quickly, perhaps startled that he had guessed her patron, but also frightened by his ire and by what she had seen him do—by what she feared he might still do. His anger led him on, deeper into the shadows. Behind them, the wooden structures of the lumber yard were engulfed in flame.

And the screams. It could have been that the thousands of golden-red tongues licking heavenward unleashed their agony, but Malachite had seen the mortals stretched out on whatever sickbeds were at hand. He recognized cries of anguish, of burning. Miriam recognized them as well. She wanted to do something about it—*needed* to do something—Malachite could tell, but she was too far gone in shock to resist him leading her away. For the moment at least, her horror at the slaughter outweighed her fear of him. She tried to give him back the boy, but Malachite refused.

"If I must fight again, I'll need free hands," he said.

Barely had he spoken the words when he heard the whinny of a horse, hooves approaching from the direction of the fire and the din. Malachite pulled woman and boy into the darkest shadows he could find amidst the rubble, shielded them with his own body and cloak, and called on the power of his blood to make him one with the night. The horse—no, too many clattering hooves. More than one horse. They drew closer… closer still….

Pressed beneath his own silent body, Malachite could hear the pounding heart of the woman, blood rushing through her body. To his ears, so close, her rapid breathing sounded as loud as the horses. He knew the sounds did not carry, but still he almost flinched with each heartbeat, each time she inhaled and exhaled. He held her more tightly, wished that he could choke off the noise without doing her harm.

The horses and riders were almost on top of them now, shod hooves striking cobbles like hammer on anvil—

—And then they were past. Still nearby, but the thunderous clomping drawing slowly away. Then stopping.

Keep moving, blast you, Malachite thought. They were still too close for him to escape, and he didn't dare attack them, two at once—not without knowing if they were mortal or Cainite, and with the woman and boy still in danger.

But the riders were taking a break from their slaughter, sighing and shifting in their saddles, which creaked beneath their weight. "Nothing this far out," said one to the other. "We should head back into the city. No use in burning cripples."

"Aye to that," said the second. "But I suppose we'll ride the outskirts until Lord Guy tells us otherwise."

"Of course," said the other right away. "I never meant—"

"I know. I know. Calm yourself. I'd rather be within the walls myself, but there's heathens and heretics aplenty out here as well. And likely those of the blood among them."

"That, I don't understand," the first confessed. "Lord Guy says give the sword to any Cainites what aren't part of the Crusade, but there's them among them that would gladly help us. They have no love for these Greeks in the city."

"But help us for how long?" asked the second. "Treacherous lot, these Greeks. You've heard about the mortal emperors, how they come to power. Poisoning each other and gouging each other's eyes out. The Cainites couldn't be much better. We don't fight them now, we'd have to fight them later. Best take care of all the killing at once. We'll stake and burn as many in the Latin Quarter as in the rest of the city, I'd wager."

They sat quietly atop their mounts for a bit longer, the first's silence likely signaling his assent. Then the two knights stretched and yawned. "We'd best be back to work," said the second. "Let's circle around and back to the fire."

"Not too close," the first said with a chuckle.

"Aye. We'll save that for the Greeks." And they rode on their way.

Greeks. Malachite snorted with disgust when he was certain the riders had moved beyond earshot. *What idiots, these barbarians. We* are *Romaioi.* Yet the barbarous Franks had captured the city that was the final vestige of what had been the glory of Rome.

"Are they gone?" Miriam whispered.

Malachite let her up. "Come."

"No," she said. For a second time, she offered him the boy. "They will pass on from here soon enough. I will hide until they do, but after, there will be people who need help, those who escaped and hid, or who didn't die in the fire."

Malachite regarded her intently. Again she did not flinch from his gaze. *Do I repulse her so, that she would rather die here than go with me?* he wondered, but he saw none of the earlier fear and shock in her eyes. It could be, as she said, that she wished to stay behind and care for the suffering. "Do you still face death so blithely, Miriam of Damascus, now that you have seen not just the aftermath of carnage but a man ripped apart before your eyes?"

"Never blithely," she said, sorrowful, shaking her head. "You killed because there was no other choice. They…?"

"The result, in the end, is the same," Malachite said.

"Ah," she said, almost smiling through the grime and tears, "but the end is not yet upon us."

Isn't it? Malachite thought.

She held out the boy, and this time Malachite accepted him. "God go with you, Miriam of Damascus."

"And God go with you."

Cradling the boy with one arm, Malachite knelt down and scooped up a handful of soot, which he then smeared across her forehead and cheeks, nose and chin, to aid in her hiding. "Lent has passed, but may the ash afford you protection."

"What is your name?" she asked him softly. "So that I might offer prayers for you."

"Malachite," he said, hoping that they did indeed pray to the same God, and that He would listen to her where He had not seen fit to hear the pleas of the Damned.

Chapter Three

It was well, Malachite decided, that the woman had stayed behind, for he was about to depart the land of the living. He felt at first that he was abandoning her, leaving her to her fate. He had done the same for the rest of those at the lumber yard, of course. And for the monk. There had been little other choice. There was no way he could save every mortal. Even in the nights before the damnable crusaders had sailed into the ports of Constantinople, mortals had suffered and died. Life, like unlife, was cruel. It could have been less so had fewer Cainites used the Dream as an excuse to further their own self-interest, had more of them taken to heart Michael's lessons of beauty and spiritual perfection. The Patriarch's guiding hand had crafted mortal and Cainite societies that could have enriched one another, the eternal grace of the latter providing a bridge of sorts, allowing transcendence, for the finite vitality of the former.

Yet the city burned.

Perhaps we did deserve this retribution, Malachite thought morosely. Rather than shepherding the mortals, Cainites had drifted toward damaging extremes of abuse and neglect. On the one hand, Bishop Alfonzo held great blood feasts in the Latin Quarter, sacrificing dozens of mortals at a time at the altar of his megalomania; on the other hand, angelic Gesu turned from mortals entirely, ignoring both the needs and the dangers of humanity.

Malachite's mood darkened as he tromped through this, the city beyond the wall—or what was left of it. This section had played the part of wasteland, caught between besiegers and besieged, suffering destruction from both as they attempted to damage and kill each other. The sight of the smoldering ruins, a patchwork of streets and rubble, filled Malachite with dread of what he would find within the city proper. Ever so often the dreamlike miasma that gripped him gave way, and he saw the blighted vista as if for the first time. The unbearable weight of reality settled upon his shoulders, pressed down on his chest as if trying to crush the life from him, more than three hundred years after his final breath.

Many of the bodies he came across were burned, charred beyond recognition. Some of them he thought carried Miriam's features, but the passing illusion was nothing more than the play of smoke and shadows and wind-whipped coals.

It is good that she went her way, he thought. He could not entangle himself with the fate of a lone mortal. Michael had seen the truth of it: that mankind as a whole was the protectorate of Caine, his birthright, his charge. Caine, like his forebears, had sinned. And as his sin in striking down his brother was to claim dominion over mortality, so too was his penance, and that of those who came after, that they should be shackled with dominion over mortals. Born in blood, thus was the legacy of the childer of Caine.

Mortals, mankind, humanity. A single woman, a Jew, was not so great a matter when thousands were perishing. *And the Dream, as well.*

Perhaps the boy, too, would perish. He had neither spoken nor opened his eyes since feeding on the blood from Malachite's wrist. *Will I know that he is about to leave me?* he wondered. *Or will I awake to dust, where last I laid him down?*

The question was pregnant with dire implications, for the boy was one of three brothers, the other two left behind when the Nosferatu had fled the city. Malachite had received no word of them since then, and if, like their brother they had somehow fallen victim to a sudden, unforeseen affliction…

Not knowing was torment. Yet, as Malachite watched the smoke rise from behind the city walls, and the carrion crows circle above waiting to pick at the bones of the Dream, he knew that certainty could be worse. Certainty could crush hope.

I will find Michael, Malachite thought. *He will set these things right. He will know what afflicts the boy. He will know how to save the city.*

The first three buildings Malachite had sought each had been destroyed. The first two had burned. The third, home to a well-to-do merchant, was little more than a pile of stone and broken masonry. Perhaps the walls had been pulled down and the cornerstones hurled from a mangonel during the assault on the city. Surely whatever wealth the merchant had not taken with him had been stolen by crusaders or desperate refugees.

The fourth building Malachite sought, a cooper's shop and warehouse, was still standing. He saw this with no small relief, for the sun was now closer than two hours from creeping above the eastern horizon. The establishment had not gone undamaged. Two of the outbuildings had been burned—they were now no more than stone foundations—but the fire had not spread to the other structures. The shop and warehouse were stone roughly to waist level, wood from that point up.

Now that he was well away from the main roads, the stream of refugees, the piteous tide of human suffering, Malachite was struck by the silence that enveloped him. Always before when he had walked these streets, even late at night, the telltale sounds of mortal habitation had called out to him: voices behind locked doors, revelers returning home, workers getting an early start on the next day, a fishmonger trying to pawn off the last of yesterday's catch on an unwary buyer. Tonight there was nothing. The residents were gone, chased away or dead. The crusaders, too, were absent—not that Malachite wasn't still on guard for the noise of horses or booted infantry. They were likely all within the city now, the majority exhausted after a night of pillaging and debauchery, while those Cainites among them sought the refuge of safe haven through the coming day. Stillness smothered the streets and homes and shops here.

This is what the world would be if left to us, Malachite thought. Silent, broken, dead. Hunter could not long survive without hunted. Couldn't Bishop Alfonzo see that—he who would slaughter the mortals like cattle for his own amusement? Or Caius and those of his ilk, who would set kine against kine to further petty goals? Or even Gesu who, despite his lauded wisdom, refused to see that the mortals must be protected from themselves? *And from us.*

Michael knew these things. *This attack upon his city will jolt him from his malaise*, Malachite thought. *He will deal with these short-sighted despoilers of the Dream.*

A sudden spasm of coughing wracked the frail boy in Malachite's arms. The elder Cainite stiffened, sick with apprehension that this might be the last—but the boy settled back into his deep, lingering stupor. Malachite felt keenly the absence of the boy's sight.

Stepping toward the warehouse, he noticed, too, the pointed absence of the cooper. Like all of the mortals of this part of the city, he was gone. Missing, fled, hiding, dead? There was no way to know.

The large wooden door that used to cover the warehouse entrance lay on the ground not far away, pulled from its track and decorated with a mosaic of smudged foot- and hoof-prints. Malachite made out cart tracks in the dust as well. He could imagine the details of the morality play that must have transpired here: the Latin pillagers ripping away the door, their eyes and hearts swelling with lust at the sight of a warehouse full of booty, only to find that the casks inside were all empty. Malachite chuckled quietly at the consternation of the figments in his mind, but the humor quickly faded. All that remained in the warehouse were a few broken barrels, smashed in a fit of pique, no doubt. The Franks would have carted off the empty barrels to hold supplies or to collect other loot in the city. So they had laughed loudest in the end.

Not yet, Malachite swore. *They have not seen the end yet.*

He had no cause to dampen the echoes of his sandals against the stone floor as he crossed to the rear of the warehouse. There, he knelt and pressed a loose stone in the lower portion of the wall, then twisted another, and then a third, all in the proper order. The click of a latch springing free was muffled enough that, had he not known to listen, he likely would have missed it. Neither did the flat stone that served as the trap door pop up and reveal itself. It was several feet away from the triggering mechanism and, though now unfastened, still appeared little different from those surrounding it. Minding the unconscious boy, Malachite lifted the hatch with one hand. Climbing through the tight opening, closing the hatch, and descending the ladder without dropping the boy took some care, but he managed it well enough.

The pitch black of the tunnel suited Malachite like a second skin. The darkness was no obstacle to his vampiric eyes, and he found that he thought more clearly without the view looming over him of the breached Walls of Theodosius II and the smoke rising from beyond them. He felt relatively safe again, certain that the Latin cavalry, even if they discovered any of the tunnels, would be useless here. This was not to say that the subterranean passages lacked their own dangers, but the *sameness* of the tunnels, in contrast to all of the upheaval above ground, comforted him. Here he could almost pretend that everything was as it had been before—before the so-called crusaders had arrived, turned away from their original purpose of recapturing the Holy Lands. These outermost tunnels were the same as they had been for years: not so finely constructed as the secret connections among the villas of the Great Palace, but roomy and straight. They were frequented most often by Fra' Raymond and his followers. The knights, monks, and healers, both Cainite and ghoul, served largely unnoticed among the mortal adherents to the Rule of St. Ladre, and the lazar houses they administered, the only refuge and solace for many a leper, stood understandably toward the outskirts of the city. The monk Malachite had met tonight might well have traveled this very tunnel or one of its fellows.

Another soul the Franks have to answer for, Malachite thought, wishing he had learned the man's name, remembering the monk's selflessness and faith in the face of death. Rarely indeed did Fra' Raymond choose poorly in those he decided to Embrace more permanently into the order. The monk's death was a loss to the Hospitalers of St. Ladre and to the city. *But does any of that matter anymore?* Malachite wondered.

Instantly he crossed himself as best he could carrying the boy. *Give me faith, Father. Forgive my lack of faith.*

His worn sandals carried him forward quickly now through the familiar tunnels. He let the darkness serve as his shield, keeping unworthy thoughts at bay. *I must look forward. What's done is done.* He could not turn back time so that Latins had not attacked the city. He could not restore to the Patriarch these last madness-clouded years. But if he could find his allies, find Michael, then they could decide how best to move forward, to save the city, to save the Dream. Chances were that the Franks would move on soon enough, perhaps on to the Holy Land at last, or piecemeal back to their French or German hovels. Even if the mortal crusaders retained control of the city, society could be rebuilt, the Dream could endure. In some ways, who sat upon the mortal throne had surprisingly little to do with how the people lived—and how those who fed upon the people conducted themselves.

Yes, that is the key, Malachite told himself. *Find Michael. But I must rally my allies as well. Perhaps Fra' Raymond could watch over the boy for the time being. And the baron. The Citadel of Petrion is not so far away. A few of his Gangrel would ensure that I reached the Great Palace safely.* There was no telling, after all, exactly how dangerous the city had become. To take for granted that the tunnel networks were all safe would be foolhardy. *From there I'd practically have reached Natalya's haven at the senate basilica, and Michael's at Hagia Sophia.* The Gangrel Baron Thomas and Brujah Natalya had been his allies in the secret covenant before this cataclysm, and they surely would rally behind the Patriarch now. Thought of saving the Dream bolstered Malachite's flagging spirits and struck squarely at the fatalistic anxiety that had dogged him all night. He could achieve one of Raymond's nearby hideouts within the hour and there weather the day.

"There is still hope," Malachite whispered to the boy, squeezing him close. But with the fading of his own quiet echo, he paused....

A faint scraping sound caught his ear—faint but growing louder, nearer, and rapidly. Nails or claws against stone. A great many claws, like a pack of dogs. *Not dogs*, Malachite realized as he now saw the forms at a distance, racing madly toward him through the darkness. *Wolves*.

His first thought was that his luck must be changing, that the baron's Gangrel had found him— but the wolves' headlong dash unnerved him slightly. As they barreled closer, snarling and angry growls became evident. Thoughts of luck changing turned to premonitions of his luck ending altogether. Alone, Malachite might have hidden from them, despite their obviously having picked up his scent. But with the boy in tow...?

They think I am an intruder, one of the Franks! Malachite stepped toward them boldly, raised a hand. "I am a friend!" he called.

His words were drowned out by snarling and the snapping of fangs as they leapt for him.

Chapter Four

Until the very last instant, Malachite could not believe that they would attack him. They would recognize who he was; they would turn aside their onslaught. But they did not. Only as the bared fangs flashed so near that he could count them did paternal instinct overcome disbelief. Malachite spun, shielding the boy cradled in his arms with his own body. The first wolf's impact bore them all to the ground. Teeth tore at his thick robes, shredded the coarse weave, made short work of the brittle flesh beneath. Powerful jaws clamped on his shoulder, his arm, his foot, shook with a fury and terrible force that would easily have broken the neck of a smaller creature.

Malachite wrapped himself around the boy, lashed out with claws of his own when the wolves darted in. But they attacked from every direction. A ferocious tearing at Malachite's arm—

Another set of jaws was ripping at his hood, then his face. Great pressure against the back of his head, his neck, fangs piercing his scalp—

"Enough!" The voice echoed through the tunnel like the clanging of the largest bells in a basilica, chasing the worst of the snarling, the snapping jaws, the crackle of dry flesh rent asunder.

"Enough!" it called again, this time followed by a yelp of pain, of a blow striking true—and the tearing at Malachite's arm ceased, the chastened wolf retreating.

Still there was the terrible pressure on the base of his skull: teeth, pin-pricks hungering for more, capable of more, yet stayed by the command. Hot spittle trickled across his scalp. Slowly the pressure eased, then was gone, and only the spittle and the punctures remained.

Moving as little as possible, Malachite tried to inspect the boy. He seemed intact, hopefully unhurt.

"Get up," said the voice that had commanded the wolves.

This time Malachite recognized the voice. He turned his head with difficulty, stymied at first by the daggers of pain in his neck. Three Cainites stood above him, where before there had been wolves. "Verpus Sauzezh. It is I, Malachite." So this was a case of mistaken identity, he saw, angry but relieved that the confusion was at an end. Verpus was one of the baron's men, a Turk, brought to civilization from the wilds of Anatolia. These Cainites were Malachite's allies.

"I know who you are," Verpus said, his words cold as a naked blade. "Get up."

Malachite's ire flared at the disrespect paid him, leader of a scion family. He held his tongue, though, as the implications of Verpus's attitude paraded through his mind. "Is the baron well?" Malachite asked sharply, unmistakably implying that the head of Verpus's family would hear of this treatment.

"I said, get up," Verpus repeated.

How dare this one order me about? Malachite thought, the Turk's threatening tone fanning his anger. But faced with three Gangrel ready to pounce, the time for debate was not at hand. He started to get up—and discovered through spikes of pain from his various wounds that he could not. Most serious, he saw through the darkness, was his left arm, savaged to the bone, numb, useless. Clutching the boy with his right arm, he could climb only to his knees, and that with great difficulty. Other wounds pained him as well: the back of his head and neck, his shoulder, his leg and ankle and foot. The vitae stored in his undead flesh could repair much of the damage, but he dared not leave himself too weak from lack of blood, too hungry. Already he was angry, irritable, and the Beast would gladly prey upon such sentiments if given half a chance. So he ignored the superficial, if painful, wounds and willed only trace amounts of vitae to his arm, his leg, enough that he could climb awkwardly to his feet without injuring the boy.

"Is this, then, how you treat the head of a fellow scion family?" Malachite asked, needing some slight release for his anger. "And in the baron's name?"

Verpus's response was to turn his back and begin walking. The two other Gangrel took up position behind Malachite and shoved him until he fell in step and followed Verpus.

Malachite's pain was as nothing compared to his outrage. Though lacking the smoke and plaintive cries and obvious destruction of the world above, the underground realm had fallen just as completely to insanity. Perhaps if he had been foolish enough to wander unaccompanied deep into the Latin Quarter, then Malachite might have expected such treatment at the hands of Alfonzo's underlings—but these assailants were the baron's men! *The Quaesitors will hear of this!* Malachite thought. There was no way Verpus could justify such actions to the three judges, one from each Trinity family. *But if the Turk has used cover of the mortal unrest to turn renegade...* He might see no occasion in which he would face the Quaesitors. *Ah, but the baron*, Malachite thought. *He would not see one of his own turn traitor. He would hunt Verpus down and destroy him, and all who followed him.*

Whether Verpus perpetrated treachery or had succumbed to insanity, though, made little difference to Malachite's immediate plight. He staggered along behind the Turk, the other Gangrel offering forceful shoves if the prisoner lagged too far behind their leader. Several times after harsh blows, Malachite turned to glare at them, memorizing the features of their faces should he ever have opportunity to seek redress from the baron, or the Quaesitors, or Michael himself. Perhaps they read the promised vengeance in the Nosferatu's eyes, or perhaps they merely tired of brutalizing their captive plaything. Either way, they left off with their rough treatment of him.

As the procession of four Cainites continued, the tunnel beneath their feet began to slope downward, gently at first, but then with an increasingly steep angle. The moat. They were passing beneath it. The stone bricks of the tunnel walls and floor smelled of dank moisture, and before long seeping water dripped from the arches that supported the wide passage's ceiling. Soon a faint glow appeared to illuminate the way—a peculiar lichen that created its own light though never touched by the radiance of the sun itself.

Like the enlightenment that we Cainites would create, Malachite mused; it was a thought he had pondered over many nights and years. Of course, he noted, the lichen also slicked the cobbles underfoot, making the path treacherous for the unwary.

At its lowest point, the tunnel was partially flooded. Single droplets of water had collected for years untold to a depth of several feet. The Cainites waded the pool without comment. It was cold even to Malachite's undead flesh.

Now the passage turned up sharply. Verpus quickened his pace noticeably, and Malachite struggled to keep up, slowed by the slight but dead weight of his childe and numerous injuries. The trailing Gangrel followed him more closely, but they did not manhandle him as they had earlier. They were passing beneath, he knew, the inner and outer Walls of Theodosius II, which had safeguarded the city for nearly eight hundred years, roughly half a millennium longer than Malachite had existed. Always in passing this way, he felt the smothering weight of history pressing down upon him, each brick and wall and tower and watchman adding its mass to that of the earth itself—to crush him, to crush all of them, to leave them dust, buried, forgotten. And the path they followed, it stretched back into the past, into darkness, far beyond what even Malachite could see. Ahead, the future was no better. That which seemed familiar was likely to have changed for the worse. The echoes of footsteps did not far penetrate the encompassing gloom and, like the ripples on the surface of the icy pool, were soon gone.

Not long after the tunnel's ascent leveled, Verpus turned aside from the main passage and into a low, narrow gap in the wall. The other Gangrel watched Malachite carefully to see that he did not attempt to flee straight ahead, continuing along the wider tunnel. *And why?* he wondered, his melancholy giving way again to anger at the disrespect and injustice done him. *Why would I flee? So that they could bring me down and savage me again? Do they think I am so foolish?* Foolish or perhaps desperate. The Gangrel knew far better than he what was in store for him. Perhaps there was due cause for desperation.

Nonetheless, Malachite stooped low and followed Verpus. This new passage was part of a honeycomb of cramped tunnels built by the Gangrel and the Obertus Tzimisce beneath the Lycus Vale. The sweeping valley, officially the district of Exokionion, was the last area afforded protection by the extended city walls. *I need to go east*, Malachite thought, frustrated and angry, *to the heart of the city*. But the likelihood seemed small that

Verpus and his companions would veer in that direction and escort Malachite beyond the Walls of Constantine, the earlier boundary of the city proper, on the far side of the vale. The first tunnel would have taken them that direction. Instead, they wound their way mostly north. Malachite wasn't as familiar with these particular routes as was Verpus, but many of the tunnels seemed to lie perpendicular to the direction the Gangrel wished to go, as they made many turns. Progress was elliptical, at best. Still, Malachite had traversed the secret paths beneath Constantinople for enough years that he kept his bearings with little difficulty. Simply negotiating the tunnels with their low ceilings and intrusive support beams was more of a challenge. In addition to having to crouch, he was forced to twist his upper body sideways to avoid braining the boy. The prolonged stance was a discomfort on top of the lingering pain of his injuries.

Soon, pangs of hunger began to creep like shadows into his awareness, slowly growing longer and darker. But there were no mortals at hand, and he was not currently at leisure to feed, regardless. Somewhere far above, he knew, the sun was beginning its ascent in the eastern sky. For him, the hunger was always worst at dawn, when his body tasted the slightest hint of what had been denied it for hundreds of years: day, sunlight, life. He could continue for a few hours still, but with each step weakness and hunger took firmer hold of him. He looked at the slack face of the boy and remembered longingly the drops of blood fed to the childe.

Verpus and the others must have felt similarly the sun's calling. From what Malachite knew of their clan, the Gangrel likely could not proceed so far into the day hours as could he—although they had not suffered wounds as serious as those they had inflicted on him, and the Gangrel might well have fed more recently.

As if to confirm Malachite's suspicions of their inability to meet the dawn, even this far below ground, Verpus turned into a yet narrower tunnel that ended in a double-barred and -banded wooden door. He opened the door and shoved Malachite roughly inside—what little there was of inside. The space was barely a closet, perhaps the size of a sarcophagus stood on end. Before Malachite could protest, the Gangrel slammed the door. The two metal bars crashing home sounded in Malachite's ears with the crushing finality of a boulder rolled across a tomb entrance.

Panic gripped him. He laid the boy at his feet, the body curled in on itself because there was not room to lie flat. Malachite pounded the door with his fists, injuries forgotten. The strength of his blood buckled the thick wooden planks, but the iron bands held.

"The baron will not stand for this!" he roared, still pounding the doors. "You'll be staked for the sun! Your burning blood will stain the earth! I am friend to your family! The baron will have your heads!"

"It is the baron who told us to bring you to him!" Verpus shouted back. "Except he wanted you in chains!"

Malachite stepped back from the door as if stung—but there was nowhere for him to go. His back pressed squarely against unforgiving stone. The shock of Verpus's words flushed the vigor from his body, and the captive felt again the pangs of hunger. He dared not look at his own childe, fearful that the Beast would seize him and sate its passions on the only blood at hand.

***

The Beast wore the face of the sun, and throughout its long, slow trek across the heavens it called to him: *Take the blood, Maleki. Take the blood.* The seductive voice was never far, but its chords wove themselves among the sounds of the final day, becoming lost, there but unnoticed, just beneath the surface of the chants and liturgical melodies that were as close to the uttered words of God as any man was likely to hear in his lifetime.

For a moment, Maleki was blinded. Rays of light streamed through the windows at the base of the great dome hundreds of feet above, and shone against marble inlaid with gold and precious stones. Lowering his sights from Heaven, vaulted arches abounded, and sparkling mosaics so intricate as to draw in the eye and mystify it with endless patterns of twisting and spiraling flowers, leaves, vines. Majestic columns lifted the spirit to God. The finest woven hangings of satin and silk ordered galleries overlooking the great expanse of the central nave, itself partitioned by ornate screens. They were a maze of tradition and meaning, and at their center, beside the holy altar, knelt Maleki.

His prelate's vestments, flowing outward from him across sanctified stone, transformed his mortal form. The rites of the divine liturgy flowed outward from him as well, through him, from Heaven above. How many hundreds of times had he knelt beside this altar, offered himself as vessel of Father, Son, and Holy Spirit? And yet still the mystery touched him each and every time. This morning, as he raised from the holy altar the glass-encased knuckle bone of St. Peter, patriarch of patriarchs, Maleki transcended his worldly office. The voices raised in unaccompanied praise were those of angels. The prescribed procession of the relic engendered the outpouring of God's grace. The dozens of priests became the heavenly saints, given their due place at the right hand of the Father. Swaying censers burned with frankincense. Maleki felt not the weight of the encased relic as he raised it and intoned the proper scripture. From the imperial gallery above, the young emperor, Michael III, among the first words of his childhood those of the liturgy, recited the response, thus fulfilling one of his responsibilities as God's chosen upon Earth. The procession continued, Maleki's every step and utterance governed by divine law.

From the galleries and aisles beyond the nave, the throngs of Constantinople looked on in reverence. Their piety infused this holy place with the spirit of humanity, where the worldly and the supernal, finite and infinite, met and became one. In glorifying God, they accepted their charge within His order, yet they transcended mortality by partaking of the Divine. The words of ritual flowed from Maleki as if of their own will, imparted to him by tongues of flame....

Take the blood.

Blinding light again, consuming the glow of lantern and taper, flaring to celestial nimbus, drawing in the chants of laymen and the shuffle of ecclesiastical feet across marble. Fire and hunger consumed all....

...Then receded again, leaving a torch crackling in its wall bracket by the door of a much smaller chamber. Two sharp raps against the thick wood of the door interrupted Maleki's vespers. Distractedly he finished his prayer, rose from before the small altar in his villa.

"Enter."

Hectorius stepped inside, bowed deferentially, his polished helm gleaming in the torchlight. Both his hands gripped the shaft of the spear before him, its butt planted against stone floor. The furrows of his callused fingers, at ease upon spear or the sword at his side, were so deep as to cast shadows. "Your Holiness," he said, "Her Eminence, the Empress and Regent, requests your presence."

Maleki placed a hand on the captain's shoulder and nodded. The message, they both knew, was less request than summons. No doubt the Emperor Michael had been visited by unpleasant dreams and wished the solace of the holy father, and any of the boy's commands would be relayed through the Empress Theodora's men and subject to her approval. For the time being, her intervention was unavoidable, but such would not always be the case. Once young Michael III came of age and ruled in his own right, the empress would be relegated to the role of advisor, one among many. Perhaps she would finish her days in a nunnery, by choice or otherwise. Maleki, meanwhile, would undoubtedly retain the emperor's confidence.

Should he live so long, Maleki thought. There was little enough chance, the bishop realized, that Theodora would have her own son murdered, but Maleki distrusted less the empress than her eunuch councilor Theoctistus. And there were darker shadows lurking about the fringes of the imperial household—one of whom had already expedited Maleki's meteoric rise through the clergy and gaining of the emperor's ear. Indeed, the imperial purple was a thin veneer barely concealing a more profound blackness beneath, of which Maleki had seen only little. *Yet I remain my own man*, the bishop thought, *and God's servant*.

As for tonight's summons, there was no real choice in the matter. "Well," said Maleki with a caustic smile, "the empress's request is my command."

Outside, he and Hectorius were joined by half a dozen more guards, hardened veterans of many battles against the Slavs and Bulgars, each man hand-picked by the captain. They were loyal to him, incorruptible, and among the most capable warriors of the empire. Three led the way for Maleki and Hectorius, the others taking up the rear as the small assemblage worked its way up the First Hill of Constantinople. As the crow flies, the villa was less than a mile from the residence of the newly enthroned Michael III. The intervening distance, however, was a patchwork maze of gardens and halls, baths, fountains, and churches, all technically part of the royal Great Palace. The sprawling collection of structures had been erected haphazardly over the centuries by preceding emperors, each wanting a testament to his greatness and largesse preserved for posterity. The origin of the various villas and baths and statues stretched back into antiquity, a tangible reminder of the history of the New Rome and its far-flung empire. Each successive emperor had constructed whatever he desired and wherever he desired it. As a result, there was no central lane through the great confluence of architecture—only winding cobbled paths snaking among marble edifices, joining to the portico of a villa that could be a palace in its own right, then turning sharply away through a garden shaded— or at night shadowed—by meticulously pruned ornamental trees. A visitor could become lost among the splendor and never find his way out. Maleki had lived among the labyrinthine acres of the Great Palace for years, since he had achieved the lofty status of bishop, and still he found himself on occasion needing to stop and take his bearings, or wandering upon a fountain or statue that he had never before seen.

Hectorius's guard showed no hesitation. The report of their boots against the cobbles echoed smartly in step as they traversed a narrow corridor between two buildings. From the soldiers' torches, the smell of pitch was distinct in the confines. The flames cast gigantic shadows on the walls to either side. At the end of the alleyway they passed through an arched gate. The path continued up the hill across a broad garden. Almost at once, the footsteps were swallowed by the infinite night, and the tiny oasis of torchlight seemed hemmed in on all sides by barely seen shrubbery and ponds, indistinct statuary poised upon the border between light and dark. With a trick of the hill's slope, the city might not even have existed, replaced instead by wild greenery.

Away from the buildings and the unfriendly ears they might conceal, Maleki spoke to Hectorius: "Did you see her, then—the empress?"

"No. The eunuch."

The dreams must have been especially frightening tonight, Maleki thought, *and the boy inconsolable*. Theoctistus generally strove more ardently than did his patron the Empress-Regent to limit Maleki's access to Michael, so if the eunuch was the intermediary tonight and still Maleki was summoned, the emperor must be distraught indeed and demanding to see *Bisop Mab-i-ki*, as the youngster called Maleki. *He is emperor, but he is still a child*, Maleki thought, *and how that must gall his mother and her eunuch, that they can't disregard the boy's every childish whimsy*. A difficult task it must be to raise an emperor. Maleki much preferred his own role as confessor and spiritual guide. It was as he contemplated the privilege and responsibility of his position that he noticed the absence of the torches behind him.

Hectorius and the fore guards must have noticed at the same time, for they all turned to look back at the same instant. Suddenly the garden was confusion—confusion and darkness.

The rear guards were gone, and as Maleki whirled back around, the remaining warriors were struggling with dark figures. Torches, dropped or knocked to the ground, were snuffed, smothered by black, snake-like tendrils that Maleki could make no sense of.

The struggle was short-lived. Hectorius stood, sword drawn, at Maleki's side, but the other guards lay dead, throats slit, hearts pierced. In the abrupt absence of torchlight, even the moon and stars seemed darkened, far away and obscured. Maleki thought to run, but he sensed the dark figures all around him, slowly drawing closer, a black net tightening. He felt, too, Hectorius's tension beside him, sword ready to strike, waiting only for a target to step close enough.

And then, as if a portion of the smothering night had parted like the Red Sea, an unmistakable form took shape amidst the darkness.

"Magnus?" Maleki was certain of the identity of his own mysterious patron, but could not comprehend the bloodshed surrounding them. Magnus's ornate robes of the Church hid neither his obesity nor his age. Beneath his peppered beard and mustache, his mouth was twisted into a sneer, and the loose folds of flesh that were his cheeks nearly engulfed his eyes.

"What is the meaning of this?" Hectorius barked, his voice thick and raw with anger at the deaths of his men.

Maleki touched his shoulder to stay the captain's sword. *There is some mistake*, Maleki tried to reason to himself. *I am Magnus's man. He has set me where I am.*

But Magnus only laughed at the captain's rage and the bishop's confusion. "Lay down your sword," the dark prelate commanded.

—And, to Maleki's shock, Hectorius obeyed.

"Th-this will be made right," Maleki stammered, trying to assure his captain and friend.

But as soon as sword touched stone, the dark figures rushed in. One slipped a garrote around Hectorius's neck, and as the captain struggled for breath another shadow warrior ran him through. The point of the blade was suddenly in Maleki's face, protruding from Hectorius's chest, the hilt pressed close to his arching back.

"Father in Heaven..." Maleki's words were choked off by the bile rising in his throat. Not even the pounding of his pulse in his ears could drown out Magnus's laughter. And then darkness...

Not light roused him this time—but pain. His feet and ankles throbbing, and his shoulders from the strange angle of his arms dangling above his head... *below* his head. He was hanging upside down. In darkness. Opening his eyes, he saw spots of color, phantasms of his own mind heavy with blood and fear. His mouth was dry, so dry that his words, when he finally uttered them, scarcely sounded. "Father, have mercy on this sinner."

"You might pray to me," spoke Magnus.

Maleki strained his eyes but could see nothing in the darkness. With his frantic effort, the colors quickened their frenzied dance. "Magnus, why do you...? I am your loyal servant."

"Loyal, eh? And obedient, no doubt."

The accusation in his patron's tone confused Maleki further. Fearful tears welled in his eyes. "I have done all that you have asked of me."

"If you are free of guilt," Magnus said harshly, "then God will free you. It is only rope that holds you. Not so difficult for our Lord and Savior. I'm not asking you to roll away a boulder and ascend into Heaven, or even to turn water into wine."

"Magnus, I... I don't understand."

"Free yourself, damn you!" Magnus shouted, suddenly furious. But an instant later his voice was calm again and quiet, and much closer: "...If you are so free of sin in this matter."

This matter? Maleki's mind was racing, but he was too frightened to form coherent thoughts. He imagined in the darkness Magnus drawing closer. Maleki saw again the garrote around Hectorius's throat, the captain's bulging eyes, the sword erupting from his chest. The peace of the imperial garden had been transformed into a bloodbath.

"And you are the gardener," Maleki muttered, unable to hold back the beginnings of hysterical laughter. Reason and sanity had no place in this darkness. He felt Magnus drawing closer still—through darkness, through ultimate oblivion—and Maleki knew with certainty what he had known all along about his patron but had refused to believe. "You are of the devil."

Laughter again now, quiet and rumbling like large stones grating against one another. "And your soul is mine," Magnus whispered, so close that the whiskers of his bearded jowls brushed against Maleki's cheek. The monster's words were rank with the scent of raw meat. Of blood. "I gave to you the emperor's ear," he said, now the magnanimous teacher disappointed with a pupil, "and you repay me with treachery."

Maleki could make no sense of the words, but menace radiated from his patron—the prelate who had appeared to Maleki the priest in darkness and secured for him advancement through the ecclesiastical orders. Fear took hold again, and Maleki struggled. His legs tingled and burned. In his frantic thrashing his fingertips brushed against the stone floor, tantalizingly near but too far to afford leverage. *Only rope*, Magnus had said. Cords binding the prisoner's ankles. But Maleki was no athlete trained for the Hippodrome to race chariots or horses. He was but a bishop, a priest who had given himself over to the devil.

"So you would rather flee than face the truth," Magnus said. "Your sin betrays you. The charge—"

"*What charge?*" Maleki screamed. "You are insane! Insane and evil! My sin is consorting with the devil. But all I wished was to do God's work."

"I see how it is."

"You see nothing in the darkness!" Maleki snapped, fearful and angry. "Magnus, cut me down. This is madness! Magnus…" His voice faltered. "I… I beg of you…."

"You are so pious and holy," said Magnus, stern, lecturing, "that by accepting access to the emperor, you were doing the empire a favor. Hagia Sophia would surely collapse in ruin were the world denied your wisdom."

Maleki screamed, rejecting this devil that twisted his words. He thrashed against his bonds until he choked upon his own fevered tears. "I sought to do God's work!" Maleki sobbed. "God's work…"

"And when I told you to support the Iconoclasts?"

The words sparked something within Maleki—a sliver of lucidity, faint hope that a reason did exist for Magnus's sudden enmity. "I supported them! I preached against the veneration of icons, spoke out against it! Not until the battle was lost did I relent, when the council ruled—"

"You defended the monastics and their common cause with the rabble!" Magnus shouted. "I will hear no more lies!"

Maleki recoiled from the rebuke, swaying in the void. His mind was racing, but he could not think straight for fear and panic. Words tumbled from his mouth in a rush: "I… I… I championed Iconoclasm until the end. I laid icons on the fire myself. I… I made no exceptions for the monastics. There were some…

yes, there were some who would have confiscated all the property of the monasteries, used the icons as an excuse to plunder the brotherhoods. That I spoke out against, for it was not—"

"And so you admit your guilt," Magnus said with a ring of finality, but no triumph. He sounded weary, almost distraught that a protégé of his should turn from the appointed path.

Maleki heard the judgment in those words— judgment that would have been rendered no matter what he had said. The realization drained away his strength. He sagged, dead weight against his bonds. "I did not betray you… did not betray… did not betray," he began to mutter over and over, surrendering again to the release of madness. Tears ran freely over his forehead and into his hair.

"You are correct that the fight against icons is a lost battle," Magnus said, "but we will use that to our advantage. We will raise Michael above all other Cainites."

Cainites. The term confused Maleki further, yet he recognized the name connected to it. "He is just a boy, you foul demon," Maleki hissed, venting his newfound loathing for this inhuman creature that would wrongly persecute him and threaten a boy as well.

"A boy…?" Magnus laughed—a cruel, mocking noise. "Not the boy-emperor, you mortal fool. The Michael I speak of is above that royal whelp as you are above a flea. But you will know soon enough."

Maleki still strained to make out the form of his tormentor, but the darkness was complete. For a moment there were only the dancing lights before his eyes and the salty smell of his own tears.

"You prayed before for mercy," Magnus said. "Mercy would be a quick death." He laughed again. "Even a slow, torturous death would be a mercy. But mercy is not yours for the asking."

Maleki did not understand. He struggled to bring his faculties to bear on Magnus's seeming contradictions—and so was surprised by the cool touch of metal against his jaw. A blade, drawn across his flesh, slitting his throat from ear to chin. He lashed out frantically but was brought up short by the heaviness of breath in his chest, by the gagging and gurgling that was his struggling for air, by the heavy flow of blood spurting from the wound, covering his face, running along the underside of his jaw, filling his ears.

Magnus had stepped back beyond reach, but he laughed nervously now, like a young lover deranged by lust, barely able to control himself. Maleki clutched his hands to his throat, trying to staunch the flow, but blood pulsed forcefully through his fingers. Like the tide it poured through, and with it he felt his strength draining away for good.

Our Father who art in Heaven, he began to pray silently, trying to calm himself, but the words came to him rushed and frantic. *Hallowed be Thy name.*

"Vasilli," said Magnus from the darkness, "now he is yours."

Thy Kingdom come. Thy will be done.

In the distance, a torch flared to life. A hunched creature crept closer, though Maleki could not see clearly, his eyes filled with blood and swaying as he was, twisting, on the rope that held him suspended above the stone, blood-bathed floor.

On Earth as it is in Heaven.

"Others will learn by your example," Magnus said. "I will not be defied again."

The hunched creature came closer. Maleki caught a glimpse of it as he twisted, a brief look, and suddenly his mind lost hold of the prayer he had uttered hundreds upon hundreds of times. The words eluded him, made slippery by his spilling blood and the sight before him. For an instant he could think only: *There is no God.* For how could God allow such a monstrosity to exist?

The disbelief passed quickly, and Maleki was left with the stark surety of his unworthiness—and judgment looming ever closer.

...Deliver us from evil, he tried to take up the prayer, but those were the only words he could conjure. His lips moved, yet no sound emanated. *Deliver us from evil.* Time stretched out, seconds into minutes into hours. Closer, the creature lumbered. Maleki smelled its fetid presence hovering over him. *Deliver-us-from-evil-deliver-us-from-evil-deliver—*

And then it was upon him. Fangs tearing at his throat, rooting at the laceration, ripping at the wound. Ravenous, lapping at what blood did still flow. Maleki beat at the creature but, from his own weakness or its strength, the fiend ignored him. Distant laughter receded behind rough grunting and slavering—then, slowly, all that subsided, fading to nothing, and there was only the furious and sporadic pounding of Maleki's heart, toiling to circulate in his body what was no longer there. Then that sound, too, was gone.

Sensing the final ebb of life, Maleki gave in to that which he could not resist. He found a deeper sympathy for other words of the Christ: *My God, my God, why have you forsaken me?*

But still anger burned within him: to die like this—*him!*—for no good reason, anonymously, in some hidden dank grotto, when he was so certain that God had more planned for him. Clarity descended upon him amidst the pain and darkness. Fear lost its hold. Very soon God would judge him for whatever sins of pride he had committed, but the demons assailing him, they could no longer terrorize him; neither Magnus nor the grunting, rutting beast at his throat. They had broken his body and stolen his life. What else could they do to him?

Maleki slipped beyond physical sensation as, strand by strand, the tether joining his body and soul frayed. Even in violent death, there was a peace, a euphoric resignation from the mortal coil....

Then fire.

Burning, drawing him back to the world of toil and pain. He was suddenly aware of his tormented body once again, blood flowing over his lips into his mouth. As in the garden so many hours or years or lifetimes ago, peace gave way to churning chaos, to blood. Gone was the fleeting fulfillment he had sensed, replaced by burning, insatiable hunger.

And a voice: *Take the blood, Maleki. Take the blood.*

Magnus? The monstrosity? Or the ravenous hunger itself?

Take the blood.

Maleki felt himself swallowing, his throat somehow healed of his deathwound. He drank down the blood that burned like Greek fire. Yet the hunger grew stronger. More, it wanted. He could not resist it. Greedily he licked at the open vein of the deformed, pox-marked creature that with Magnus had murdered him, and still the hunger grew, took on a strength all its own, filled that place where before had resided Maleki's soul. Quietly he wept, whimpering, knowing truly now the emptiness and desolation of God's forsaken. But that did not stop him from feeding the hunger—and never was it enough.

With each drop of unholy blood that passed his lips, Maleki cursed himself. All that he had lived for was proven a mockery, faith subsumed by ambition. He had entered into a covenant with the devil—knowing and not knowing—and now the covenant was sanctified with his own blood. God was justified in casting him out, rejecting him.

With each swallow, Maleki confirmed his guilt. At one point, he realized that someone had severed the bonds that had held him, but he did not consider flight. Instead he fed, wallowing in blood and filth and darkness with a creature so vile as to rival the vileness taking hold within his own breast. And whereas before physical sensation had fled, now it rushed back with a vengeance. Though the hunger was far from sated, the creature's blood was denied him. Like a tanned hide, his skin began to grow tight. His teeth grew to fangs, so sharp that they dug into his own flesh. He tried to cry out but heard only the snarling of a wild beast. Maleki writhed in mounting agony. He felt wet stone against his face and took to lapping his own blood beside the pathetic creature that was his creator. He lost himself to the blood.

***

Yet still the hunger burned. It burned like the light of day, God's gift of the first day, and that which forevermore was forbidden Maleki.

Forevermore.

The light of day. This was not all that was stolen from him. The Beast taken root in his belly denied Maleki also the true presence of God, for never again would he, unworthy of the cloth, set foot on sanctified ground. His life, and everything of his life, was destroyed, leaving him quivering and sobbing, his body twisted and grotesque.

Nonetheless, human history ran its course. It did not pause in sorrow or farewell. Those who wondered at Maleki's absence grew old, died, and were buried. The waters of the Golden Horn flowed into the Bosporus, and the sun traced its path across the heavens.

Ponderously. Tauntingly slow. Miles above. Unseen but driving the Damned to quiescence. But the Beast did not truly sleep.

Take the blood, Maleki.

Maleki. Malachite. A name and a life taken, a bleak existence left in its place.

He lay crumpled in a heap. There was no room to straighten his legs. Another body lay beneath him, cold, unmoving. That flesh held blood, however slight—unseen, like the setting sun, but Malachite sensed bane and boon alike. Why, then, had he not already fed? Why had he not heeded the hunger that gnawed him from within seeking release? Slowly he reached for the unmoving boy, wrapped spindly fingers about the wrist, so close, and drew it to his mouth.

Take the blood!

But memory was not completely crowded out by hunger. Something of reason remained, and of compassion. It was this boy Malachite sought to save. *My own childe, bless the saints above*, he thought. One childe of three brothers among Malachite's brood of five, and a family of ghouls and mortals who looked to him for guidance.

Within him the Beast raged. It had tasted victory—a coppery, sanguinary taste—but the blood of an entire army would only whet its thirst.

Malachite pushed away the boy's hand. The Beast tore at his dead heart and he reached again, but held back finally. "Michael," Malachite muttered, calling on the name of the founder of the Dream: not the boy-emperor who had grown to a drunkard and died in his bejeweled goblet, but the Cainite of such power and glory that he was like unto the Divine. "Give me strength." Malachite closed his eyes and turned his face from the boy.

I am no animal to devour my young. I am here to save my race, Malachite reminded himself, *not feed upon the weakest of them.* He was here to find Michael and to salvage what he could of that which the Patriarch had engendered. They must pull what remained of the Dream from the wreckage of the city burning above. Remembered purpose gave the Cainite strength and held the Beast at bay—at least for the moment. Malachite opened his eyes, though the cramped tomb afforded him no view. He did not recoil from his childe, but tenderly stroked the sparse, stringy hair of his head. Beside God in His Heaven, the sun inched toward the western horizon.

Chapter Five

Eventually there came scrabbling noises at the bars against the outside of the heavy wooden door. Malachite heard but did not stir. His prayerful attitude was a tenuous balance against the baying Beast. Even when the bars were lifted and the door opened, he maintained his position curled in a heap with the boy.

"Two peas in a pod," Verpus said. Something struck Malachite, something small, and then another. "A gift worthy of the head of a fellow scion family," added the Turk.

Two rats, freshly dead, lay among the two entwined Cainites. Malachite wanted to cast them back at Verpus—instead, he drew them greedily to his mouth, bit into the flesh, and feasted upon the blood of rodents, first one and then the other. Despite the indignity, he sucked at the carcasses until he had extracted the last drops of blood. Verpus and his two clanmates waited impatiently, though it was not long until Malachite was done. He wiped his face and licked his long fingers. Only then did he deign to rise, the boy in his arms, and follow those who would dare hold him captive.

They continued through the cramped honeycomb tunnels for perhaps another hour. The going was rough for Malachite: injured, weak with hunger, crouched awkwardly, and struggling again not to brain his undead childe against the hewn stone walls. He refused even to consider handing the boy over to his captors, who likely could have managed the body more easily between two of them. Not only did Malachite harbor doubts as to the boy's safety in the hands of the treacherous Gangrel, he was determined also to show them as little weakness as absolutely possible. They had watched him reduced to feasting upon rodents. He would not now give them the satisfaction of appealing for mercy or succor—not that they would be willing to lend aid.

When finally Verpus led them from the tunnels, they climbed stairs into an abandoned villa near the Church of St. John in Trullo, on the north slope of the Lycus Vale. Even before the onslaught of the so-called Crusade by which this preeminent Christian city had fallen to barbarous Christian warriors, the number of abandoned buildings throughout had been increasing for many years. Cynics suggested that the New Rome's day had passed, but Malachite had always argued otherwise. The most enduring ocean had its ebb and flow; so too with a city that was to be a center of culture and knowledge in perpetuity. Mortals were such a fragile lot, after all. The odd war or famine or plague might cull their numbers, but they were resilient as well. Afforded the subtle guidance of Michael the Patriarch, the mortals and the city would thrive.

Tonight, however, seeing again the smoke lying over Constantinople and more destruction than he had believed possible, Malachite could not frame the argument so assuredly, not even to himself. A fog hovered over him, a lingering haze, a pall cast by the dreams visited upon him that day. After so many years, he had nearly forgotten the glory of Hagia Sophia bathed in sunlight, forgotten too the terror of that final night of mortality, forgotten his own pride and mighty ambitions, and the vast depths to which they had been laid low. There was a difference, though, and one that he chided himself he must keep in mind. His own plans, though lofty in his own mind and ultimately directed toward service to God, had sprung from the mind and heart of mortal man, who was little more than dust.

How much greater was this endeavor, this Dream of angelic Michael, most enlightened of Cainites?

Such thoughts rattled like crossed steel against the reality of Malachite's current predicament. *In chains.* Verpus had said that the baron wanted him brought in chains. Impossible. The Nosferatu might as well have been shackled as they marched onward, the boy in his arms as unresponsive as he had been most of the recent nights. Despite Malachite's burden, Verpus set a brisk pace. Only once did they pause, and then not to rest but to keep out of sight from a passing band of mounted knights. Verpus's companions seemed poised to leap to the attack, but the leader forestalled them with a silent gesture, and the Cainites held their position until the knights were gone. Malachite considered making a sound, giving his captors away—what loyalty did he owe these treacherous ruffians?—but after last night's attack on the hospital, he was loathe to take his chances with the Latin knights, even for the opportunity to slip away during a bloody melee.

The party of Cainites continued up the rough and rocky slope. At the bottom far behind them, the Lycus River crossed from the Walls of Theodosius II to the west and ran beneath the Walls of Constantine to the east. Ahead, along the northernmost edge of the city, rose an ancient castle, the Citadel of Petrion. Was it possible, Malachite wondered, that Verpus spoke the truth, that they were in fact taking him to the baron? The citadel had long been abandoned by the mortal defenders of Constantinople, the city and its walls having spread over time up river. Baron Thomas and his Gangrel had appropriated the castle for their own. Based there, they had enforced Cainite Law, as set forth in the Codex of Legacies, throughout the city—excepting the Latin Quarter. That portion of the city practically had been given over by the Trinity families to the Venetian vampire Narses—and later to his creature, Bishop Alfonzo—and the Latin Cainites, a decision to which Thomas had not taken kindly.

The citadel was pressed against the city walls, which comprised its riverward defenses. Beyond those walls lay the Golden Horn itself. Once merely the Horn, the river had been named Golden, not by a romantic poet basking in the glory of sunset, but by the merchants who had accumulated fortunes many times over, buying and selling their wares along the bustling wharves. The citadel's inland walls loomed ever taller as Malachite climbed. Six towers rose from the crenellated line of the walls, though in truth the battlements and towers had seen better nights. In places, the stone had crumbled away, and clinging vines had taken hold, some grown thick enough perhaps to serve as scaling ladders. To mortal eyes, the citadel appeared an abandoned husk, well past its prime, but Malachite spied the red gleam of eyes atop the walls, measuring his approach.

It was interesting, he thought, that Verpus had brought him to the citadel thus, aboveground to the front gate, despite the risk of roving Latin crusaders. *Do the Gangrel think I am unaware of the underground passages leading into the heart of Petrion itself?* Malachite scoffed, loudly enough to draw Verpus's threatening gaze. *I'd wager I know more ways in and out of their own citadel than they do.* For Malachite and his kin were ever vigilant in such matters. If not for the sake of secrecy, perhaps they led him this way for reasons of security, he decided. *Perhaps they have closed off the tunnels, so that they might spare fewer guards and man the walls against the Latins.*

Whatever the reason, Verpus led him to the central gate. Aged and seemingly decrepit, the large door swung open. Malachite suspected that it remained solid and strong. They passed through the entry tunnel lined with murder holes for arrows and boiling oil and into the main courtyard, where they did not tarry. Crossing the broken flagstones, Malachite felt the eyes from the walls and towers marking his progress. How many fierce Gangrel warriors manned the defenses? he wondered. These Cainites had long been his allies and made common cause with his family, yet tonight they looked on him as enemy.

It is the enemy who has breached the walls of our city! he thought, his anger again kindled as he neared the end of this forced march.

A lone sentry manned the entrance to the keep, an Anatolian by his dress, perhaps from Trebizond, or as far as Caesarea or Edessa. The baron had many followers from lands as distant as Egypt on the one hand and Greece and Dalmatia on the other. The Gangrel roamed all that land, though, and only ever a score or so seemed gathered at once in Constantinople. Malachite glanced back toward the walls beyond the courtyard once again. The crusaders obviously had seen no need to scour this corner of the city, when great treasures lay in wait for the taking farther in. But how long would the citadel stand against a concerted attack?

A rough shove from behind reminded Malachite that he was no general arranging defenses, but a prisoner. He crossed the threshold into the keep, not knowing if the view of the night sky he left behind might be his last.

A series of halls and descending stairs soon brought them to a dirty, narrow corridor lined with doors, one of which Verpus opened, indicating that Malachite should enter. This cell was more spacious than his cramped prison of that morning, but a cell nonetheless.

A disheveled bed of straw and rat-nibbled cloth was against one wall, and there Malachite laid the boy, still oblivious to all that had passed since the attack upon the hospital. With the crash of the door closed, only a thin line of lantern light at its base reached into the room. Malachite sat in darkness and listened to one set of footsteps retreating down the corridor.

***

Within the hour, he heard more footsteps, approaching this time, two individuals. Malachite stood and shielded his eyes from the lantern light as the door opened. It was Verpus, carrying the lantern. He hung it on an iron hook on the wall. Alongside the hook, Malachite now saw, were other iron rings, rusted, and from them hung chains and manacles.

Behind Verpus entered Baron Thomas Feroux. He stood half a head shorter than Malachite, yet there was about the Gangrel something of barely restrained violence—more so tonight even than the many times Malachite had seen him in the past. The naked sword in the baron's hand did naught to dispel that notion, nor did the deep scar that ran the length of the right side of his face, from hairline to stubbled jaw, crossing over his eye, which he was fortunate not to have lost. The eyes themselves were remarkable: green and slit like those of the ferocious large cats paraded on occasion at the Hippodrome. Like those cats, and much of the rest of his Gangrel clan, the baron was a hunter, a vicious predator, but unlike the others, his huntsman's form concealed the heart of a scholar. It was this that had brought him and Malachite together.

"So," said the Baron Thomas, tapping the tip of his sword lightly against the stone floor, "he returns home, the prodigal son. Forgive me if we do not slaughter the fatted calf for a feast. Though there has been slaughter aplenty."

"The prodigal son squandered his inheritance," Malachite reminded him. "I took next to nothing with me, and I left in obedience with the wishes of the Patriarch."

The baron's narrow cat's-eye pupils suddenly grew wide, and he rapped his sword tip against the floor, cracking stone. "Speak not to me of *inheritance*! You faithless coward!"

Malachite felt as if he were plunged again into dream and vision—a supposed ally inexplicably turning on him—though he did not flinch at the baron's outburst. Without appearing to do so, he kept careful note of the sword. *This would not be the time for analogy and dialectic*, he decided belatedly. The baron was in no such mood. And Verpus—the Turk stood behind his master, not in contest against him. If treachery were at work, it was by the hands of the Baron Thomas himself. "The last time we stood together," Malachite said in quiet but strong voice, "it was as friends."

"It is as you say," said the baron, again conversational, his fury of a moment before gone—for Malachite, though, not forgotten. "But much has changed in so few weeks. Calamity has befallen us— disaster more voracious than locusts, more destructive than earthquake. Or had you not noticed?"

"I noticed. And I have wept tears of blood that a city of such magnificence should be laid low. As of yet, I have seen but little—"

"You have seen *nothing*!" the baron shouted, the sinews of his hands and wrists straining, so tightly did he grip his sword. "You have seen nothing, or you would have given yourself to the dawn for having deserted us! Not that the destruction of a coward and a traitor would atone for much, you leprous turncoat! I should have known better than to have depended on a gaggle of diseased—"

"There are lepers among my kin," Malachite said tersely, "each of them a virtuous soul, and I will hear no one speak otherwise of them. Not even you, baron."

The baron's pupils flared wide indeed, and Verpus started forward. Malachite, even if he were strong and well fed, which he was not, would have dreaded fighting either one of these Cainites, much less the pair together. For a moment, all seemed lost, but suddenly the baron jerked to a halt. He raised his face to the ceiling and closed his eyes. Verpus held his ground.

See how close he is to the Beast, damnable fool! Malachite cursed himself. *Curb your pride and your haughty tongue, or he'll raise your head on a pike above the citadel walls at sunrise!*

But while Malachite, outnumbered, injured, and weak from lack of blood, stood poised to receive as best he could whatever attack the Gangrel offered, the baron maintained his assumed stance: face upturned, eyes closed as he focused on a fierce internal struggle, fingers gripped about the hilt of the down-turned sword before him. He stood like that for what seemed forever, grimacing, hands beginning to lift the sword as if by a will of their own, then stopping. Malachite waited like one of the defeated gladiators in the Coliseum of the Old Rome, awaiting the judgment of the emperor, thumb raised high or turned downward. Verpus watched too. His hostility was plain to see, as was his anger, his embarrassment, that another Cainite should witness his master's battle for control.

The baron's jaws worked as if he were rending flesh from bone. His fangs glistened in the torchlight. His throat convulsed, caught in the throes of a silent scream.

And then it was over. His face eased of its anguished contortions. With trembling hands, he lowered his sword, slowly. Even now he maintained complete control of the blade. The tip clicked lightly against the floor once and then was still. When he opened his eyes, they appeared almost normal, the vertical slits of his pupils wide enough to seem human, but not the full black pits of the wild hunter.

"Forgive me, Malachite," he said at last, voice rasping, the words an effort. "I would not wish for the worthy deeds of all my kin to be discounted should I prove faithless."

He has heard nothing that I have said! Malachite fumed, angry despite his relief that the baron's rage seemed to have subsided.

For the first time, now, the baron noticed the boy lying still upon the straw bed. Malachite instinctively stepped between them as the baron moved closer. For a long moment the two Cainites held each other's gaze—both fierce and proud—and then Malachite stepped aside, a gesture of consent granted rather than acquiescence.

The baron knelt, touched the boy's ash-white face. "What has befallen him?"

"I do not know." *What has befallen all of us, my friend?* Malachite thought. "That is what I must find out."

The baron remained there, silent, kneeling beside the boy, fingers stroking the dead cheek. "It is all destroyed," the baron said at last. "Everything."

A chill gripped Malachite. A premonition flashed before him of his worst dreams realized: the entire city reduced to rubble, looted, burned; the surviving Cainites forced to begin the whole affair anew; Michael's hand guiding the mortals—such erratic agents of the Divine—in the creation of an eternal city. *But it can be done*, Malachite thought, in a feeble attempt to buoy his own spirits. "We will start again," he said.

The baron, still kneeling, stiffened. He turned from the boy, and Malachite saw that the Gangrel's eyes were rimmed with blood tears. He spoke through clenched teeth: "They burned the Church of St. John Studius."

The chill returned. It froze Malachite where he stood.

"They burned the monastery," the baron said, fighting the tremor in his voice. His face twisted again, as if from physical pain, and his words were transformed to guttural snarls. "The library... they burned the library!"

Malachite was too paralyzed by shock to react when the baron raised his sword. Visions of books and ancient scrolls consumed by fire clashed in Malachite's mind with the onrushing doom of his childe. The blade flashed through the air—

—crashing against the far wall, where the baron had flung it.

"Burned!" he shouted once more, then slumped forward, his rage spent but not his sorrow. "Burned," he mouthed, barely audible. "Burned. The knowledge and wisdom of centuries, that which I was sworn to protect. Destroyed. The Dream is destroyed."

His will restored by the sudden fear for his childe, Malachite lurched forward. The baron was leaning over the boy, as if in an attitude of prayer, but not harming him, not feeding. Of the tears welling in the Gangrel's eyes, a single scarlet droplet fell onto the boy's pale forehead.

The Dream is destroyed. Malachite felt the anguish in those words. The baron had pledged himself and his scion family to safeguard the Library of the Forgotten, that depository of ancient wisdom and esoteric texts gathered together by the Obertus Tzimisce at St. John Studius. The crusaders, then, had not been satisfied with secular pillage. They had burned the church, the library. *And they claim the mantle of Christ!* Malachite thought. Righteous indignation kindled strength in him. He stood more resolute in the face of the baron's despair than when confronted by his own.

"The Dream is not so fragile as all that," Malachite said.

The baron whirled around, with feline speed and grace was on his feet, pressing close to Malachite. The feline eyes were wide and black, the hunter prepared to spring. The baron hissed, fangs bared. Malachite held perfectly still. Unwittingly, he had stepped to the brink of violence with this, his old compatriot—and violence, here, in his state and with these Gangrel, could have only one end.

"Then it was for nothing," the baron snarled, "that we conspired to remove tomes from the library and smuggle them out of the city to safer places?"

"No, not for nothing," said Malachite, careful with his words lest they topple him into the abyss. "Do you not remember that I was there with you from the beginning? Whose people hid the bundles in the old disused cisterns until your followers could take them beyond the walls? It was not idleness that led me to join the New Trinity with you and the Lexor Brujah. We all saw the danger—that the city was not as strong as it should be, that the self-absorption and pettiness of our kind weakened it—and we all saw that the knowledge housed in the library would survive more readily elsewhere if the worst befell the city." Malachite stepped back from the baron. The Nosferatu felt again the weight of the destruction he had witnessed—and now he knew that the Latins had not spared the churches. If St. John Studius was burned, what then of the others, what of Hagia Sophia, crown jewel of all sacred places on Earth?

Is he right, then? Malachite wondered. Was the Dream destroyed like so many leatherbound tomes consumed by fire, like stone walls thrown to the ground? The boy had put it differently, if no less bleakly: *The Dream is dead.*

Malachite shook his head. *The boy is ill, delirious. And the baron is little better.* The need to find Michael, to reach through his madness of recent years, gripped Malachite with renewed urgency. *If I can reach him, he will set things right. The Dream needn't die!*

Yet here was the Baron Feroux, who must first be dealt with: cajoled, or appeased, persuaded, outwitted.

"None of us thought it would happen so soon," Malachite said in earnest. "We thought we would have centuries, not just a few short years. Maybe even the city could be restored to its rightful glory, and our precautions proven unnecessary. But that the New Rome should fall so soon…"

"And you so conveniently gone!" The baron stalked across the chamber and retrieved his cast-off sword.

"I have told you…!" Malachite checked his anger. To challenge the baron would be to fling himself onto that sword—and though he might not in the end be able to save himself or the boy, he had to try to find Michael and plead with the Patriarch not to abandon the Dream. So Malachite denied the words that came most readily to his tongue: *I have betrayed no one, you fool!* Instead, he spoke evenly, in measured tones: "Thomas, before you judge me, will you hear me out?

For all that our endeavor and the library meant to you, will you listen?"

Baron Thomas glared. Slowly the wide hunter eyes narrowed, the vertical slits less crazed. He sheathed his sword. "Speak then." Behind him, ever poised to leap to the attack, Verpus waited.

"It is not as you seem to think," Malachite said. He was angry still, but with the immediate danger past, his strength drained away. The injuries the Gangrel pack had inflicted pained him: shoulder, arm, neck and head, leg, ankle. Hunger gnawed at him from within. He took only a moment to collect himself—for the baron was not in a patient mood—checking on the boy, folding the small hands across his chest, posed like the carving atop a sarcophagus.

"Many weeks have passed," Malachite began, "since Michael called me to him. You have experienced it, I know. There is no messenger from the Patriarch, no parchment summons, but a quiet voice… here." He pressed a hand against his chest. "Like whispers from the tongue of an angel, speaking to your heart… as if he knows your wishes and fears better than you know them yourself. I was surprised. Michael had grown so remote for some time. He had long since ceded night-to-night authority over his family to Petronius. I had not seen him, Michael, the Patriarch, for… over a year it was." Malachite paused to reckon the interval, but he still felt keenly each night of the separation; he remembered it as a different type of hunger, one more profound and sorrowful than his insufferable longing for blood. For it was Michael had set Malachite free from eternal madness after Magnus's treachery; it was Michael had redeemed Malachite from damnation and showed him the Dream.

"I went to him at once. He was in his sanctum beneath Hagia Sophia, where he had taken to spending so many nights—in prayer, resting, lost to madness? I don't know. But that night…"

Malachite groped for words that could encapsulate the ineffable glory of the Patriarch. "There was no light in his chamber, no torch or lantern—only that which emanated from him. It shone as if an inner sun, and looking upon him was like a mortal staring at the sun. I could do naught but avert my eyes. But you have stood in his presence, Thomas. You know. You know how his body glistens like the most brilliant stained-glass masterpiece. Michael, the Archangel, the Sword of God, brilliant and terrible and beautiful. To be in his presence is to feel the warmth of the sun upon your face; it is to…" He stopped, eyes closed, willing the memory of radiant glory to fade. These were thoughts that Malachite had never before confided—not to anyone. His weakness and hunger had gone to his head, had sapped his discipline. Yet to open his heart was to hand a deadly weapon to the recipient of the tidings, and the baron had far from earned such confidence.

"I went to him," Malachite continued more guardedly. "He did not speak, but his message to me was clear." Malachite again placed hand to breast, remembering the sadness he had sensed in Michael on that occasion, the deep regret. "He wanted me to leave, to flee. He wanted me to lead my family from the city. I did not understand. He must have know the city would… I could not… I could not do other than obey. Do you doubt this, Thomas? I obeyed the Patriarch. I gathered together my childer and my followers—and, yes, what of the secreted books from the library that we could manage—and took them away, as Michael wished. For I felt that he knew of our industriousness, baron. I never spoke a word of the library, yet I doubt there was a part of my heart that he did not know. He must have known... if he knew that the city would fall..."

Mention of the library, though, renewed the baron's agitation. His hands moved to his sword hilt, and his eyes grew suddenly black and dangerous. "You suggest that he knew the city would be attacked, and he did not lift a hand to save it, that he let the library burn? You seek to share your treachery with the Patriarch! You are a liar as well as coward and traitor!"

"His madness!" Malachite insisted angrily. "You have seen it as well as I. Perhaps this world can no longer contain all that he has become. Come with me, Thomas. Come with me to find him. If we can reach through his madness and save the city—"

"He is destroyed," said the baron.

Malachite staggered backward, steadied himself against the wall. For a third time, his hand clutched at his heart. "This is insanity," Malachite whispered. "It is you who lies."

"He is destroyed. At whose hand," the baron shrugged, "I do not know. But what matter does it make? The Latins have looted the palaces, the churches. What they do not take they burn or, worse, defile. They placed a harlot upon the altar in Hagia Sophia. Some say that they rutted with the whore right there, while they ate and drank of the sacraments. A whore! Would Michael have allowed that, I ask you? Could that ever have happened were he not destroyed?"

Malachite did not answer, could not. Nor could he feel the cold strength of the wall at his fingertips—only the unforgiving stone beneath his knees as he crashed to the floor. The baron ranted on. Malachite could no longer make out the words. Michael destroyed, blessed Hagia Sophia defiled... "Lies... lies," said Malachite's voice from somewhere far away from him.

But the end is not yet upon us. Who had said that? The woman, the Jew. She was wrong, could not have been more wrong. *The end washed over us like a flood, and none of us realized we were drowning. None of us knew,* Malachite thought.

He slumped against the wall, his hand brushing against the foot of the inert boy. Malachite stared at him in horror. *He knew.* It was the boy's gift: to see what could not be seen, to know what could not be known. *Damn him! Damn him for being right! Damn him for knowing!* A bottomless gulf opened beneath Malachite; crushing tentacles reached for him, coils of truth from which he could not defend himself. The confining walls of the cell might as well never have existed. The solid earth above and beneath him was fleeting and ephemeral, reduced to vapor in the void. Perhaps the sun had ceased its motion about the world. And what matter did it make?

There is naught but blood! roared the Beast within Malachite. *Blood!*

All that he had striven for since Michael had tended Malachite's horrendous body and broken mind—destroyed, dead.

The Dream is dead.

Lies... lies... lies....

Blood! Naught but blood!

The Beast was growing stronger, twisting the truth to its own ends. *Why not fling yourself over the precipice into the abyss? Is that not preferable to the void? If the boy and Baron Thomas tell the truth, then all you believe and love is ash, emptiness. If the baron lies... then take his blood!*

It made a certain sense. What could be the harm? Though the baron would doubtless prevail, a final lashing out would put an end to the pointless drifting of existence beyond both Patriarch and Dream. And if the failing Nosferatu somehow managed to best his captors…

Blood! Blood! The Beast screamed for it.

Malachite felt his fingers balled into bony fists. He lacked the strength to call talons that would rend flesh. He must pound until he met his doom.

Blood!

But a niggling of doubt—of denial—seized an unraveling thread of hope and held him tottering on the brink. *What if the baron does lie?* Malachite thought desperately. *And the boy is wrong? I must be certain!*

The Beast roared boiling rage. *You are certain! Take the blood!*

A hand clutching at Malachite's sleeve, twisting tired fabric and dead, brittle skin as well. He started to launch himself at the baron, to embrace the end—but the fingers digging into Malachite's arm were not those of the baron, nor of Verpus the Turk. The baron still ranted, hurling abuse at Malachite and Latins and scheming Ventrue. The Gangrel's curses crashed like surf against the shore. They pulled Malachite back from the void, banished the tentacles, which withdrew beyond the periphery of certain truth. The hand on Malachite's arm held him back from the abyss, from throwing himself into the attack and self-destruction. But if the hand belonged to neither of the Gangrel…?

Take the blood! the Beast screamed. *It matters not whose! Blood is blood!*

The boy. The hand was that of the boy. Malachite staggered back from the brink. In rapid succession, he became aware again of the here and the now: the boy's gaping eyes; stone transfixing the horizons of the immediate world; flickering lantern light powerless, try as it might, to alter reality, moment to moment.

The Beast, after a final bellow, furious, mad with lust, retreated gracelessly to the cave that was its own darkness. Malachite clasped his hands to either side of the boy's face, showered his childe with despairing kisses.

The boy's wide eyes flitted heavenward, rolled up into his head. He spoke: "Even here we are under attack."

The words sliced through Baron Thomas's ranting, which ceased at once. Silence. Then a moment later from the hallway sounded footsteps, long strides, hurried. One of the baron's men rushed into the cell.

"What is it?" The venom in the baron's words disputed the boy's claim.

"The fore defenses are assaulted," the man said. "A patrol of the crusaders has summoned reinforcements."

The shadows in the cell cast the baron's scar in sharp relief. He glared at the boy and at Malachite. Malachite tried to gauge the eyes: Were these the eyes of a noble, a scholar and a leader of men; or of the Beast? A permutation of that question was likely playing out in Baron Thomas's mind as he decided what course to follow.

"Engage them," he said. "But lead them away from the citadel."

"We attempted that already, baron. They would not follow. They are intent on taking the walls."

A brief tremor took hold of the baron, an enraged grimace creasing his scar. Eyes and nostrils flared. From the floor, Malachite looked up at the sword, contemplated the blow that might fall at any moment—

And then the baron's palsy passed. He was again in control, steady. "Keep a guard at the door. We will deal with the crusaders first, and then with traitors." The decision made, the baron turned on his heels and stalked from the room with the force of a thunderhead sweeping across the Bosporus. His two sworn men followed in his wake, Verpus taking the lantern.

As the door crashed shut and plunged the cell back into darkness, the light seemed to linger on the eyes of the boy: white, fluttering as if with seizure. Malachite reached for him, clutched at the frail body with bulbous-knuckled fingers, and in the darkness embraced him.

Chapter Six

Captivity and indignation lay less heavily on Malachite than did despair, there in the darkness of the cell. What use was offense at indignity and maltreatment when the world was shaken to its foundations?

Michael destroyed.

And to think that Malachite had been perturbed by his rough handling from the Gangrel. What difference was any of it? So the baron had proved himself faithless—

No, Malachite stopped himself. *Thomas is suffering his own torment.* The baron had mistaken the means for the end, and now the objects of his obsession were no more. *But the books were not the Dream. Can he not see that?* Malachite reflected for a moment on his current predicament, and his question answered itself: *Apparently not.*

Yes, the loss of the Library of the Forgotten was a tremendous blow, an unconscionable disaster, but the library was but one manifestation of the Dream, not the Dream itself. All of the lore that the Cainites had been able to gather over hundreds of years—philosophy, metaphysics, history, theology, prophecy—and most of it lost.

We did not begin soon enough, Malachite lamented. That which had made the library so valuable, such an immense concentration of knowledge, also rendered it vulnerable. With the tacit approval of some of those who kept the library—perhaps Gesu himself—Malachite and the baron had acted to safeguard the stores of learning, but they had removed no more than several hundred volumes. Malachite did not know where all of the books were taken after being spirited out of the city by the Gangrel. That was not the most important detail, though. It was enough that the tomes were scattered, sent to different places far from the burning and looting.

We should have saved so much more. If only there had been time.... But events as dictated by mortals moved ahead with untidy haste. The crusaders were in the city now. There was no more time, not for the library. And for the Dream? If Michael truly was destroyed?

It is not so, Malachite thought determinedly. *Baron Thomas is wrong. Rumors, hearsay, ravings of the desperate and frightened.*

And the boy, too, was wrong? Malachite could not believe otherwise. The boy, whose sight, a gift from God, had preceded and survived his Embrace into eternal night—he was wrong. He knew that Cainites lurked among those who attacked the hospital. He knew that the citadel, as well, was under attack. *Acute hearing, or a penetrating sense of smell,* Malachite told himself. Those were not the same thing as knowing the ultimate destiny of the Dream. Not the same thing at all.

The boy was silent again, motionless. Malachite held the body against him. His own injuries were but a dull ache now, the pain of them crowded aside by the trauma of widespread destruction, of friends turned foe by madness, of the suggestion that the Patriarch was no more. Lurking beneath the anguish, hunger waited. The Beast bided its time.

***

The noise beyond the door seemed at first the stuff of a waking dream, delusion. No footsteps announced the approach of interrogator or torturer. Instead there was the sudden ringing of steel against steel, savage growls of strife, struggle for lifeblood—

Awash in brittle hunger and grief, Malachite could not place the sounds. Darkness and despair skewed his reckoning of time. It rushed past him, a great confused torrent: Hectorius's guard ambushed; murderous riots throughout the Latin Quarter; shouted accusations at the Council of Trinity Families; a lumber yard *cum* hospital set aflame; avenging wolves streaking along the tunnels, leaping, attacking…? None of it fit.

Shadows danced through the thin line of light beneath the door, their motions accompanied by savage screams of rage, defiance, pain. The scent of blood caught Malachite's notice, set his nose to twitching, and stirred the prowling of the Beast deep within him.

Then silence.

Hushed voices did not quite escape his hearing. The jarring rattle of keys, quickly muffled. Metal against metal, no combat this time, but the slow scraping of a turning key, a bolt sliding ponderously free.

Malachite shielded his eyes against the light as the door opened. Dark shapes approaching, reaching for him.

"Can you stand?"

He resisted briefly as they took the boy from him, but found he hadn't the strength to hold on.

"Here," said the same voice, abrupt but concerned, gravelly, as if from inconstant use.

They held out Malachite's hands cupped together, poured something into them—

He fell upon the blood at once, the scent instantly vanquishing any other sentiment or concern. Greedily, he licked his palms and fingers, heard himself grunting like a dog at carrion. Human blood. Another quick splash elicited groans of ecstasy. Even so, his tongue felt like ancient parchment. He grabbed the wrists of the figure kneeling before him, but the other was too strong and resisted. Malachite caught a glimpse of a heavy blood-laden bladder handed back to another figure.

"Soon," Malachite's benefactor assured him. "We do not know for certain what we have unleashed on the citadel or how much time we have. Come."

Unseen hands helped him to his feet, ushered him out of the cell. The hallway beyond was littered with bodies. Undead knights wrapped their fallen brothers in torn cloaks and whisked them away. One pair brushed dust into a sack and collected seemingly discarded accoutrements: hauberk, gauntlets, sword. Lying almost forgotten among the bustle was a Gangrel sentry, eyes glaring hatred, three wooden stakes protruding from his chest—the attackers had needed several attempts to strike true, and they had paid the price.

"You are strong enough to travel, Malachite?" asked the gravel-voiced knight who had spoken in the cell.

Malachite now saw clearly his face: eyes sunken so deeply in his skull as to be nearly invisible; flat, broad nose; ashen skin marred by open blisters and boils; and a lower jaw recessed so severely as to make indistinguishable chin from neck.

"We must be away from here at once," his rescuer said with restrained urgency. "Are you strong enough?"

Malachite ignored his inner voice, the snarling Beast, which wanted more blood. Always more. He nodded. Another knight, with the boy in his arms, ducked down the tunnel into darkness. Malachite fought back a twinge of panic. He knew these Cainites, trusted the leper knights of St. Ladre more intimately than ever he had his Gangrel allies. The leader of this attack force, he who had given Malachite blood, was called Ignatius. He was a long-serving, faithful follower of Fra' Raymond.

"What of this one?" another Nosferatu knight, equally deformed, asked Ignatius. They both scrutinized the fallen Gangrel, conscious but held immobile by the stake through his heart. Ignatius scowled, looked to Malachite deferentially.

"Leave him be," Malachite said. "If the city is to survive, it will need the strength of the baron. Perhaps he can come to realize that we are not the enemy."

"Very well," said Ignatius. He gestured curtly and the other knight moved off down the corridor. "But at present he knows no such thing. We must go before his warriors return—or the besiegers of the citadel win through and venture this way."

Malachite was beset by questions, but Ignatius was right. Aside from two knights flanking the elders, the other Nosferatu were already gone. Malachite fell into step behind his rescuer. They quickly left behind the cell, the staked Gangrel, and the Citadel of Petrion. They bypassed blocked tunnels—evidence confirming Malachite's suspicion that the Gangrel had attempted to wall themselves in—but there were more hidden ways known to the Nosferatu than any other clan could ever hope to seal. Their route took them beyond the perimeter of the citadel, to the south and then east. Malachite thought they might slacken their hurried pace, but Ignatius showed no such inclination.

We do not know for certain what we have unleashed on the citadel or how much time we have, Ignatius had said. Yet they were away from the citadel now, and still they pressed rapidly ahead. How far away was far enough for an armed war party of Nosferatu? The knights' urgent determination to increase the distance did not bode well.

Malachite saw little choice but to follow their example. He had been away from his home of centuries for but a few weeks, and all had changed. Nothing was as he had left it. The order that had long been established—the order that God ordained for his Creation—was in ruin, ashes.

And always there was the hunger. What strength and concentration remained to Malachite, he required to keep the Beast in check.

He gave himself over to his rescuers. He felt naked, so accustomed had he become to holding the boy next to him, yet they had taken the boy. *I trust them*, Malachite thought. They might not technically be part of his scion family, these leper knights whose presence in the city was a little-known secret, but they might as well be. Whereas he and Baron Thomas had shared common purpose—purpose that had been twisted, distorted, turned against him—these Knights of St. Ladre shared with Malachite ties of blood. They had suffered as he had suffered. Many in life had been soldiers of Christ, Templars or Hospitalers of St. John; most, but not all, had become lepers. God had chosen to test them.

We are the clan of Job, selected to suffer pain and disfigurement so that through our steadfastness we might glorify God, Malachite thought, for the agonizing ruination of body and mind induced by the Embrace of their clan made leprosy seem a kindness.

Family or no, they were of Malachite's blood. He staggered onward as a blind man, Ignatius's grip on his sleeve leading him. Stride after stride after stride. The offering of blood sustained him but did not satisfy; the coppery taste in his mouth taunted, called to him like the street merchant's hawker, the butcher, the harlot.

They have more blood but will not give it to me, Malachite thought as he stumbled along the black tunnel, through the darkness he could not penetrate.

Then, panic coupling with his own desperate desire: *The boy... they have taken him to render him down for blood. They would steal what is mine!*

Snarling—so loud that the others must have heard it. Malachite fought it down, willed himself to study the progression of his footsteps shuffling across stone. *I trust them. My blood is their blood.* He told himself that over and again, lest the ravenous, ill-tempered creature within him win out. With every step, it grew in strength, its murderous hunger seeming more and more reasonable. Yet Malachite denied it, drew more tightly its tether.

At some point, he realized that they had passed beyond the Walls of Constantine, those which protected the bulk of the city. *Surely we are far enough from the citadel....* But they continued forward at a relentless, furious pace. He became aware of words spoken in the darkness, clipped tones, sentries and scouting parties reporting to Ignatius, scattering in all directions, reporting back only to scatter again. They buzzed and flitted about like flies to Malachite's clouded awareness. The motions of his legs grew increasingly labored, his forward motion a thing beyond him, separate from him. When finally Malachite's legs failed him altogether, Ignatius lifted him and laid him over one shoulder with care. The flight continued. For innumerable steps, Malachite felt each impact in his chest, as if his very body were a prison, and the prisoner grasping the bars of his ribs, shaking, rattling, bellowing for release, for—

Blood!

Down Malachite delved into the darkness. There were those, he knew, who embraced oblivion as a lover, who did not return for nights or years or centuries. He heard the siren call now, not simply of hunger but of utter exhaustion, unimaginable weariness of the spirit. Such retreat was another stratagem to deny the grasping claws of the Beast, yet there was so much that needed attending to….

Though the details eluded him at present….

There was the boy. Yes, the boy… but he was among friends, among blood kin. Surely they would care for him. Was anything truly so urgent? What harm could come of peaceful respite, of fathomless serenity?

And then…

Something…

Something pulling him back.

Blood scent. The return was not gentle, no gradual floating to the surface. The Beast raged, a wild horse straining madly at its tether, landing a kick at his head that left him crippled, stuttering, nauseated. The creature's screeching obliterated the soothing, rhythmic wash of oblivion.

Dear God, let me rest.

Blood!

He was over no one's shoulder now. Cobbled stone pressed up against him. And a body—radiating warmth and the smothering aroma of blood, heart beating out *pom-pom pom-pom* to the time of shallow, panicked breath. The loosed creature animated him, claimed him, claimed the blood. The tender resilience of flesh gave way before him. Mortal screams, screams of mortality, thick and wet, gushing across his face with arterial splendor. His throat burned as if laid open to the morning sun. He reveled in the agony, in the welling, spilling life. His spirit, engorged, lusted—arched, pressed against the ecstasy, finger nails digging furrows of flesh along his back—achieved fulfillment, fell back spent only briefly before rising again for more.

Pom-pom, pom-pom.

The water of life spat across his face, free-flowing, growing sticky beyond the reach of his tongue. The cries now were devoid of conviction, a shutter clattering in a weak wind, reflex without meaning or hope. They mingled with his own bloated whimpering. The Beast gave a thought to rearing, tearing free of its tether—but, sated, it could find no purchase. It sank into the crimson mire and was lost, finally, to viscous bubbles and silence.

Malachite lay still, ruddy-faced, atop a sprawled corpse. Stirred from indulgent stupor, for an instant he recoiled in horror, fearing the worst: that he had consumed his childe. Then he remembered the beating heart, the mortal frailty, and he looked questioningly—with tired anxiety rather than trepidation—upon the body.

"A captive," said Ignatius, his rasping voice betraying neither triumph nor contempt. "One of the Latin crusaders."

Malachite saw now that the dead Frank was much too large to have been confused for the boy. The corpse's slack muscles were those of a trained warrior, though his hands were bound behind him. Malachite did not try hard to see the savaged throat, the wide-eyed expression of death—a hollow mask that would haunt his daylight hours. To kill a man in combat was one thing. In feeding… it was not necessary, not desirable. *A waste*, he thought. *A tithe to the Beast and its gluttony*.

"You should have stopped me," Malachite said.

"You required sustenance. And he was one of the destroyers." Ignatius's judgment was unequivocal.

One of the destroyers. This one had been taken at looting or defiling, then.

The baron's words haunted Malachite: *They placed a harlot upon the altar in Hagia Sophia*.

Ignatius's attitude was clearly that such a heretic deserved whatever he got—though it was less the crusader's fate and more his own succumbing to the Beast that troubled Malachite. He climbed to his feet, resisting the heady vertigo of so great a feeding. The corpse on the floor was a thing apart, lifeless, a discarded vessel. Malachite did not deign to notice it as it lay in silent accusation.

Ignatius made a shrill chattering noise through his teeth, as might a rat in the sewers. Two leper knights appeared, hoisted the crusader's body between them, and returned to the darkness. His strength and awareness rushing back like a spring flood, Malachite probed their surroundings, eyes piercing the veil of black. The vaulted ceiling of a stone-crafted grotto rose above them, tunnels leading away in the four directions. He and Ignatius stood in an underground basilica, of sorts. Fragments of the divine liturgy cascaded unbidden through Malachite's mind. He cringed, for his piety and faithfulness were beside the point. He was of the Damned, anathema to that which was of God. The holy places and the liturgies practiced within were forbidden to him. Was his participation in the holy rites any less blasphemous than the Latins placing a whore astride the altar of Hagia Sophia?

We are chosen to suffer, exiled from that which we most desire, he thought. *I am Moses, wandering lost in the wilderness… Moses, who saw the Promised Land but never entered into it. Yet Moses was a leader of his people….*

Malachite gazed into the vaulted shadows above him, imagined the glorious light of the sun streaming though stained glass crafted over mortal generations. He took hold of the image, banished it—that which was as dangerous to him as was the Beast.

…And here I wallow in self-pity.

Flush with blood, he felt the warmth as the fire of shame, of condemnation.

No more. Not from this instant onward!

Yet even as he resolved to move ahead, he felt in the back of his mind the chill touch of pernicious uncertainty—collapse of the ordained order—reaching out to take hold of him, to sink poisoned barbs of mourning and angst into his soul.

"I'll not allow it!" he hissed. "I shall not despair." His words grew to fill the silence of the vaulted chamber.

Nearby, Ignatius said nothing.

Does he think I still speak of the crusader? Malachite wondered, studying Fra' Raymond's lieutenant. *He is observant, this one*, Malachite thought. Quickly, he pressed forward, unwilling for the inertia of fatalism to crystallize and paralyze him. "Where is the boy?"

"He is being cared for," said Ignatius, "though there is little enough to do but wait."

Malachite felt a flash of anger, its heat like that of the blood filtering through his dead flesh. "Have your people make a litter and bring him here. I will keep him near." If the boy was to perish, then Malachite at least wanted to be present, and he might yet find some sort of cure for... whatever the ailment was.

Ignatius nodded deferentially. More chattering and, in a moment, the boy was brought. He lay as still as death.

"And we must send word to Fra' Raymond that I have returned," Malachite added.

Ignatius paused, looked away. "Fra' Raymond's exile has ended."

For a moment, Malachite did not comprehend—the words so close to his own thoughts—then the full weight of loss struck him. He steadied himself. Sorrow and fury churned within him until he thought his newfound blood would boil. Control. The very cosmos might rebel against divine order, but he determined to remain master of himself. "How?" he whispered.

"One of the cisterns collapsed." Ignatius seemed to retreat into his dark hood. His words were like a thin mask concealing grief. "The other boy was with him."

Malachite let the news wash over him. Slowly, it filtered through his skin and blood and bones, becoming part of him. *The other boy*, second of the three brothers, of Malachite's five childer. "You are sure it... it was the end for them?" He knew already how useless was the question.

"I am sure. The boy was ill... like the one with you. Fra' Raymond wanted to consult a work removed from the library but still in its hiding place in one of the surplus cisterns. He took the boy with him. He always had the boy with him. While they were there, the cistern collapsed."

Treachery? Malachite wondered.

"The crusaders had already breached the walls and entered the city, but the cave-in was unrelated," Ignatius said, anticipating his fellow's thought. "There was no war damage to the cistern—simply aged masonry."

Simply.... The word stuck in Malachite's throat. *Not treachery. Simply a cruel jest of fate.* Another manifestation of the entropy that had seized the world.

"We dug them out. It seemed likely that we could save them, that with time and blood they would... but Raymond was..." Ignatius faltered for but a second. "...He was... dust."

"And the boy?"

Now Ignatius cocked his head, a quizzical attitude coming over his morose features. "We found the boy, and he seemed unhurt. He was buried, but in a hollow space amidst the rubble, not crushed. For several nights before that he had been…" He paused, searching for the correct description, for an explanation that was beyond him. "He had been sleeping like the truly dead. When we found him, though, and uncovered him, he opened his eyes. I do not know if he understood where he was and what had happened. But he said, 'I would like to have seen the moon rise above Mount Erciyes.'"

"Mount Erciyes?"

"Yes. Likely he was raving."

"Perhaps," Malachite said, though more often than not over the years he had found that it was his own understanding rather than the sanity of the boys lacking when doubt arose. "Mount Erciyes." He had always concerned himself more with Constantinople itself than with the far-flung territory of the empire—these nights sorely diminished from its expanse of preceding centuries—but he believed Mount Erciyes lay many leagues to the east in Anatolia, in the heart of the old land of Cappadocia. "Then what?"

"Then," Ignatius said, "as I lifted the boy from the rubble, he was silent again and crumbled to dust in my arms."

Malachite closed his eyes. *And I did not know!* he thought. *Blood of my blood, and I did not feel his passing.* He looked down at the boy beside him, lifeless. Was such to be his fate?

"So much destruction," Malachite muttered. He felt himself spiraling inward again, drawn by the weariness of spirit that even blood could not lift from him. *I will not give in*, he thought defiantly. He crouched down beside the boy that, for the time being, was still with him. Sire ran his fingers across the scabs and pox marks of the childe's scalp, the delicate neck, frail arms, took solace in the immediacy of the boy, in the fact that he had not fallen away to dust. *Not all is yet destroyed. I will not give in.*

"What then of your order?" Malachite asked, seeking any link, any distraction, that would save him from his personal despair.

"I direct the Knights of St. Ladre," Ignatius said. "Fra' Raymond had sent us out into the city when the attack fell, so that we might give comfort and protection where we were able. We had no hope of turning back the attack. The time was long past for that. We have been leading the crusaders away from innocents when possible; other times herding the mortals out of danger's way. We fight the Latins when odds warrant, but not often. I carry on as I believe Fra' Raymond would have."

"Fra' Raymond would have taken on Baron Thomas?" Malachite asked.

Ignatius seemed briefly disgruntled at this, then regained his stoic bearing. "Even as the city was under attack by the Latins, the Gangrel were assaulting our patrols."

"The baron thinks I am a traitor."

"He thinks we are all traitors," Ignatius said.

"I left the city. I returned after it was in flames," Malachite said, pressing. "You do not find this suspicious?" *Better to know now*, he thought. *If I cannot rely upon blood…*

"Fra' Raymond never doubted you," said Ignatius. "I do not doubt you."

"The Patriarch ordered me away from the city."

"As you say, then."

Malachite felt welcome relief. If Raymond was destroyed, at least he was succeeded by a fellow stalwart. Raymond did not extend the Embrace without careful consideration.

"You saved me from the baron," Malachite said. "How did you come to know that I was in the Citadel of Petrion?"

"One of our scouts followed you from the fire beyond the outer walls."

The hospital. I did not know that we were followed.

"He did not realize who you were, unfortunately. Our problem at first with the Gangrel was that we did not expect them to attack us. We have grown very cautious in approaching Cainites directly. Not until you were waylaid in the tunnels did the scout hear your name and know you. He followed you and the Gangrel, and sent word as soon as he was sure where they were taking you. We came as quickly as we could."

"And the attack on the citadel: a diversion," Malachite said.

Ignatius hesitated. "A dangerous one, and not what I would have chosen if left to my own. We led a patrol of crusaders to the citadel, and then made sure that they came into conflict with the Gangrel." The admission disturbed him.

"And it got out of hand," Malachite surmised.

Ignatius nodded. "The Latins had reinforcements quite close, it turned out. There were Cainites among them."

Malachite remembered his own run-in with the vampiric knights outside the burning hospital.

"I would not have chosen to press the Gangrel so sorely," Ignatius said, "despite their demonstrated ill will toward us. I received reports during our trek here that the battle still raged at the citadel. More and more crusaders were flocking to the tumult. There is a duke among them—of the blood—Guy of Provence. He is now leading the assault."

"I have heard his name," Malachite said.

"He is perhaps the worst of the Latins. He cuts down anyone who strikes his fancy, man, woman, mortal, Cainite—even those of the Latin Quarter, whom others among the crusaders see as potential allies. I tell you that unholy bargains are being made."

"What of the rest of the city, then?" Malachite wanted to know. He had seen too much of smoke rising beyond the battlements. His ignorance of events on the ground tugged at him like a millstone about his neck. "What resistance is there to the invaders?"

"There is no resistance." Ignatius shook his head, dismayed. "It is chaos. Of the mortal rulers, Murzuphlus, who as emperor took the name Alexius V, has fled the city. Of the father and son co-emperors he deposed, feeble, blinded Isaac died of his own after the coup. The son, Alexius IV, was less graceful. He survived several attempts of poisoning, so Murzuphlus had him strangled. The Latins control the city, though they have yet to impose order. Of the crusaders, Baldwin and Boniface are content for their men to loot, supposedly gathering riches to be divided equitably among the faithful. The venerable doge of Venice, Enrico Dandolo, it is he who subtly maneuvers the others, I believe. He likes nothing better than to see the city bleed."

It was as catastrophic as Malachite had imagined. Perhaps worse. No truce, no parley among leaders; instead, destruction, pillage. Constantinople was the richest city upon the face of the Earth. Unrestrained, the barbarians from the West would pry apart every mosaic, scour the gilded domes bare, and carry the wealth of emperors home to their pitiful, grimy dukedoms and baronies.

"There are Cainites among them, as you have said," Malachite suggested. "I have seen some of them. Can not Caius come to some agreement with them, have them use their influence to halt the pillaging?" *And what of Michael?* Malachite wanted to shout. *He could stop all of this! None could stand before him!*

"The mortals are like a plague of locusts," Ignatius said. "Who could stop them now that they are loosed upon us? As for Caius, he has not been seen for many nights. It is whispered that he has fallen. Of the families loyal to him, only the Lexor Brujah might prove of use, but Natalya is missing as well—destroyed or fled the city."

Malachite shook his head violently, as if seized by a spasm or a palsy. "The other families, then!"

"Gesu burned with the library—"

"No!" The cry tore itself from Malachite's cracked lips. *Not Gesu!* The mystic destroyed, childe of the Dracon, himself partner with Michael in creation of the Dream. Gesu, better than any, could perpetuate the spirit of enlightenment if something had happened to Michael—*No!* Malachite stopped himself. *It cannot be that. Michael will set all of this aright.*

"As for Baron Thomas," Ignatius continued his macabre litany, "you have seen that he will not parley with the Latins—no more than he would listen to reason from us. I have heard tell, also, that Magnus was taken in chains to his clanmate, Bishop Alfonzo."

Malachite was too distraught to take more than the slightest satisfaction from that news. Alfonzo had ruled the Latin Quarter as his own fiefdom since the Eighth Council of Trinity Families. He was a beast and a tyrant. Magnus, though also of Lasombra blood, was subservient to Michael, as was Malachite. *It does not surprise me that the Lasombra would devour their own*, Malachite thought. *Magnus forced the Embrace upon me so that I might suffer his wrath throughout eternity*. It was an act that had angered Michael, who had taken

Malachite under his wing. Yet still Magnus had venerated Michael—had led the way, in fact, for a burgeoning cult that exalted the Patriarch. *And did that worship do anything but add to Michael's madness? Good riddance if Magnus is tortured and destroyed. A thousand sunrises would not be justice enough for him.* Malachite recognized the unworthiness of his harsh thoughts, yet he was helpless before them.

"Then there is no one," he said, ticking off the names of the major families in his mind. "They are all destroyed or gone or mad or impotent in matters of state."

Ignatius watched him closely, did not say that which would have sent Malachite spiraling again within himself, searching for peace, for escape, for an end to his weariness: *None but you, Malachite.*

Malachite flinched under the weight of meaningful silence. *Is this, then, why Michael sent me away? So that I might return and save the city? Who else is there?* There was one, he realized. There must be.

"In his madness," Malachite said, "the baron spoke of Michael's destruction."

Silence. Ignatius did not meet his eyes. "It is whispered," spoke the leper knight at last.

"Whispers! Rumors! Lies!" Malachite's words echoed throughout the vaulted darkness so that the world was filled with thousands of lies.

Movement by his feet—the boy stirred, opened his eyes. Malachite's rage grew suddenly chill in his breast. The boy yet survived, yet Malachite knew only fear. He grabbed the boy. Surprised by his own ferocity, Malachite shushed the boy with quiet, frantic words, placed a finger of silence over the boy's lips. "Quiet, my childe. Quiet, now. Save your strength," he half whispered, half hissed, as he stared into the eyes that seemed to say, *Would you call me a liar?*

Do not tell me that I am wrong in this! Malachite entreated silently. *Do not say that he is destroyed! I cannot bear it!*

"You say this thing but you do not know it for certain!" Malachite turned his accusations on Ignatius.

"I have not seen it," said Ignatius, unperturbed. "Nor do I know any who have."

"Then I will hear no more of it."

"As you wish."

Malachite felt a twinge of guilt. *Did not Michael begin his descent into madness by believing only what he wished to believe?* But the Nosferatu was decided on his course.

"Send out messengers," Malachite instructed Ignatius. "Call all your brethren to gather here. Tomorrow when the sun sets, we march to the Patriarch's haven beneath Hagia Sophia. We will seek his counsel and reclaim the Dream."

***

I will find Michael, Malachite thought during the porous hours that, far above, were the province of day. *He will set all of this aright.* As the sun climbed, memory of that first night, long since passed with the youth of his unlife, leached to the surface—that first night in the presence of ineffable glory.

He remembered kneeling at the base of a dais, staring up at an ornate stone sepulcher from below. Bright light emanated from atop the dais and through magnificent stained-glass windows lining the immense dome above. This was not the great church of his mortal days, but it almost could have been... if he had not been spirited by Magnus, creature of Hell, into a world of blood and darkness and torment.

He remembered himself as Maleki, fallen bishop, punished for his transgressions, cast out by God, marked with unspeakable hideousness, despised by all creatures living and dead.

The light from atop the dais grew brighter until he looked away. Still he shielded his face from the radiance, as if a thousand suns burned beyond the windows. He felt, then, instead of seeing, the presence of the Cainite Michael. Basking in the glow, Maleki's skin grew hot to the touch, yet he did not burn. The warmth was painful in that it cleansed him of all pretense and hubris, as the desert sandstorm scours the bones of flesh—for even as a leprous Nosferatu he retained the shaken pride of his mortal days; therein lay the horror and humiliation. But here his unworthiness was accepted not as curse but as blessing: Only thus, as an empty husk, could he receive the gift of divine grace.

The very air around him grew warm and crackled as the Patriarch's feet touched step after step, descending so that lesser creatures might partake of his holiness. Maleki trembled. Not even in the divine liturgy of Hagia Sophia had he ever felt so touched by supernal glory.

And then touch him it did.

Hands of molten glass lifted him to his feet. Maleki cried out, but as righteousness enveloped him, he knew nothing more of fear, of pain and self-loathing. His suffering, he saw, was an opportunity to further glorify God! Wise Michael made this clear without the utterance of a single word! Maleki carried the words within him already.

Blessed are the poor in spirit, for theirs is the kingdom of Heaven.

Blessed are those who mourn, for they will be comforted.

Blessed are the meek, for they will inherit the earth.

Blessed are those who hunger and thirst for righteousness, for they will be filled.

Blessed are the merciful, for they will receive mercy.

Blessed are the pure in heart, for they will see God.

Blessed are the peacemakers, for they will be called children of God.

Blessed are those who are persecuted for righteousness's sake, for theirs is the kingdom of Heaven.

Blessed are you when people revile you and persecute you and utter all kinds of evil against you falsely on my account. Rejoice and be glad, for your reward is great in Heaven, for in the same way they persecuted the prophets who were before you.

In that instant, buttressed by the glory of the Patriarch, the vile wickedness of Magnus was clear to Maleki. To Embrace out of hatred, to inflict an eternity of suffering for cruel amusement—there could be no justification for such as that. Righteous indignation flowed from the Patriarch through Maleki, but also the knowledge that anger could be tempered by mercy. Basking in Michael's radiance, the deformed Cainite stood tall and knew the security of acceptance. For the first time since his mortal death, he had no cause to dread Magnus, nor would he ever again.

Salvation was at hand. Redemption.

Suddenly undeniable hunger took hold of Maleki. Michael felt his need and provided for it. Hands of pure light were at Maleki's face. As the fingers unfurled, shafts of blood red poured from fiery stigmata. Maleki drank of the light, and with it, the Dream. Michael's vision filled his being, gave purpose to his eternal night, and Maleki was christened Malachite in the blood of the Patriarch.

I will find him, Malachite thought. *He will set all of this aright.*

Part Two:

Constantinople

Chapter Seven

The hunched figure rushed frantically up the Second Hill of Constantinople toward the expansive structure of the Hippodrome in the distance. He struggled against the burden of a bulging sack tossed over his shoulder. Luxurious villas, empty and silent tonight, lined both sides of the wide lane. From the darkness, the clatter of horses' hooves drew closer. A cry sounded. The fugitive was spotted. He redoubled his efforts.

But the stallions carrying mail-clad knights were swift and strong. They quickly caught up to the man, surrounded him, put an end to his futile flight.

The foremost of the knights reined his horse within a few inches of the cowering robed figure and spoke in Germanic-accented French: "To flee from soldiers of the cross marks you as a heathen."

"Have mercy, Knight of the Temple," said the man afoot, for the knight towering above him wore the cross of the Templars.

"A petty thief," said one of the other knights.

"Hand over the sack, old man," said another.

But the man did not shift his burden. He turned in a fitful circle, the hood of his robe jerking this way and that, like a nervous bird looking from predator to predator, but his face remained hidden in shadow.

The first Templar leaned closer. "Are you deaf, old man?" A steel gauntlet buffeted the old man's head then reached for the sack, while the other knights laughed among themselves. "Holy Jesu!" the knight shouted as the weight of the sack nearly pulled him from his saddle. The bag slipped from his grasp, crashed to the ground and fell open, spilling rocks across the cobbles.

Some of the knights laughed at their compatriot. Others muttered curses. A few thought to wonder how a hunched old man could have shouldered a load too heavy for an armored knight—an awkward angle from which to hoist a load, no doubt, leaning forward from the saddle.

"I hear cries of 'petty thief,'" said the old man. He drew back his hood.

Breathless curses streamed from the knights, who leaned back in their saddles and turned their mounts to distance themselves from the pox marks, scabs, and festering boils of their prey. The Templar stared, horrified, at his gauntlet, as if the metal might rot and fall away right there.

"Petty thieves," the old man said, nodding. "I would not have been so bold as to openly name you such, but I cannot argue."

For an instant, they regarded him with shock and befuddlement—then he had in hand the short broadsword of an infantryman, drawn from the folds of his robe, slashing at the Templar's mount, severing one of the forelegs with a single, vicious stroke. The stallion screamed and fell, tumbling its rider to the cobbles.

At the same instant, dark figures like birds of prey swooped down, leaping from the surrounding villas and bearing knights and horses to the ground. Armored warriors rushed out from the shadows, swords at the ready, making quick work of the dismounted riders. The struggle was fierce, bloodthirsty, and brief.

Malachite stood up from the corpse of one of the Latin knights and wiped his blade on the dead man's cloak.

"They are all mortals," Ignatius said, then corrected himself: "Were."

Already the leper knights had hustled away the surviving horses, silenced the wounded. The bodies of the knights, too, were dragged and carried out of sight. There was blood to claim. Sand was scattered over the cobbles to obscure what had spilled. "Dead crusaders would bring cruel vengeance down upon whatever mortal *Romaioi* were unfortunate enough to be nearby when the bodies were discovered," Ignatius said. "If the knights simply go missing…"

Malachite nodded, turning to the one surviving Templar, who was bound and gagged and being dragged toward the shadows. His eyes were wide with shock and incomprehension. The lane behind was as ever it had been: quiet, undisturbed, revealing no sign that it had been the scene of a furious bloodletting but moments before.

Safely in the shadows, Malachite motioned for the Templar's gag to be removed. The Nosferatu carrying him, Zoticus, who had played the part of the old man, obeyed.

"Our scouts told us that Latins were pillaging the Church of the Archangel Michael," Malachite said. "Strange that you, a knight of the Temple should be among them, leading them, in fact. Tell me, how is it you hope to recapture the Holy Lands by peeling the gilt from the domes of our basilicas?"

"Perhaps," said Zoticus, "they hope our holy relics will transport them to Jerusalem. Is this it? Or perhaps the *Poor* Knights of the Temple of Solomon have tired of their vows of poverty and wish to change their name?"

The Templar stared dumbfounded at the creatures looming above him.

"Speak, man!" Malachite barked.

"We… we hope to preserve the relics," the Templar forced out.

"An admirable intent," Zoticus said. "Your mission must be an urgent one. No doubt you thought the old man had raided the reliquary before you could, and thus you chased him through the streets."

"We were done at the church!"

Malachite reached for the man's throat. "Done, were you?"

Ignatius approached. "One of them had several pack mules," he said. "It was loaded down with altarpieces and crucifixes, priests' vestments, icons, coins, shards of stained glass. They even chipped away bits of the green marble from the walls."

"It seems all the wealth and glory of the Church needs preserving," said Zoticus.

Malachite resisted the urge to squeeze the man's throat until neither breath nor lies could pass. "See that all is hidden—where these religious bandits will never find it."

"It will be done." Ignatius disappeared again into the night.

"You are not men but demons," the Templar whispered.

With one hand, Malachite lifted him by the throat. "Demons, are we? Creatures of Hell? Though it is you and your kind that profane the holy places of our city? You rummage through our places of worship like they were a merchant's back room. How many priests and monks have you struck down for decrying your sacrilege? How many old men have you ridden down and robbed? Tell me!"

The Templar's feet now dangled inches above the ground. He choked and wheezed as Malachite, in his rage, shook him like no more than an unruly child. Something fell from the mortal's cloak, clattered to the stone cobbles.

Malachite paused in his throttling and looked down at the object, no larger than his hands held side by side. It was white amidst the darkness of night—an ivory tile. Suddenly he cast the knight to the ground, lunged for the tile and scooped it up in his fingers. He held it gently, more gently than even he had held his own stricken childe. To Malachite's eyes, a radiant nimbus surrounded the painted figures of the icon: the Archangel Michael, wings spread; in one hand, upright flaming sword; the other hand placed upon the shoulder of the ascendant Christ. One corner of the tile was chipped. A crack ran across its surface, threatening to separate the two divine beings.

Malachite managed somehow to hand the icon to Zoticus, to make sure that it was safely in his grasp—then fell upon the Templar with the speed and fury of a leopard.

The mortal was too terrified to scream. His brief and piteous wail quickly gave way to a moan of both fear and ecstasy.

"You do God's work?" Malachite snarled through blood and flesh at the man's neck. "I could show you God! I could give you pain and pleasure so great that you would love me above all others, that you would worship me! I would be your God!" He clamped down with his fangs, felt the Beast stirring admiringly within his belly.

Malachite pulled his face back from the bloody mess, held the face of the Templar so that he could not look away. "You are a saint, and I a creature of the Devil? Then know this: Your Hugh de Clairvaux, leader among Templars here, he is one of us. And Guy of Provence. They are like me!" A clinging sinew fell from his blood-smeared mouth. "Are they saints or devils? Servants of darkness or soldiers of God? And what of you?"

He leaned down closer to the knight, who was now shaking uncontrollably from shock spiritual and physical, whispered: "There are more among you, you self-righteous, hypocritical fool! Which of them? Baldwin, Boniface, Lanzo von Sachsen, the doddering doge? I'll leave you to wonder—to wonder who and what have given the orders that rule your life."

The delirious, muttering creature that was the Templar thrashed as Malachite leaned down again, roughly licked the worst of the neck wound, then shoved the mortal away from him, into the dust.

"Replace his gag," Malachite said, grabbing the icon from Zoticus. "Take him as a blood hostage. There will be those among us who will need to feed."

The man's eyes rolled up and fluttered closed. His throat still bled but was no longer the gaping death wound that it had been moments before. He had not the wits to protest or struggle as Zoticus again gagged him and dragged him away.

Malachite hardly noticed the Templar's passing into darkness, fixated as he was upon the icon he had snatched back from his fellow Nosferatu. He held the tile close to his face, pupils stretched wide, thirsting for absent light, as he drank in every detail of the image.

He envied artists the ability to make real and tangible the holiest of divine personages. Even as a mortal when—as Magnus had instructed him—he had supported the Iconoclasts in their quest for the destruction of religious depictions and the veneration accorded them, he had done so with a heavy heart. For a time after his torturous Embrace, he had thought that perhaps that had been his unspeakable sin: He had been insincere in debate, committed intellectually but without heart in his exegeses before the ecclesiastical magistrates. Magnus had been right to condemn him.

The fault was his own, and he deserved eternal damnation. In time, Michael had helped him see the foolishness of such thought and the truth of the casual brutality that Magnus had demonstrated.

It was natural, then, that Malachite's eyes would be drawn first to the representation of Michael the Archangel, commander of all the warriors of Heaven. There were those Cainites in Constantinople who worshipped Michael the Patriarch *as* the Archangel. Magnus was foremost among them—*had been* but likely would no more, if what Ignatius said of his apprehension by Bishop Alfonzo was true. *Bishop!* Malachite scoffed. There was another sacrilege: bishoprics of the Cainite Heresy, which set vampires above mortal men like gods. *Is Clan Lasombra entwined within every foul blasphemy upon the face of the earth?* he wondered. *Obscenities within obscenities within obscenities.*

The very fact that he could not view an image of the Archangel without being reminded of the vile schemes of the magisters grated upon Malachite—and the fact that he could understand the impetus for Magnus's cult grated still more. Perhaps Magnus had been sincere in his veneration of the Patriarch. In Michael's presence, Malachite was likely to forget himself, to be awed by the glorious essence. *Yet he is a Cainite like us.* Malachite caught his error at once. *Not like us—like us made perfect, but Cainite still: cast out, Damned.* And, more each year, subject to madness. The cult of sycophants had helped this not at all. Malachite resented that Michael had never dissuaded that veneration—and felt profound guilt for the resentment of so perfect a creature, architect of the Dream.

All of this ran through Malachite's mind as he held the icon to his face. With one long finger, he traced the line of the flaming sword oriented toward Heaven.

Then he followed down the length of the Archangel's other arm to where his hand rested upon the shoulder of the ascending Christ, welcoming Him to the Heavenly Kingdom.

Thy will be done on Earth as it is in Heaven, Malachite recited silently.

The crack that the icon had suffered in its fall to the ground ran cleanly through the Archangel's forearm and above the head of the Christ, through the nimbus that encircled Him. *As if the thievery of this brigand of a Templar could vanquish the Son of God from Heaven*, Malachite mused. *He ascended into Heaven and sitteth on the right hand of—*

Malachite balked mid-scripture. He drew the icon closer to his face, until knife-thin nose touched the tile, his face screwed up in consternation, unmindful of the sheaths of skin that cracked and peeled away.

"The face…" he muttered. "The face…!"

"Malachite?"

Malachite whirled at the touch of a hand his shoulder and the quizzical rasping voice at his ear.

Ignatius drew back his hand, held it palm-out before him to show that he meant no harm. "Forgive me. I called you and you did not answer."

The sight of his friend struck a discordant note. Malachite stared uncomprehendingly for a moment, then returned his gaze to the icon—and the face of Christ. *I know that face*, Malachite thought, *the face of human perfection. I know it. For almost a hundred years I knew it!* He laughed at the sheer happenstance of it all: that he should see that face again. But the laugh caught in his throat, died there.

Did happenstance truly exist in this order that was Creation, that which God had rendered?

"Malachite?" Ignatius said again. The puzzled concern in his thick voice was evident. "The scouts bring news that the Citadel of Petrion has fallen to the Latins. The Gangrel are scattered. They are scouring the city in packs—hunting for us."

Malachite heard the words, recognized the dire portent contained therein, but he could not tear his gaze from the divine countenance rendered upon the icon: *I know the face of the Dracon!*

"We must return to the tunnels. It will be safer," Ignatius was saying somewhere far away.

Still Malachite stared at the icon. Gazing upon the face, he felt a light beginning to shine into the dark place where he thought only the imprisoned Beast resided: *Cainite created in God's image, or God's image given Cainite form?*

"We must go. Now."

Is this what Gesu's monks feel after starving themselves of blood night after night? Or the desert fathers in their stark caves, stripped of all worldly distraction? Illumination slowly banished the darkness.

Yet Malachite could not cast off the here and now, could not completely ignore the wisp of breeze that still carried the taint of mortal blood, could not ignore the hand again upon his shoulder.

With a single quick motion, so that his heart did not break, he turned from the icon, wrapped it in the folds of his cloak, out of sight.

"Where is the boy?" he asked. The childe's plight was like sand ground into an open wound. *Gesu retreated from the world, and he burned with the library*, Malachite reminded himself. The Dream did not exist in a void, but in relation to men, in the relation between sire and childe.

"The boy is with Basil," Ignatius said. "He is safe—which is more than I can say for us." His sunken eyes scanned the dark streets and surrounding villas.

"The others?" Malachite asked.

"Below ground, where we should be. The rearguard remains here with us."

Malachite surveyed the darkness himself, strained for any sign of leper knight, found none. "The Gangrel would do better to chase the wind."

As they turned to slip down through the drainage sewer into the world below, Malachite was caught by the desire to look again upon the city. The pillaging knights dealt with and the icon out of sight, he noticed again the pall of death that hung over Constantinople, as thick as the smoke of burning buildings. The villas and mansions were empty, their wealthy owners having fled with what they could carry. Street lamps were unlit, patrols long since run off to fight or flee from the invaders.

It is a dead place, he thought. *All that we have worked for…*

"This way," Ignatius said gently, not blind to the pull the city maintained on Malachite.

"Fate is not fickle," Malachite said. "She is cruel, to cast away such perfection."

"Pearls before swine," Ignatius agreed. "This way."

And Malachite did not resist. They left the night sky and the worst of the smoke above, crawling into the darkness of the tunnels.

Chapter Eight

Fingers laid against the boy's face evoked no response, no acknowledgement, neither defensive nor affectionate. Malachite watched this impassively, wondered wryly what else he had expected.

"It is not unusual, the deep sleep, for our kind," said Basil, who had been watching over the boy since the gathered Nosferatu had begun the night's journey.

"Is it usual," Malachite said, suddenly cross, "for the deep sleep to claim one of our kind mid-sentence—no injury, no wearing down of the blood over time?"

Basil flinched at the rebuke. Malachite saw this and regretted his words instantly. The hand he had put to the boy's face he laid on Basil's shoulder. "Forgive me, Basil. You have cared for him tonight as tenderly as would I have myself. I owe you gratitude, not harsh words."

"There is naught to forgive, Malachite. Our lot is to serve."

To lessen the suffering of others, Malachite thought, *for we have taken it upon ourselves.*

He patted Basil's back. "Stay close to me." *One of my childer has passed from this world. I would not have this one leave with me unawares.* There was some comfort in knowing that his two elder progeny were at the camp near Adrianople. Malachite had taken them there, along with numerous ghouls and mortal hangers-on, after Michael had commanded him to leave Constantinople. The nights of fleeing were like a fevered memory: spreading the word; gathering a few necessities, including as many of the tomes from the library as they could manage; passing hurriedly beyond the city walls; turning from well-traveled roads and following half-formed tracks to the northwest; settling finally in a sheltered vale several miles shy of the city of Adrianople. All the while, Malachite had felt himself in a trance, despondent to have been cast out of Eden by his Patriarch, but helpless to do other than obey. Then the Latin crusaders had besieged Constantinople, breached the walls, and the tide of the displaced—mortal and Cainite alike—had begun to flood the camp. Malachite had felt drawn to return but unwilling to risk his entire family. He had brought the boy who had accompanied him into exile, and the boy was struck down.

Of the three boys, Malachite now knew, at least two had been stricken by the sudden illness, and the third…? *If only there were time to find him. If only this boy would wake long enough to tell me of his brother.* In their strangeness, by their sight, the boys maintained a sense of one another; they were able to know each other's minds though they be separated by leagues. Their gift had been a great boon to Malachite over the years. One of the boys had stayed with him, another with Fra' Raymond, so they were ever able to contact one another. The third roamed the sewers and tunnels that, more and more as the years passed, were the province of the Nosferatu. The third boy was still out there somewhere, perhaps stricken like his brothers.

But there is no time, Malachite thought mournfully. *Even should I find him, I cannot save him without Michael's aid.* The same was true of the city, of the Dream.

Malachite turned from Basil and the lifeless boy. "Ignatius, are you ready to proceed?"

Not far away in the tunnel, Ignatius raised his hand for patience as he listened to one of the returned leper scouts. The Nosferatu had moved rapidly this evening, determinedly, more so after the ambush of the brigand crusaders. Aside from the boy, Malachite had left his family at the camp, but the leper knights numbered some two score, and with their ghouls and sympathetic humans initiated to varying degrees into the mysteries of the night, another score. Yet they traveled in companies of no more than a half dozen, snaking through tunnels and hidden ways, skittering through darkened streets above ground to regroup at predetermined rendezvous.

Ignatius finished listening to the scout, bade him wait, as well as the few others who had already reported, and then came to Malachite.

"The Gangrel press close behind us," Ignatius said. "The rearguard are making feints and diversionary attacks to slow them down, leading them astray and then fading away."

"But the Gangrel are skilled hunters," Malachite said.

"Yes," Ignatius said. "We are fortunate that only a few packs seem to have taken an interest in us. Our outrunners tell me that, after abandoning the citadel in the face of the crusader onslaught, the Gangrel scattered across the city and are leaving trails of blood wherever they go. It seems they are not so much searching specifically for us, as we first assumed, but for anyone on whom they can pour out their fury."

"Grave as the news is, I am glad it has not come to open war between our clans," Malachite said. He could not shake, though, the image of madness in Baron Thomas's eyes, the Beast lurking so close beneath the surface.

"There are other concerns," Ignatius continued. "The Forums of Theodosius and Constantine are thick with crusaders. They are using them as staging grounds for their patrols and collecting many treasures in those places as well, so that their leaders may divide the spoils, no doubt."

"We should drive them before us," clamored one of the young firebrands among the leper knights, "and reclaim what belongs rightly to the people of Constantinople!"

A general muttering of approval quickly died away in the face of Ignatius's obvious distemper. "Would you become the most quickly destroyed knight in the history of the order, as well as the most foolish?" He turned back to Malachite.

"Then we will not stray to the north," Malachite said.

"To the south," Ignatius said, "the Venetians hold the Palace of Bucoleon and the harbor there. Luckily they do not seem as inclined as the Franks to push into the city and delve for treasure."

"There is no need. With the Franks so deeply in their debt, much of the stolen wealth will find its way back to Venice. The old doge is no fool. So," Malachite added, "we can swing south if need be, since the Venetians can be expected to hold to the palace and the coast."

He pondered for a moment the lay of the city. "The Forum of Augustaion, the senate basilica—those will be gathering places for the Latins as well, both to satisfy both their greed for loot and their pride that they control the institutions of the city. I am correct?"

Ignatius nodded. "The scouts' reports bear out what you say."

"The villas and halls of the Great Palace are still subject to looting?"

"Yes. The Franks keep a close watch on their troops there, so as to make sure that every coin and candelabrum is accounted for."

Malachite considered that. "We could likely steer clear of them, but if trouble arose we would risk being caught between the Franks on one side and the Venetians and the sea on the other."

"The Hippodrome, then?"

"Yes," Malachite said. "It is the most direct route and, it would seem, the path of least resistance."

"As you wish." Ignatius gave terse orders to be passed along through the various patrols: selected routes, order of advance, rendezvous points and backup rendezvous locations. There was no questioning of his and Malachite's decision, no more agitating for confrontation with the crusaders. Even those leper knights not in the know could guess at least the destination if not the exact purpose of tonight's quest. They were to remain unseen as much as practicable as they traversed the tunnels beneath the great open arena of the Hippodrome and pressed on to the catacombs beneath the Church of Hagia Sophia—where lay the chambers of Michael the Patriarch.

Malachite heard the whispers among the leper knights:

"He's going to rally the Patriarch to drive off the invaders."

"They say the Patriarch is no more. I say Malachite wants to claim the mantle and city for himself."

"We'd be the lords of the city, then."

"There's an army of crusaders you're forgetting about."

"Not to mention the Cainites of the Latin Quarter. Alfonzo won't stand down without a fight. He's been eyeing the rest of the city for years."

The muffled chatter ended abruptly as Ignatius ordered the knights on their way. Remaining with him and Malachite were Basil, with the boy, and two others, one scouting ahead, the other bringing up the rear. When they were underway again, Malachite drew next to Fra' Ignatius and pitched his voice for that Nosferatu alone: "What word from our spies among the slave pens beneath the Hippodrome?"

Ignatius's head jerked to face Malachite, the sunken eyes taking him in.

"There were no secrets between Fra' Raymond and me," Malachite said.

"I can see that it is true."

Yes, he begins to see, Malachite thought, *that we are blood kin, and all that we do is for a larger purpose. There is room for neither pride nor jealousy if the Dream is to survive.*

"Now that they are busy trying to save their own skins," Ignatius said, "the Ventrue do not visit their playthings so often as they did before. There was a time when the patricians gloated over their caged warriors before pitting them against one another or the wild beasts brought from the ends of the empire. No more. Since the attack on the city, even the jailers have fled— but they did not free their charges. We have set guards of our own."

"Are the slaves near riot?" Malachite asked.

"They receive little enough news from beyond the pens. We have provided them food." Ignatius shrugged. "They are better off than they were. The combats are not being held."

"It is time they were set loose," Malachite said. "At least for the time, the power of the Ventrue is broken. Amidst the confusion there will be no repercussions."

"There are criminals and killers among the slaves," Ignatius pointed out. "Not all are imprisoned on the whim of senator or prefect."

Gherbod Fleming

"Their judgment is at hand," Malachite said, stalking along the tunnel, which in this portion of the city was wide enough for two to walk abreast easily. In the cause of secrecy and out of a profound distaste for open flame, the Nosferatu carried no torches, depending instead on their own supernal vision to pick out the way. They kept up a determined pace. Malachite allowed himself no time to dwell in gloom, to debate the necessity of abandoning the third boy for the time being, nor to mourn the state of the boy close at hand.

Forward. Ever forward.

No time for reflection. He clutched the icon tucked in his robes but refused to contemplate for more than a passing second the image of the Archangel, the face of Christ. *Of the Dracon!* He could not give in just now to the presentiment that tugged at his awareness. There was too much that might strike at his resolve now that he had determined his course.

Forward. Once they reached the nether levels of the Hippodrome, then Hagia Sophia would be very near. *I will know the truth of Michael. He will see through the madness this time. He will recognize the peril of the city—of the Dream!—and he will be moved to intervene.*

When need required, the Nosferatu were capable of moving as stealthily as the chill draft that haunted the tunnels. Even Basil, his arms full with the boy, stepped surely and silently. When the advance scout returned, his scarred and disfigured face creased with grim concern, he appeared as if out of nowhere, disgorged without warning from the darkness.

"Keep to the right up ahead," he said, reversing his course and matching the others stride for stride.

Instinctively they increased their pace. Malachite saw that the scout strode with naked blade. Ignatius noticed as well, and the two elders drew their own swords. Very soon they came to the split in the tunnel, and from the left heard the crash of steel against steel, faint, far away if the deceptive subterranean acoustics were to be trusted—but growing closer.

Ignatius shot the scout a questioning look.

"Gangrel," said the scout. "A small pack. Be it accident or design, they would have cut us off. One of our patrols intercepted them."

The group paused at the split so that the leper knight in the rear could catch up.

"And here is Armand," said Ignatius, a moment later when the rearguard arrived. "Stay close from here on. The Gangrel may have been ranging wide, but they will have found what we have: that the forums along the Mese and the coastal defenses are held in strength. Any of the baron's people who are south of the Mese will be funneled this way."

The muffled noise of combat was gradually growing closer. The Nosferatu patrol was giving ground, if slowly. As snarls and belabored grunts became distinguishable among the echoing clang of swords, Malachite considered rushing to the patrol's aid.

Ignatius must have read something of his thoughts. "It is why we have the patrols," he said. "So that we may win through."

"Then let us go now, at once, and give our knights more ground to surrender, if need be."

Ignatius nodded. "There may be other of the baron's people about—and at some point it is likely that the Franks, in their enthusiasm to find riches, will stumble upon one of our tunnels. Let us hope it is not tonight. Press on, Theodore."

The scout obeyed, and the rest followed along with no little urgency. The wide, smooth tunnels were no obstacle. These passages were among the oldest in the city and had been improved over patient centuries.

"The Ladder of Septimius is just ahead," Malachite said.

"A guard is stationed there," Ignatius said. "I called all those of the blood to us, but left a contingent of ghouls to watch over the pens."

They turned a sharp bend and came to the ladder—stairs really, carved into bedrock, steep and treacherous despite hundreds of years of attention.

There was no guard.

"This is the path I would have chosen," Ignatius said, "but there may be some trouble."

"We will climb," Malachite said, sheathing his sword so as to attack the ladder with all fours. "Guard the boy well, Basil. Take time as you must. Armand, stay with him."

They ascended into darkness. Theodore, Malachite, and Ignatius quickly outdistanced Basil and Armand. The ladder rose from the lower tunnel at times at an almost imperceptible angle, a narrow shaft that never widened, so that a traveler, if necessary, could catch himself by splaying his limbs and pressing against opposite surfaces. The stone walls crowded close. Malachite purged thoughts of the tomb-like enclosure in which Verpus had imprisoned him during the day.

"There is a light above," Theodore called in a low voice.

"That is the level of the pens," Ignatius said, as he labored to peer through the arms and legs of those before and above him. "But there is another passage, and a locked, guarded door. We should see no light."

They climbed onward, upward, and not long after they had noticed the light, Malachite felt moisture beneath his fingers. His first thought was that he must be sure of his handholds and footholds, lest he slip—then almost at once the scent penetrated his senses. Darkness could not hide from him the smell of blood.

"Christ and Caine have mercy," Theodore muttered, and Malachite could hear the struggle to maintain control in his voice.

"Steady, lad," he said. "There may yet be blood aplenty at the end of this climb." Yet Malachite, too, felt the stirring of the Beast. It was impossible that they should come upon blood unexpected—and much of it; the ladder was growing heavily wet now—without feeling the urgency of its call.

As if to explain the presence of the blood, a drawn-out scream reached their ears from above—not a pained cry of combat, but rather a lingering, hopeless, tortured plea. Despite the treacherous footing slick with blood, the three climbed more quickly. The thought of falling was less distressing than the continuing scream, joined by others.

The steps seemed infinite in number, as if Septimius had substituted Jacob's ladder, and they climbed all the way to Heaven. But the sounds above were not of Heaven.

And always there was the blood. So close. Right before his face. Malachite climbed almost in a daze. For a moment, he forgot the place and time of his exertion, the reason for his journey. The screams seemed those of the Beast. But he held it in check, mollified by the blood recently offered it as tribute, restrained by bonds of purpose—

Yes. I must find Michael. The boy… the city… the Dream…

He felt, too, the unwelcome stirring of enlightenment. With the Beast cowed, blood called to buried knowledge as well. But neither could he give in to it. Not now.

Forward! Malachite told himself. *Climb!*

They stumbled out of the shaft before he knew they had reached the top. Blood pooled thick on the floor of the corridor, drained into the opening of the shaft from which they had emerged like deformed babes into the world. Ahead the screams echoed from stone. The Nosferatu rushed ahead toward the slave pens, drawn by the appalling sounds of torture, swords ready, primed to the taste of violence by so much blood.

A dizzying mélange of sound and smell assaulted them: caged animals—lion, mastiff, panther—many injured and slain, dung and offal mingled with molded straw, screams of animal and man, mortal bodies, gritty dust scattered by boots. A few torches mounted on iron brackets cast the scene in hellish relief.

And then more voices raised, yelling, shouted battle cries: "St. Ladre!" The sound of battle joined rang close by now, just ahead through the open doorway to the slave pens.

Our own knights, Malachite realized. *They are attacking!*

A restraining hand grasped Malachite's shoulder, Ignatius: "More patrols will be arriving."

The suggestion was clear enough: *We can press on to Hagia Sophia if you so choose.*

But Malachite was wound tightly after the climb—so much blood!—and this was no small pack of Gangrel to be diverted. The battle in the next room was a raging melee among dozens at close quarters—and among them, striving against the newly arrived leper knights, were men wearing the livery of Bishop Alfonzo.

"We make this stand or the city is not worth saving," Malachite said.

The three Nosferatu slipped into the mayhem unseen. Malachite paused briefly to take in the scene, rather than charging in heedlessly. The chamber was wide and low-ceilinged, lined with metal cages on either side. Many of the cages, pens filled with slaves trained to combat, were open, and the fighting had spilled into them. The central corridor was packed tightly with bodies: dead and dying, maimed, flailing with sword or spear. The Nosferatu patrol had entered from the far end. The attention of Alfonzo's men was turned that direction.

Malachite was not a warrior trained, yet he had seen his share of martial strife, ambush and battle, death and dismemberment. The fighting did not daunt him, yet around the edges of the milling fray of Cainite, ghoul, and mortal, signs of Alfonzo's horrific intent were apparent.

Among the corpses in the pens lay numerous bodies, recently dead, writhing in the agony of the Embrace, their bodies still relinquishing the mortal coil, yet the shared blood of Caine held them to this world. These men, trained to die by the sword for the entertainment of others, contorted in the throes of death denied, stolen. They did not know the pain and disfigurement that Malachite had suffered, but no Embrace, not even at the hand of the Lasombra, was kind.

Alfonzo would create an army to swarm across the city, Malachite realized. *And the slaves would be his unwilling fodder.*

He grabbed Theodore's arm. "Those who are in the midst of the change—destroy them!"

Then Malachite and Ignatius waded into the fray. They used surprise mercilessly, striking from behind, hacking off limbs, disemboweling, rending head from body when possible. A single deathblow might fell ghoul or mortal, but a Cainite might rise from heinous injury whole of body, redeemed by the grace of blood. Better not to chance it.

In the opened pens, some slaves cowered, silent or screaming, from the demonic creatures besetting them on all sides. Other slaves seized the weapons of the fallen, defended themselves, or lashed out at whomever was closest. In the closed pens, men climbed the bars and yelled, huddled in corners, dug at the stone walls with tattered, bloody fingers. Interspersed with it all, the dance of swords spun out of control. The Lasombra, at least a score all told, were largely ghouls, but deadly Cainites passed among them. Warriors slashed with weapons, gouged at eyes and mouths with claw and fang. Bloody chortles of triumph were accented by lingering wails of agony.

The overwhelming chaos worked to the advantage of the Nosferatu. Malachite and Ignatius struck down a half dozen or so men each, before the Lasombra realized the danger to their rear. A hasty resistance formed, but another patrol of leper knights arrived just then. They stepped from an opening, that a moment before had been indistinguishable stone wall, into one of the locked cages. The foremost Nosferatu produced a key from his tunic, unlocked the cell door, and he and his three brethren leapt into the battle.

There the tide seemed to turn—until one of the few torches in the long, low chamber went out. Then another, and another, snuffed by inky black tendrils extending from the shadows. And as the shadows grew darker, so did the black tendrils, taking on more distinct form and solidity. Malachite shuddered at the memory of the garden on the night of his own forced Embrace:

the dark shapes and tentacles murdering Hectorius and the rest of his guard.

Like the cracks of whips, they struck, crushing leper knights left and right, leaving scattered bodies, broken swords, crushed helms, in their wake. Advantage shifted back to the Lasombra with their shadow magic. The men-at-arms regrouped, formed a cohesive wedge against the now hard-pressed lepers and another opposing Malachite and Ignatius.

Which one is it? Malachite tried to see. *Or which ones?* Who was calling the shadow tentacles into existence, controlling them, pitting them against the Nosferatu?

Protected between the outward-facing phalanxes stood two armored men—Cainites whom Malachite recognized from public gatherings of the city's undead. One was shouting orders to the remaining soldiers. *Marco*, the name came to Malachite. The other—Gregorio—was just as intensely focused on the battle, but silent, maintaining concentration, gesturing in ways that might correspond with the lashing attacks of the tendrils.

Him! Gregorio!

Either way, they were favored among Alfonzo's followers, sent here to Embrace a small army. Both deserved destruction.

Malachite signaled to Ignatius. Ignatius nodded, ducking beneath the thrust of an enemy as he did so, then skewering the man with a short, brutal stroke of his own. The two elders moved in concert, Malachite darting in after the swift, sure slashes of Ignatius, striking with his own blade or raking claws across an enemy's exposed face or neck. The Nosferatu maneuvered furtively amidst the chaos of melee, striking here, slipping from view before their befuddled opponents only to strike again from a different direction.

The Lasombra men-at-arms had numbers, though, and the roving tentacles of shadow tempered somewhat the greater concentration of Cainites among the Nosferatu and their ability to vanish from sight. Malachite and Ignatius drew closer, step by blood-drenched step, to the opposing commanders, to the shadowmancer. Across the chamber, the tendrils were taking a terrible toll among the leper knights.

Malachite was almost close enough to strike Gregorio, to render impotent the shadows. Two more contested steps, driving the men-at-arms before them. Feint. Slip around unseen to the other side. One more step…

The opening he was seeking—Malachite swung, his blow endowed with inhuman force!

—But the other Lasombra, Marco, anticipated his attack, parried it. A mortal or a lesser Cainite would have lost his arm to that blow, but Marco met strength of blood with strength of blood. The clashing steel thundered like great ships colliding. Loose masonry fell from the ceiling, crashed to the floor among the throng, showering them in dust.

Malachite found himself suddenly off balance, overextended. Barely, he fended away a blow that would have cleaved his head from his shoulders.

The men-at-arms redoubled their attacks, pressing their advantage. Malachite fended off a glancing blow that sliced into his forearm, tore through robe, peeled skin, chipped bone. If not for Ignatius's skill, the two would have fallen many times over. As it was they retreated, losing hard-won ground a step at a time.

And now Gregorio turned one of the shadow tendrils against them.

If that will allow the others to advance... Malachite thought hopefully, but the remaining tendrils kept back those leper knights still fighting. Though formidable, the Nosferatu were better suited to ambush and diversion than to standing battle—especially against the black arts of the shadowmancers.

Pushed back, step after step, toward the door through which they had entered. While parrying attacks, Malachite scoured his memory for details of the tunnels behind him: There could be no retreat down the Ladder of Septimius; an orderly withdrawal down the corridor past the animal pens was possible; then flight into darkness.

But Alfonzo cannot be allowed these killers from the slave pens, Malachite thought. *We could harass them all the way back to the Latin Quarter. Fewer of them would make it... but we must press on to Hagia Sophia!*

Alfonzo would have to be dealt with later. Then Malachite realized: *Once we alert Michael, he will deal with the Bishop Alfonzo!* As he prepared to signal the withdrawal, Malachite consoled himself that at least he and the others had lessened the number of fledgling Lasombra Alfonzo would have at his disposal until Michael made amends.

At that instant, Malachite caught sight of Theodore. They had completely lost track of him during the fight, after sending him to dispatch the Cainites-to-be. Now he was sneaking in from the side toward the Lasombra leaders. Malachite saw only the flash of steel, a headlong attack—

Again Marco intervened. But at a price. The blow that would have severed Gregorio's head sliced instead into the face of the other. He crumpled to the floor, out of the fight if not destroyed outright. Two other men-at-arms, however, turned to face Theodore, at least one of them Cainite, judging by his speed and strength of arm.

Theodore gave up ground quickly. And it was fortunate that he did so.

The snarling beast leapt from behind Malachite, over his shoulder—a flash of fangs, golden mane, lashing tail. With a deafening roar, the lion fell upon Gregorio, bit into his neck and shoulders, shook him until the plaintive screams ceased.

The tendrils of shadow suddenly disappeared.

For a moment, the battle ceased—then the men-at-arms succumbed to confusion and fear. A few realized what was happening and attacked the lion. The beast turned from the pieces of Gregorio and set to rending the Lasombra fighters limb from limb. Those whose armor forestalled its claws, it mauled and batted aside.

The Nosferatu resumed their attack, also, against their distracted opponents. The patrol knights made rapid progress. Malachite and Ignatius ran through warrior after warrior. The lion pounced on the nearest Lasombra at hand, seeming to take special pleasure in dismembering those who revealed themselves as Cainites.

Amazingly quickly, it was over. Pleas for mercy fell on deaf ears, and then there were only stunned, mouth-agape slaves and bloodied, hideous Nosferatu, standing among bodies—in some places knee deep—and amidst all the carnage crouched a crimson-muzzled lion, eyes wild, tail slashing back and forth through the air.

The Nosferatu watched the beast as a desert mouse watches a hawk that has just snatched a serpent from nearby: glad enough to be rid of one threat, but painfully aware that all was not safe. Did the lion have a taste for Lasombra flesh—or merely Cainite?

It turned its back on the bulk of the leper knights, sauntering toward Malachite. He drew back his sword—but then held the blow, unsure why he did not strike. The lion stopped before him, dropped from its mouth an arm that landed at his feet, and then the cat continued past and through the door.

For a moment, Malachite stood stunned, then he forced himself to follow the beast. It made its way back to a cage, stepped within, lay down. Before the cage, eyes closed, the boy clutched in his arms, sat Basil, still as death. A moment later, his eyes fluttered open. Malachite knelt before him, but Basil stared off into the mid-distance. Only gradually did any amount of recognition cross his face, as if he knew Malachite's face but could not recall from where, and the name that went with it was gone as well.

Ignatius had followed. Very gingerly he closed the lion's cage, and only after fastening the latch did he relax in the least.

"Basil, you are back," Malachite said. "Do you remember what you did, casting your soul into the body of the lion?"

Basil did not resist as Malachite lifted the boy from him. The leper knight seemed confused still. He wrung his hands, as if trying to clean them of blood that was not there. "I... I... remember," he said, "but... it is more like I have been a lion who has now cast his soul into this body."

One of the knights behind Malachite laughed quietly, relieved—until he realized that Basil did not jest.

They helped him to his feet and away from the cage, though he seemed absently reluctant to leave it. In a quiet corner of the slave pens, they set him to rest and collect himself.

"Ease your mind, Basil Lionheart," Malachite said, "and know that you turned the tide this night. We have you to thank that Bishop Alfonzo will lack this army of trained warriors at his beck and call."

Malachite and Ignatius moved away from him. All around them, the leper knights tended their fallen and wounded, while others herded the surviving slaves back into pens—at least those slaves who were not balled against the wall, sobbing openly at the madness of inhuman creatures and bodies ripped limb from limb by rampaging lions and animate shadows. The armed slaves grumbled menacingly at the return to captivity, yet even they hesitated to resist these monstrous knights whose call wild animals answered.

"Did spies survive among the slaves?" Malachite asked Ignatius.

Ignatius scanned the crowd, nodded. "A few."

"Good. There will be no more slaves here. Place a good man in charge. Those slaves whom the spies identify as true criminals—those who have murdered or maimed or raped—put them to death. The others are to go free."

"As you wish." Ignatius moved away to pass on the command.

Malachite thought that he should have felt more satisfaction at the outcome of the battle. He and his people had thwarted a nefarious plot of Alfonzo. The obscene bishop would still hold court in the Latin Quarter; he would still enact blood feasts, indiscriminately torturing and killing mortals as lightly as a proper noble would play chess or drink wine—that all was true. But Alfonzo would not have a readily available cadre of trained killers, newly brought to the blood, with which to terrorize the city.

Alfonzo has doubtlessly collaborated in the Latins' attack on the city, Malachite thought. *Maybe now Michael will consent to have him put down... and perhaps evict all of Clan Lasombra from Constantinople.* The empire would be much better off, Malachite thought, without the bishop, or Magnus if he still survived, or any of their kin.

There should also have been the satisfaction of undermining the noble Ventrue, the family founded by Antonius, third founder of the Dream with Michael and the Dracon. Now nominally led by Caius, they held themselves in high regard, above all others: they who set mortal generals and imperial pretenders against one another; they who made sport of others' suffering in the blood matches of the Hippodrome and Kynegion Amphitheater, with their gladiators and ghouled beasts and blood-deprived Cainite criminals.

I should have destroyed the slave pens long ago, Malachite thought, *even if it meant my own banishment, my own destruction!* Yet he had hidden behind the edicts of the ruling families. He had shown no moral leadership, only distaste, cowardice.

And now in the hour of his triumph, he felt next to nothing. *We have succeeded here only because the city is laid low—because we have failed the Dream.*

Every moment he spent here was another moment's delay in reaching Michael and the city's salvation.

"Ignatius, we must go onward with those who are able," he called. "Spare as few as possible to tend the injured and deal with the... former slaves." Excited whispers spread through the slave pens, those who had heard passing the news along. Tears of joy joined those of the maddened few.

Ignatius approached. "More patrols have arrived now that the fighting is done," he said wryly.

"There was little enough room for more bodies," Malachite pointed out.

"True," Ignatius said. "There are still Gangrel lurking," he continued, "and some of the crusaders—Templars by all telling, led by those of the blood—have begun delving below the churches. They have found a few of our tunnels and likely think they lead to caches of buried treasure."

"All the more reason for us to be on our way," Malachite said. To linger any longer was to risk being overwhelmed by countless dangers, both external and internal. He needed to move forward. And so they did.

Chapter Nine

After the Hippodrome, Malachite entrusted the boy to Theodore. The scout had suffered a terrible wound to the head after attacking the Lasombra commanders. Blood from a condemned slave had helped re-knit his fractured skull, but one ear was gone and he complained of a constant ringing noise and blurred vision. Still, he had refused to be left behind. The boy was a light enough burden, Malachite thought, and, though injured, Theodore had proved his worth.

Along with Ignatius, Armand to the fore, and Zoticus in the rear, Basil traveled in the company. He responded to direct questions, but still seemed slightly dazed. Though Malachite could communicate with some animals on a very basic level, he had never attempted to cast himself into the body of another creature. He had heard tales of those who had taken control of a beast only to find themselves trapped within it, or who returned to their own form tainted by the animal, unable ever to shake it completely from their thoughts and instincts. Like Theodore, Basil had proven himself, and Malachite felt he owed them his protection, his loyalty.

They made good progress from the Hippodrome, through the wide, straight tunnels, in places lined with marble as pure as that used in the halls of the Great Palace not far above. Outrunners and scouts checked in with Ignatius frequently. They kept a close watch for the Gangrel, but saw and heard nothing.

It was with quite different news that Armand returned from the point, his expression perplexed, verging on fearful.

"What is it?" Ignatius demanded.

"There is a woman…"

"Go on, lad. A woman, here in the tunnels?"

"Yes."

"And…?"

"And she would speak with Malachite." Armand's hideous face twisted into a sort of queer, apologetic smile.

Malachite and Ignatius exchanged concerned glances. "The baron might have spread word that I am in the city," Malachite said, "but how would she have known to wait for us in the tunnels—even if she knew we were heading toward Hagia Sophia? There are at least a dozen routes."

"I thought you likely wanted to keep your whereabouts your own business," Armand said, "so I made that I didn't know what she was talking about. And she says, 'I am the Lady Alexia Theusa.' Then she says, 'You are traveling with Malachite, leader of a scion family to Michael. You are traveling with several others of your clan—interesting, that, since you have no permission from the Council of Families to be in the city.' I told her that I knew nothing about any of that. I was just a humble knight doing my duty, and she needed to be on her way."

"I suppose it would be too much to ask that she agreed," Malachite said.

Armand grew more agitated at this, almost angry. "She laughed at me, m'lord. Laughed! And it was the strangest thing. It… it…"

"Spit it out, lad," said Ignatius. "We've only a few hours till sunrise."

"Something about the way she laughed… it made me feel… well, embarrassed, if that makes any sense. Embarrassed that I had tried to tell her her own business. And then she says, 'Tell your master that the Lady

Alexia would speak with him. Be quick about it, for I sense he travels with some urgency.' That's what she said."

A chill foreboding gripped Malachite. He felt the pull of the illumination that he refused to face—and in the dark places the Beast writhed; it would see him back to the slave pens, where he could revel in the blood and feed beyond contentment. Why should the demands of Lady Alexia affect him thus? She was a Cainite of elder years, perhaps one of the eldest in the city. *But she has never wished me ill that I know of*, Malachite thought. *Of course, neither had the baron....*

Then he remembered the mortal woman, the Jewish physician at the hospital, Miriam of Damascus. *The woman was spying for Alexia and told her of my return to the city!* Even so, how did Alexia of Clan Cappadocian intercept him so precisely here in the labyrinthine tunnels?

"There are other ways," Ignatius said. "Let us turn from this path and leave her waiting in the darkness."

Malachite nodded. "Yes. It would be better." He clutched a hand to his chest as if to physically restrain the Beast, and in doing so felt the line of the icon tucked safely amidst the folds of his robes. Suddenly he felt compelled to turn to Theodore, to make sure that the boy was still with them and not crumbled away to dust.

Something in the movement caught Basil's attention. He flinched, as if about to leap forward and pounce, checking himself at the last instant.

"Quickly, then," Ignatius said. He pointed out the route, Armand again leading the way. They backtracked for perhaps a hundred yards, turned into a side tunnel, hurried along, made several more turns.

Nebulous dread was growing in Malachite, churning within him. He vaguely recognized that the troop had circled about, swung wide of their previous route, but that they were again bearing in the same direction: toward Hagia Sophia. Toward Michael.

They traveled swiftly and in silence, so the voice, when its sing-song tones sliced through the darkness, jarred them as might have a sudden cave-in of the tunnel.

"I see that you received my message," she said as they turned a corner, nearly running into her.

They were close on Armand's heels and had no warning except her dulcet words. The Nosferatu stopped suddenly, poised between fight and flight, wavering momentarily.

"I would speak with you, Malachite," she said, the Lady Alexia Theusa. Her skin was so pale as nearly to shine in the darkness. Draped in a flowing gown of damask, still she was slight—though she seemed to bar irrefutably the intersection of tunnels where she stood, this crossroads of the underworld. A rigid beauty clung to her features, enhanced by her regal bearing, that of a queen carved from crystal.

"Come," she said, holding out a delicate hand to Malachite.

He hesitated. Ignatius moved to step before him, with Armand to shield Malachite.

Alexia laughed, her amusement the sound of water from a fountain, moonlit diamonds gently splashing. "Do you, a band of warriors, have so much to fear from a lone woman who would seek aid?"

They paused, hands upon the hilts of their swords, and Malachite felt the embarrassment of which Armand had spoken, concentric ripples from her laughter, spread out to encompass them.

"I would speak privately with you, Malachite," she said. "If you wish it, I shall extend my word that I offer you no harm… though it seems more fitting that I should seek assurances from armored knights."

The undercurrent of quiet laughter, of absurdity, tickled Malachite's pride. "We shall not be the first to offer grievance," he said, stepping past Ignatius and Armand. "The Lady Alexia has never provided offense against my family. I shall hear her."

Alexia nodded graciously, gestured to the side tunnel where they might parley in confidence. Malachite followed her.

"You seek the Patriarch," she said when she had stopped. The casual lilt of her words belied the lengths to which she had gone to find Malachite.

Malachite was acutely conscious of being in the presence of a Cainite of elder generation, a creature whose origin was shrouded by the mists of history. Her easy manner did little to comfort him. *No elder speaks his or her mind openly to another*, he thought, knowing this to be the case, for he had learned that lesson well as his own unlife had stretched from years to decades to centuries.

"You have heard the rumors," she said, "the nervous whispers on the lips of cowards."

Malachite held his peace, did not speak, but he felt himself nodding. *Yes*, he thought. *The rumors that Michael is destroyed. Worse than rumors—lies!*

"You, however, are no coward," Alexia said. "While the others tremble and fret, you would know the truth of this thing."

It is not true that he is destroyed! Cannot be true! This I shall prove!

Alexia regarded him intently, and suddenly Malachite was uncomfortably aware of the hideous beast he must appear to her with his deformities and torn, blood-stained robes. He shrank back, ashamed, cowed by how easily she read his intentions. Of what use was his silence? What could he conceal that she could not know?

"It is as you say," he told her.

Her tight-lipped smile was cool kindness—yet in her expression was nothing of pity, which would have offended Malachite, enraged him.

She knows me so well, yet we have seldom exchanged words before this night. She is so old... that must be the way of it. She has had countless years to observe and learn. What emotions has she not seen play themselves out hundreds of times over? Tell her nothing else, fool! He clenched his hand to his chest, remembered the icon, the images of the Archangel and the Dracon-faced Christ.

"If you consent," she said, "I would go with you, Malachite. I, too, would know the truth."

She is asking this of me, then? Malachite thought. *Not demanding, not threatening?* He felt himself again standing erect, unwilling to shield his visage for anyone, proud that such an aged Cainite would actually seek his assistance—and then suddenly, clutching the icon, he was too aware of his own stature, of the way in which Alexia played him like a harp that did not even feel the harper's fingers but sang nonetheless.

Fool! You who have stood with emperors and patriarchs, flattered by the wiles of a woman! he thought, and then blurted out: "It is not possible. You may go where you like, of course, but not as part of my company." *I cannot trust myself to measure her words. She knows me well enough, but the words she speaks of herself—nothing is as she says!*

Wrinkles tightened the corners of Alexia's eyes. Her smile now was the knowing look of the forum merchant, certain that the haggle would turn in her favor, counting beforehand the sale as complete.

"You think I reject you so as to sweeten the contract between us," Malachite said, genuinely surprised. "This is not the case. I would have you leave me to my own business."

She nodded and smiled as if accepting his words, yet her eyes said that she saw through his charade. "I understand, Malachite. All know that you are loyal to Michael." She place a hand to her own chest. "I, too, would know that he is well. Who else might save our city from the ravagers?" Now the worldly street merchant was gone, and she spoke as the wronged woman, victim of war waged in the streets. "For the sake of the Dream, Malachite…"

She was soft-spoken, not pleading, yet it was as if a powerful entreaty struck directly at Malachite's heart—as if her hand was with his, cradling the holy icon.

Why does she bother ask what I cannot refuse her? he wondered, flustered. He had risked the wrath of this elder Cainite by refusing her, yet still he could not manage to extract himself from her requests. In the face of one such as this, words and deeds were but fragile light split and scattered through the heart of a prism.

"I have seen many things this night," she continued. "I have seen Baron Thomas Feroux vanquished from the Citadel of Petrion. I have seen his Gangrel rampaging through the city, seeking vengeance against crusaders… and others. I have seen Bishop Alfonzo's underlings slaughtered. I have seen the slaves of the Ventrue prefects turned free."

She was none of those places! Malachite thought, then realized: *She said nothing of being there—only seeing.*

"If the rumors of the Patriarch were true," Alexia said, "not that they could be, mind you—yet if they were, then the old order is crumbling before our eyes, Malachite. Trinity, scion families, Codex of Legacies..." She scooped dust from the stone floor, let the fine sediment sift through her fingers and drift away. "One could do worse than to strike at his rivals when opportunity avails."

Rivals...? Malachite required a moment to make the leap that Alexia had spanned. *Succession... warlordism... is that what she thinks this is truly about? And this is her true purpose: to offer her services in the factionalism she sees devouring the city.* Another implication struck Malachite, shook him: *She thinks Michael destroyed, then—or else she is playing both sides of the coin and will deny that which was not said outright. Very well... I shall choose my side of the coin!*

"Come with me, Lady Alexia. We travel to Michael's crypt beneath Hagia Sophia."

Alexia's satisfaction was genuine, Malachite thought. He could have lost himself in the glow of her countenance. *Let her think that I aspire to be the Cainite warlord of Constantinople, and perhaps she can be of help if indeed Michael is... not well. But let me match her in mercenary spirit. She will expect as much and be suspicious otherwise.*

"In return, I require one thing of you," he said.

"Oh?" She feigned silk-thin surprise, yet her eyes were those of the bartering flesh-merchant.

Malachite cast about for a suitable demand. Normally from such an elder of influence and means, an unspecified favor to be consummated in the future would have sufficed, but just now a distinct unease about the future gripped him. A price more immediate in nature seemed preferable. But what? Then he latched on to it. "The woman physician, Miriam of Damascus— she studies with you."

"I seem to remember the name."

"She will become the responsibility of my family. You must relinquish all claim to her."

Alexia hesitated. She seemed almost pleased, perhaps amused, by this unexpected turn of events. "Your leper knights will find few converts among the Jews, I think," she said.

"It is my price."

"I thought perhaps thirty coins of silver."

"The night wastes away," Malachite said.

"Very well, very well. She is yours."

How quickly her talk of the Dream rings hollow, Malachite thought. *It was but cheap fodder for a 'loyal' beast of burden.* "Then let us be on our way."

Chapter Ten

"The Lady Alexia will be joining us," Malachite told the other Nosferatu. They regarded her skeptically, warily. "Let us go. We have wasted enough time already," he said, at the same time signaling secretly to Ignatius: *Watch her*.

Alexia said nothing. Having made her bargain with Malachite, she paid little heed to the others of his company, and they seemed disinclined to penetrate the armor of aloofness which encompassed her. And so they continued onward: Armand, Malachite, Alexia, Ignatius, Theodore with the boy, Basil, and Zoticus.

As they proceeded, Malachite could feel Alexia's eyes upon him. When he glanced behind, she did not look away, did not feign disinterest, but rather held his gaze—intently, inscrutably. Her eyes were black as the deepest tunnel shaft and burned dark fire against her chiseled ivory countenance. Over her shoulder, Malachite could see Ignatius, watching, prepared for any threat she might offer—but it was not the dagger in the back that Malachite feared. That was not the way of one such as the Lady Alexia. Would she not have attacked him when they were alone, if she wished to carve the heart from his body? And why would she want to? For then her mercenary bargain would be wasted. *She thinks I desire to rule the city in Michael's stead*. Malachite did not believe her interest in the Patriarch's welfare—no more than he believed tenderness drew the vulture to carrion. *But it may be that she can aid him somehow*. If in reaching Michael they found that she could help him, she would do what was necessary—out of fear if not devotion.

Still, the apprehension gnawed at Malachite. The feeling was entangled with all that he denied through his forward flight toward Michael: the icon with its Dracon-Christ, the fluttering presentiment that would not give him peace but which sought to illuminate the darkness within him better left undisturbed.

Michael will restore the balance that I cannot reclaim on my own, Malachite thought. And so he trudged on, fatalistically ignoring the Cappadocian threat behind him. *If it is my heart she desires,* he thought, *first she will make me love the knife, plead for it, so that in the end I will thank her as she takes my blood and I crumble to dust.* Yet still he felt, somehow, that he might turn her toward the Dream.

"Careful, now," Ignatius said.

Then Malachite, too, heard the sounds from ahead: voices, mournful cries, wails of desperation.

What torment and bloodshed have I come upon now? he wondered.

They were close to the church of Hagia Sophia, he saw—much closer than he had realized in his distraction. *I will know the truth.* The steps of all that had come before—a mortal lifetime; almost half a millennium of bloodstained undeath—had brought him to this juncture. *I will know.*

They had delved deep into the hill, yet through the countless tons of packed earth and rock, from beyond the crypts and tunnels and catacombs, he could sense the holiness of Hagia Sophia. *The Latins might defile the altar, they might pillage the relics and the sacred golden vessels, but they cannot separate the* Romaioi *from the grace of God the Father!*

This sudden sliver of contentment, of trust in the ordained divine plan, could not, however, dispel the tortured cries that emanated from the lighted chamber ahead.

"The antechamber of the Patriarch," Ignatius said, his words tinged with no small amount of awe.

He has never been here before, Malachite realized. The leper knights of St. Ladre had committed themselves to the Dream, but that through Malachite's proselytizing alone. They had never been recognized by Michael nor formally accepted into the city. *But Michael must have known*, Malachite thought. *The same as I felt he must know how Baron Thomas and I tried to preserve the Library of the Forgotten.*

Malachite stepped in front of Armand as they approached the antechamber, but suddenly it was as if his legs would not go on; they grew stiff and hard like pillars of salt. Ahead, the moans droned on. Chanting underscored the more piercing cries, voices raised in unison, the uttered sounds of ritual, accented by grace notes of agony.

She knew we would find this, he realized, wanting to turn to face Alexia, to look into her black eyes and cold smile. *She feared to pass through on her own.* Another layer of her machinations opened to him, and he wondered how many more lay beneath. But he could not face her, could not turn any more than he could go forward on his trembling legs. Was the chanting that of the divine liturgy he had led as a mortal bishop? Did the words descend from above, from Heaven? Or even from the great basilica above, through stone and earth and the bodies of the saints?

The screams put the lie to his vision. They pricked the Beast. If he was to deny what his inner vision had to show him, then perhaps the creature would run free.

Then someone was beside him, a hand on his shoulder. Ignatius spoke quietly: "The sun will rise soon."

The sun. It would shine its light across the earth, no matter protestations, while creatures of the night scurried for cover.

"Yes," Malachite said. "We go."

He led them into the antechamber, a huge torch-lit hall no more than twenty yards wide but easily thrice as long. Interlocking arches atop marble pillars rose into domes carved from living rock. The chamber sparkled white in the firelight—and red, bright crimson against dry red-black, fresh blood flowing over old.

The floor writhed, a sea of humanity, naked bodies thrashed raw, faces smeared gray with ash. Rent, discarded sackcloth littered the room. Quivering hands raised knotted cords embedded with shards of glass, paused while dry lips uttered prayers to the Archangel, then fell with all the strength that remained to them, lashing self or fellow. Throats swollen from lack of water spat anguished groans to mix with the ongoing chant.

There were Cainites among the throng as well, Malachite saw: corpse-white bodies crisscrossed with barren slashes, torn skin that did not bleed.

At the head of the assembly, atop three wide, shallow steps, stood a scarred Cainite before two massive doors. The torn vestments of a priest lay at his feet. Hair shorn and eyes closed, his dead flesh a maze of open, pale slices, he raised his fists to the heavens in entreaty: "Deliver us from evil, most favored of God's chosen, Michael the Archangel."

"Deliver us from evil," chanted his followers. "Deliver us from evil!"

Whips bit into flesh. Here a woman, breasts mutilated, fell to her knees. There a man lapsed into stupor and lay as if dead. The muttered prayers continued: "Jesu, Jesu, Michael, Michael, Archangel Michael!"

And the chanting: "Ours is not the power nor the worthiness, but by your grace shall we endure."

"Ours is not the power! Ours is not the power!"

Woven cord snapping against flesh. Glass claiming its prize. Battered penitents pleading though their very blood poured out, an orgy of torture and torment, all in the name of—

"Michael! Archangel Michael!"

"No!" roared Malachite. He could bear no more.

Whips raised to strike paused in the air. The multitude turned as one, away from the priest. Malachite stepped from the tunnel at the rear of the hall. The bloodied and exhausted throng parted before him. The mortals among them had seen Cainite tricks in the guise of miracles, no doubt, but they had never beheld the unmasked hideousness of the Nosferatu. Yet Malachite sensed as he stalked toward the false priest that the people made way from fear of his own will as much as his gruesome visage.

They are sheep, he thought, *and this charlatan would lead them through torture of body and soul to their doom!*

"No more!" he shouted. "Not in the name of Michael, you wretched blasphemer!"

The priest rose up, tall and terrible in his self-righteousness. "It is you who blasphemes!" he answered, incensed at this challenge. He raised his arms as if to call down the fury of Heaven. The people drew back—but Malachite marched unhesitatingly, glaring murder. The other Nosferatu and Alexia followed in his wake less enthusiastically, aware that the wave could break and carry them all away.

Malachite drew out his sword. "Speak those words again, and I shall flog you with your own tongue." Coming closer, he realized the priest's identity as he had not at first with the countless lacerations and severely cut hair. "Libanias! You are a trained bird of Magnus's, and Embraced only recently, while Michael's attention has wandered. You foul these chambers with your mimicked lies. Begone. All of you!" he bellowed, turning to the onlookers. "Begone!"

They shied away, but fear or exhaustion or piety held them to their places.

"Your threats," said Libanias, "are no more dire than the swords of the crusaders. They steal and kill… and Magnus is taken away…."

Malachite heard the slight tremor in the priest's voice, self-doubt, trepidation. *He believes!* Malachite saw. *He is Magnus's man, yet he is no charlatan, but dupe!* "Pitiful wretch," said Malachite, and he turned away from the priest.

Libanias's rage kindled anew. "We call on the Archangel Michael to strike down our enemies: those who persecute us with swords, those who spread lies among the faithful! All the wrongs that have been done will be set aright!"

Malachite drew back his sword—then faltered. *All the wrongs that have been done will be set aright!* Had he not said much the same thing? Had he not clawed his way to the haven of the Patriarch so that Michael might have mercy upon the faithful, save Constantinople and the Dream from enemies without and within?

The bloody throng stared in rapt silence at the priest and at Malachite. Then, quietly at first, the muttering began in low voice, indignant questions, pleas for intervention, threats against the blasphemer:

"You can see by his face that he is marked by the Devil."

"What other master could so foul a beast serve?"

"Michael will strike him down. We are the faithful."

"Pray, and the Archangel will deliver us."

They are so blind, these mortals, Malachite thought. *But so are the Cainites among them. They are fools, each one, as big as this priest, or Magnus, or... or...* He could not follow the revelation where it led. He clenched his fists. First he must expose this heresy. How many dozen mortals lay naked and bleeding upon the floor in the name of Michael? How many Cainites mutilated themselves in the cause of redemption?

"Is your suffering so much more noble because you inflict it upon yourself?" he shouted at them. "Do you think Michael is pleased that you tear your clothes and peel the flesh from your bones? Does this glorify him? Does he answer your call?"

Malachite turned and pointed at the great doors. "How many nights and days have you labored at this folly? And still he does not answer. Fools and hypocrites!"

He took his sword, flung it end over end into the crowd. "Who thus do I strike down?" he cried. "And how much worse is his lot than those who die at the hands of the Latins? How much worse is his lot than the rest of you, destroying yourselves for a false hope?"

Angry murmurs rose from the throng. Like the first turning of the tide, they began to press forward.

"Go ahead! Tear me limb from limb!" he shouted. "If this is what has become of the Dream, then it is what I deserve. It is what we all deserve."

"Deliver us, Archangel Michael," intoned Libanias. "Deliver us from evil."

"There is no Archangel!" Malachite shouted. He found suddenly in his hands the icon, the face of the Archangel, and of the Dracon-Christ. "No Archangel, save in Heaven beside God the Father!" With unholy fury, Malachite slammed the icon to the stone floor, felt as much as saw the ivory crack, fracture into pieces.

At that instant a beast was loosed upon the crowd. Snarling, it pounced left then right, rending with fang and claw. Screams echoed from marble. Penitents tried to run, slipped in their own blood, and then were trampled underfoot.

Basil! Malachite saw.

The Nosferatu's deformed face was contorted almost beyond recognition. In his fury and brutality, he resembled nothing so much as a wild animal. Ignatius stood near Malachite, sword drawn in case the penitents came closer. The Lady Alexia's black eyes took in everything from behind her ivory mask.

"No, this is not what I wanted," Malachite muttered. Then he was struck from behind and staggered, stumbled on the steps.

Libanias was on him, gouging at his face, tearing brittle dead flesh that crumbled and fell away like an escarpment of sand. "Deliver us from evil! Deliver us from evil!" the priest screamed with each swipe of his claws.

Malachite struggled to defend himself, managed to raise one arm before his face. Claws ripped through his wrist, through tendon and into bone. Another frenzied blow slipped past his guard, caught soft flesh, tore free.

The pain came an instant later, searing his mind as if the path the claw traced through his face was all that existed in the world.

Not in the name of Michael! he raged. Pain made him stronger, focused the faithful.

He fought back with his own claws, plunged them deep into Libanias's bowels, churned muscle and desiccated organs. Malachite felt the priest's body spasm and knew that the blow had penetrated the crazed fury.

Still they thrashed and rolled. Malachite struck with snapping, tearing fangs, claimed a prize. Bone caught between his teeth. He wrenched his head and jaws like a jackal, felt the crunching, grinding—a *pop!* He spat from his mouth one of the groping fingers that had ripped at his face.

Shout of pain—

Bone-jarring impact—

And then suddenly Libanias was gone. No weight pressed down on Malachite. No claws sought to rend his face. His tattered hand, raised defensively, met no resistance. He became aware of the hard edges of the marble steps beneath his back. Something blocked his field of vision. He could not see clearly.

Hands tugged at his arm—but not roughly. Ignatius helped him to his feet.

"I could not strike him without hitting you," the knight said. Malachite was forced to turn his head to see the other Nosferatu properly.

The echoing screams drew their attention now. Mangled bodies lay sprawled throughout the antechamber, limbs scattered, blood pooling on marble. Cultists of the Archangel Michael crowded at the tunnel entrances, climbed over one another in their panic to escape.

Basil-the-Beast fell upon them, one after another after another, pulling them down from behind, striking deathblow after deathblow. Several Cainites lay hamstrung, throats torn out, unable to flee or even scream. They pulled themselves across the floor by their fingers or merely writhed in silent agony.

And there was another beast.

A dark wolf. It tore at a ragged body—what was left of Libanias: bone, blood-stained like the marble; portions of limbs; spilled entrails, dried leather straps; and staring, unseeing eyes beneath a jaggedly torn scalp of shorn, blood-matted hair.

Malachite could not place the wolf, could make no sense of its being there. The carnage of penitents dominated his strangely restricted vision. *This is not what I wanted!*

"Enough!" he roared.

The wolf looked up from Libanias's carcass, curious. Basil started, turned toward Malachite, glowering feral menace.

"Enough!" Malachite bellowed again, crossing toward his clanmate, stepping across ruined bodies, wading through slick blood. He wiped at his face, trying to remove whatever obscured his sight.

Ignatius was at his side, sword ready. Malachite stalked fearlessly toward Basil, who hesitated before his elder's wrath.

"Is this what we have become?" Malachite hissed through clenched teeth. He grabbed Basil by the shoulders, shook him. "We exist so that mortals might endure! Not be slaughtered like animals! Not... not this!" Malachite gestured vaguely at their surroundings, at the destruction of life and limb.

Basil stood transfixed, and in his eyes Malachite saw the reflection of his own face, torn open to the bone, one eye destroyed, slashed and hanging half from the socket.

Seeing the Beast receding within Basil, Malachite turned to the other monster in their midst. Where the wolf had been stood Verpus Sauzezh slapping dust from his hands—all that was left of the rapidly decaying Libanias. Malachite faced the Turk, asked him: "Would you add to the carnage?"

The faintest hint of a smile crossed Verpus's lips. "I merely pulled this one from you." He pawed with his boot at the dust on the floor.

"And what would you do now?" Malachite asked. "Slay me? Take me in chains to your lord?" He felt Ignatius stir at his side.

"The baron charged us to hunt down the enemies of the city," Verpus said. "Here lies one, destroyed."

"Would not your baron include me among the enemies of the city?"

"Perhaps," said Verpus with a shrug. "He did not mention you by name, and if he does consider you an enemy… I differ with my lord in this matter."

Malachite regarded him skeptically, listened for the lie in the words, but found it difficult to focus. He touched a hand to his face and felt the trickle of jelly that had been his eye.

Verpus. My captor turned friend—instead of the other way around this time?

Terrified screams receding down the tunnels distracted Malachite, as did the blood, so much of it spilled. The Beast stirred, demanded its due.

"Malachite," said Alexia calmly from where she had observed the chaos, "we dally while the sun draws near the eastern horizon."

Malachite nearly staggered under the weight of her words. *There is no time*, he thought. *My enemies circle like sharks, and above the city burns. Perhaps already the Templars delve beneath the church.*

"Ignatius," Malachite said, "we have won through to Michael's chambers. The Lady Alexia and I shall go within. The rest of our people must weather the day nearby... not here," he added. *Too much blood has been shed here. Innocent fools. Sheep led to the slaughter—and us wielding the blade, God forgive us.* "Forward," Malachite muttered to himself.

"Return here at sunset," he said to Ignatius. "I will do that which I should have done long ago: I shall present you and the rest of our people to Michael. We will hide like shamed criminals no longer."

Hearing quiet whimpering, Malachite turned to Basil. He had fallen to his knees, his whole body trembling.

"The Patriarch is beautiful and terrible," Malachite said, "but he is kind, just. Do not fear." Perhaps Basil took some comfort in that. His trembling eased. With the Beast cowed, Malachite saw only the leper knight who had saved them at the slave pens and who had cared for the boy—who himself lay as if asleep, oblivious to the bloodshed, in Theodore's arms. Malachite went to him, took the boy.

The time is at hand, childe. You will be restored.

"And you," Malachite said to Verpus, "if you are true to the Dream this city might yet become, then come here tomorrow night. Michael will have need of the faithful. If you return with the baron and those who would do us harm, then we will know where matters stand." *And Michael will deal with it.*

Silence fell over the antechamber. The weariness of morning pulled at Malachite, the desire for strife to be at an end; hunger pulled at him also. He made his way back to the steps, to the doors, to the icon he had smashed against stone. It lay in three pieces. The crack that had seemed to separate the Archangel from the Dracon-Christ had become an open fissure. Another break ran through the image of the Archangel as well.

Gently Malachite laid down the boy, and just as gently gathered the fragments of ivory tile and tucked them safely within the folds of his robe. He felt faint, sick with the destruction he had wrought.

Lady Alexia stepped toward him.

"First, I shall feed," said Malachite. "Then we will go forward."

Chapter Eleven

Blood. It was due the Cainites—a tithe, of sorts, for their shepherding of mankind. Yet the shepherds neglected their flock. Worse, they fleeced their charges of lifeblood.

We serve no purpose but to steal blood, Malachite thought. *I see it, yet still I drink.*

Blood flowed down his throat, worked its wonders on his abused body. He knew the titillation of lust, the awe of sacrament. The torn wrist grew whole and strong again. His dangling, lacerated eyeball quivered as of its own accord, drew back into the socket and began to mend. Slowly, vision returned, a horrible blur at first, but gradually he saw. The Beast grumbled at Malachite's restraint—so many bodies! But he chose only one.

The woman was on the verge of death when he found her. Among the dead and dying, she lay naked in blood and excrement. Nearby, Malachite found two young children: lashed raw, dead, hands and wrists bound to ensure their piety.

Did they belong to her? he wondered. *Did she think to save them? Did she think to save herself?*

He sought answers the only way he knew how: in the blood, searching for any hint of recognition as he drank in her fading life, but all he tasted was her fear, her despair and desperation. Or perhaps his own.

"Shall we?" Lady Alexia asked, when he was done.

Malachite wondered at her veiled urgency, and at that moment he hated her for it. He wanted more than anything to step beyond the huge bronze doors, to find Michael. *Yet I fear the final step.*

Alexia's impatience revealed his own faithlessness.

He looked to the body at his feet. *This woman had more courage and faith than I—this poor fool of a woman.*

"Malachite," Alexia called; not unkindly, yet he glared hatred at her. She stepped back from him.

He took up the boy, his own childe, and moved toward the doors. They towered above him, but when he grasped the handles, the doors swung open easily. Malachite felt sickened. He could not turn to face the bodies strewn throughout the antechamber. *They did not dare to try. Damnable fools! They would torture themselves and perish in hopes that their Archangel would come out to them—and to enter through the gates was in their power all the while!*

"There is only danger in worship," Alexia said sternly, "for the believers and for their god."

"Michael never asked for their worship," Malachite said.

"Nor did he turn them away."

The sputtering torches from the antechamber cast the Cainites' shadows before them through the frame of the doorway onto the stone. And thus, at the end of this, the third night since his return to the city, Malachite entered the haven of Michael the Patriarch. Alexia trailed silently behind, her shadow covering him.

The chamber rose into darkness. Malachite knew from earlier visits what it was that they did not see: the magnificent carved dome, converging arches, at the base separated by forty arched stained-glass windows. When Michael was awake, the windows shone as if by the light of the sun, never mind that they were far underground.

Now the dome was black as pitch.

The first time Malachite had been here, he had thought himself in the nave of Hagia Sophia. The similarities were striking—and by no means coincidental: the vast dimensions of the dome; the windows, number and design; the cascade of semi-domes on both east and west sides; galleries and marble columns, north and south; fine gilding and mosaics of precious stones, identical to the last detail to those in the great church. Michael had taken hundreds of years, employed artisan after artisan, to create his divine paradise.

Stepping inside, Malachite's step crunched. He paused, saw fragments of glass on the floor—stained glass. Instinctively, he looked to the dome but could see nothing in the heights. Looking back to the floor, he saw that the very marble beneath his sandals was blackened, scorched as if by fire. A sick feeling gripped his insides. The Beast began to stir.

They continued forward, each step grinding glass underfoot, beyond the projection of torchlight from the antechamber. At the center of the darkened pseudo-nave stood a sepulcher upon a dais, both carved of stone. Otherwise, the vast chamber was empty. Malachite moved toward the dais, an altar of sorts to Michael. Each step was labored, halting, as if Malachite were drawn forward by chains wound onto a giant rusted winch.

Closer… closer….

The dais was much larger than it seemed from the doorway. It rose above his head to at least twice his height. He wavered momentarily before placing his foot upon the first step. Only the unyielding presence of Alexia pressed him forward.

Would I have the strength for this without her? Does she know that? She had known, he felt certain, of the blood cult poised at the gates. *What else does she know? Does she know what we will find?*

But whether she knew or not, Malachite would know. He summoned the courage to climb the step, and then another, and another. Around him, beneath him, the nave spread out into darkness.

Forgive me, Michael, for disturbing you, Malachite meant to say, but his lips and tongue were struck dumb. *It is not for me, but for the boy, for the city, for the Dream.*

He rose step by step. All the world was only the dais, the sepulcher, the boy, the ivory-masked Cappadocian. All else was darkness, the silence of death. Malachite stepped forward, gazed into the open sepulcher of the Patriarch....

"Dust..." Alexia whispered.

The word ascended into shadow, thundered in Malachite's ears until he feared the entire city would collapse atop them.

"No."

"It is true," Alexia said, her dulcet voice suddenly dry, coarse, a confused mix of shock, awe, fear, anticipation. "The rumors are true."

"No," said Malachite. "It cannot be."

He sagged against the stone. *It cannot be!* Michael rendered to dust; the most beautiful city on the Earth, an eternal testament to the glory of God, in ruins; the Dream...

"It cannot be."

Malachite laid his face against that of his childe, wept tears of blood—blood shed twice this night in hopes that Michael would wield his fiery sword and smite the despoilers of the city.

"My brothers are both gone," said a quiet voice in his ear. He felt the cold lips of his childe move ever so slightly against his face. "They are both gone. You cannot bring them back."

Malachite jerked up, searched the boy's blood-smeared face for signs of vitality—yet the jaw was slack, the eyes closed.

Did I hear it? Did he speak?

Malachite looked to Alexia, but she was transfixed by the ridge of dust within the sepulcher—dust that once had walked the darkened streets of Rome, many miles and years ago; dust that had crossed seas to a backwater settlement and helped transform it into a golden city.

Whatever had happened before, the boy now was silent. Michael now was...

"We must be certain," Alexia said. "We must be certain it was him."

Only slowly did the meaning of her words creep through Malachite's shock.

...*Certain it was him.* The utterance echoed throughout the darkened heights and, in Malachite's mind, entwined itself with churning impossibilities: *Dust... gone... cannot bring them back.*

"It could be a hoax," Alexia was saying.

Hoax... dust... certain.

"Or a test," Malachite whispered. "He is testing us." His own words hardly escaped his lips. As with the boy a moment before, Malachite wondered if he had indeed spoken. But whether his words fled into the dark or were smothered by it, he latched onto the idea that Michael was testing him. There was still hope for the boy and the city, for the Dream.

Cannot bring them back...

"There is a way," Alexia said.

...*Bring them back.*

"What is it?"

"It is said that you... that you have drunk of his blood." Alexia's face became more of an ivory mask at that moment than ever he had seen it before. Only her eyes gave her away, staring so intently that Malachite thought the mask might crack and break like the painted icon. Her voice was flat, perfectly controlled, yet the black eyes burned, envious, that so horrid a creature could have partaken of the blood.

Malachite raised himself upright, his pride pricked by her unstated sneer. "It is true," he said.

Her reaction was somewhere between disbelief and satisfaction. "If so, then all I require is a drop of your blood."

If... Malachite recognized her goading. *It is a trick*, he thought. *She will make me love the knife, plead for it, so that in the end I will thank her.* But the chance to know the truth...

He knew he would walk that path, though she lead him into sunrise itself.

Alexia smiled. She reached within the folds of her gown and produced a small golden cup, scarcely larger than a thimble. From the sepulcher she scooped a tiny fraction of dust—of Michael, perchance.

"I would know the truth," said Malachite. He held out his hand to her.

She began to whisper—almost imperceptibly. Malachite strained to hear, but her words were nothing he could comprehend, not the Greek of the New Rome nor Latin of the old. No barbarian tongue of the West, no nomadic speech nor learned dialect of the East. Something older, something that reached as deep as the roots of the earth, nourished by blood.

In her other hand now she held a silver dagger. With a single, forceful motion, she sliced across Malachite's palm. He allowed the blood to come, to well up in the gash. A single drop stretched down toward the golden cup, hesitated, resisted the call of dust, stretched farther...

...Then dropped.

In the cup, blood and dust disappeared in a hiss of steam. Alexia's arcane incantations took on a sharper edge, grew more pronounced if not more easily decipherable. They grew more real—while the rest of the world became distinctly unreal, faded, distant. The bloodsmoke filled Malachite's senses; crowded out the darkness of the shadowy dome; filled his eyes, mouth, nose; dissolved the cold solidity of marble beneath his fingertips.

The chanting was louder, though Malachite had not noticed the increasing volume until now it seemed to emanate from within his own mind. Each syllable stretched out like the blood clinging to his hand—stretching, resisting, stretching, breaking—giving way grudgingly to the next. He tried to mimic the texture of each sound, but the feel of them eluded his tongue. They held him rapt, as time-sense wrinkled, lost meaning, lost relation to any context of here and now. The sound elongated until surely a single word exceeded the cycle of birth and death, season shifting to season shifting to season.

From the chanting and smoke emerged light, warm, bright, and cleansing.

And God said, "Let there be light."

Malachite knelt at the base of the dais—watched himself kneeling at the base of the dais. He saw through his eyes, yet simultaneously existed outside of and beyond himself. This duality of vision was mirrored by overlapping tides of thought, one wave's perspective receding as the next crashed onto the shore of consciousness.

He knelt, staring up at the sepulcher from below. He remembered standing beside the sepulcher, leaning against it. Bright light emanated from atop the dais and through the magnificent stained-glass windows lining the immense dome above, yet part of him knew the dome was cloaked in darkness. He awaited the first glance of the Patriarch.

Yet I have seen the ridge of dust.

Time-sense was hopelessly jumbled, roiled by the crashing waves of perspective, cloudy with sediment.

Dust.

He slipped into the then-self—Maleki, the self so naïve as still to think in mortal hours—in days!—though he had been dead for nearly a year, tortured by Magnus and by his own conscience.

The light grew brighter. He looked away, shielded his face, felt the presence of Michael. The very air around him grew warm and crackled as the Patriarch's feet touched step after step, descending so that lesser creatures might partake of his holiness. Maleki trembled.

And then supernal glory laid hands upon him.

Salvation was at hand. Redemption.

Then the undeniable hunger. Hands of pure light were at Maleki's face. Shafts of blood red poured from fiery stigmata. Maleki drank of the light, and was christened Malachite in the blood of the Patriarch.

"So it is true," said a voice, a woman's voice. "You drank of the blood."

A wave of addled time-sense crashed violently over Malachite. The undertow took hold of him, dragged him from his epiphany, the most blessed moment of his existence. Desperately, he wanted to go back, but he could not navigate the dark waters, could not even make sense of his own body suspended between then and now.

"You drank of the blood," the woman said. "Now we will know the truth."

Malachite cared nothing for truth. He desired the precious vitae above all else. The Dream shone through his pores like bloodsweat. To feel the light receding was pure agony.

Yet recede it did, to be replaced by a different light—if a candle can be said to replace the sun. The illumination was enlightenment of a different sort, less primordial than the epiphany born of the Patriarch, but still it burned. This time Malachite had no preoccupation with which to steel himself.

Now we will know the truth. The woman's voice…

Who is she? He could not remember. Her name and face escaped like sand through his fingers. Malachite knew, though, that she could see within him. His blood had opened this door for her.

Yet she could not enter through the door without showing herself to him—even the trailing edge of a shadow. He followed her words, the sound of her chanting, softly, rhythmically, in some incomprehensible tongue that felt of musky earth, of mountains rising from the sea and falling again to rubble, of love and death, but mostly death.

No—there was love—driving, tumultuous, torturous—tucked within the decay of flesh and spirit—lost love—love that was promised at some time to return.

"Can the time be at hand when my Andreas will return to me?" she wondered—

But then she realized Malachite's knowledge of her; she withdrew behind an ivory mask so that not even a portion of her shadow was revealed to him.

Darkness.

A ripple of time-sense, and light again—the telltale radiance of the Patriarch as he lay within his sepulcher. And the pathetic light cast from a single torch. Two figures entering through the bronze doors, dwarfed by the black heights of the unlit dome. The man on the right wore the squint of countless years of reading by candlelight. He was attired in the plain robes of a monk. A step behind him, a smaller cowled figure pulled back its hood, revealed the face of a young girl—young and not young. Her body was slight, with wrists like fragile reeds, hands delicate as crickets' wings. Her skin was dark: not sandy dark of the Turks, nor the creamy chocolate of Egypt, nor the darkest hue from the far southern reaches of Africa. She was dark as though she had been burnt, a clay-fired vessel formed in the shape of a girl.

And the eyes—there was nothing young about her eyes.

"Put out the torch, Peter, you simpleton," she hissed.

"He will not stir," Peter sniveled. His eyes caught the light, danced spasmodically, constantly shifting with the fabrications of insanity. "The visions are upon him. He will not stir."

I know this one, Malachite realized, *this Peter— another of Magnus's underlings, and not a favored one. A babbling sycophant. Worse than Libanias is... was...* Malachite found himself caught upon a cusp of time-sense, a bubble, an eddy in the churning waters. Though he was not here, he saw the man and woman advancing, a twisted mockery of his own pilgrimage—that which still occupied him, that which had not yet occurred.

"He knows we are here," she said.

Peter grinned maniacally, strangled a laugh in his throat. "Of course, he does, Mary. But he will not stir. The visions are upon him."

"The light..."

"The light is ever with him, never extinguished."

It is extinguished! Malachite wanted to shout. *It will be!* He wanted to rush to the top of the dais, retrace his own unstepped steps, shake Michael, warn him.

"You are certain?" Mary asked.

The laughter forced its way out now, squeezed like the wrung neck of a cat. "I told you I would bring you to him helpless, unable to resist you. You have no faith in me. Like Magnus, damn him! You have no faith in me. Am I certain? I am as certain of this as I am of the hand before my face. Would we still walk and speak and gaze upon him if it were not so?"

Slowly, Mary nodded. "I agree. And if he is not to stir, and if the light is ever with him, then we do not need the torch... nor do I need you."

Her sword flashed through the air with a speed and violence that put the lie to her frail body. The torch fell to the marble floor, and beside it, Peter's head.

Mary moved forward, set foot to step.

Malachite could no longer see her. The wind and the waves carried him away, wracked with vertigo, spinning, spinning....

He was Michael. The world was a magnificent dome overhead, the brilliance of forty angels of fiery light. They awaited him, hands outstretched, with heavenly trumpets prepared to greet him. He stared up at them—then at the black face staring down at him from a much closer vantage, the black face that was to intercede on his behalf.

"Greetings, lover," she said. "It has been... many years."

Many years. The words could not encompass the scope of lingering hatred in her eyes. Centuries upon centuries, thousands of years, simmering, boiling over. And if ever that venerable girl had known love, the capacity now was less than the whisper of an ancient memory.

Yet he remembered their love of so long ago. He remembered the touch of a beautiful lithe girl, swept away by the millennia. He remembered the agony of awaking that night to find that his followers had smuggled his body out of the besieged city of Ebla. He remembered the heartache of knowing that the girl would die, that she was taken from him by fate.

Now destiny had returned her to him, and he smiled.

As if from far away, Malachite remembered these things, knew them, felt them—impossible memories of blood. He wanted to shout warnings to Michael, to stop what was about to happen—what had already happened. They were one and the same, joined by blood, and Malachite could see the hand of God descending upon the Patriarch, could see the divine inspiration—and yet knew it for the madness it was.

"What vision is it that you see," Mary asked, "that you would smile at this, the time of your undoing? I would that you could scream and squirm and know something of the torture I have endured for all these many years." She glared down at him in the sepulcher, black eyes in a black face, a stain surrounded by a brilliant nimbus of vibrant colors.

I am Father to the Dream, thought Michael, thought Malachite. *By my passion I am become also the Son.*

Mary held a sword before his face, her fingers wrapped around the shaft. "Your blade," she said, her voice dripping evil, sweet honey. "I threw myself upon it… found it centuries later, took it from a trader whose heart and entrails I devoured." Slowly, she squeezed the blade, its edge slicing into her flesh. A trickle of black blood ran down the sword, and from her wounds crawled bone-white maggots.

With the sound of metal grating against bone, she snapped the blade in two, threw the pieces down on top of him.

"I know you see me. I know you *know*," she hissed. "But Peter was right. You will not stir. You are too entranced by your visions, by contemplation of your Dream. But know this: It will crumble with you! Nothing will remain!"

With her bare hands, she rent the robe that covered her, revealing charred black skin, barely formed breasts. She set fingernails to her forehead, rent flesh down her face, neck, chest. More maggots crawled forth from the wounds.

"My suffering will be your suffering!" she cried, leaning closer—then paused. "And what is this?"

From his chest, she raised a crucifix, held it before his face. "Your God and your Christ are useless and impotent. They will not help you. They cannot help you."

You do Their work, he thought. *My will be done*.

Malachite could not separate himself from the passion play in which he was ensnared. He wished only to tear himself from it, to shake Michael to action. *The city burns! You can smite this demon as easily as you can smite the false crusaders! The Dream needn't die!*

But his fury was distant, weak like cheap wine that has been watered.

Mary regarded the crucifix with contempt, but he saw it for what it was. He saw the ecstasy of pain, torture and sacrifice, release—and he saw the face of the Christ, the arch of the supernal son made flesh, flesh made spirit, rendered so that generations upon generations would worship Him... the Dracon-Christ, lover of Michael the Patriarch, co-equal to him in all things of the Dream.

Then Mary's fangs were at his throat. There was the searing pain, the ecstasy of the kiss, explosions in the heavens, rain of colored glass.

Do not do this! Malachite screamed without voice, knowing that it was already done.

Michael had found redemption in the hatred of a lover, too far beyond the Dream to return. Malachite tasted the madness of the Patriarch's blood, even as Mary tasted it. His defeat was nearly as bitter as her victory.

And Michael smiled.

In the end, there was a searing blast of fire, liquid glass imploding, then flinging outward, a hundred times over, the heat that had forged it. Mary cried her vengeance to the ages.

Then silence.

Chapter Twelve

Darkness. Malachite was alone. The frail body of the boy lay beside him on the dais, but Malachite was alone. Somewhere nearby in the darkness, Alexia hovered, a vulture poised to alight, but Malachite was alone. The raging tempest of perspectives was a calm ocean. The cusp of time-sense was receded, the bubble burst. The inner light, now gone, had showed to him that which he had so greatly denied and so ardently resisted seeing: Michael was destroyed. Malachite was alone.

The sleep of oblivion called to him. How tempting to close his eyes, perhaps to wake up when years or centuries had sorted through the chaos of the world; perhaps not to wake at all. If not for the press of jagged shards of stained glass beneath his shoulder and the charred, pungent scent of fire-scorched marble so close beneath his nose, he might already have given himself over to the sleep. Michael was destroyed. The Dream...?

"There must be another to carry on," Alexia said.

Wearily, Malachite held her words upon his tongue. He tasted something in them... but what? His guesses about her intentions, her motivations, had proven so inadequate thus far. Perhaps she had wanted him to see her past the penitent cultists, and that had been the all of it. Perhaps she wished to back him in taking the reigns of Cainite leadership and restoring the devastated city. Perhaps she had known what they would find within the haven of the Patriarch. Perhaps, even, she had known what they would see if Malachite allowed her his blood.

But what use did she hope to make of him now?

He tried to remember what he had seen of her as she had stepped through the door into the light of his inner eye: long-denied desire, love lost but destined to return, someone named Andreas.

How am I part of her plans? He shook his head. *Does it matter? Do I have a choice?* Whatever secrets drove her, Alexia had made possible his seeing what otherwise would have haunted him throughout eternity. *I know the truth of Michael's fall—Michael's ascension.*

"He is gone," Alexia said, "but it may be that the Dream will endure."

"And how is that?" Malachite managed, unable yet to give himself fully to defeat.

"It matters little who sits on the mortal throne," she said. "Constantinople will survive—damaged, yes, but it will survive. You have the strength of your conviction. All know that you, above all others, were faithful to Michael. You could take the mantle of Patriarch, bend the city to your will, oversee a restoration that would glorify God and enrich humanity until the end of days."

"I am content to serve," he said, shaking his head.

"Do you seek your own contentment, or fulfillment of the Dream?"

Her barb struck deep, yet Malachite could sense the more lethal snares she laid all about with her questions and advice.

"I am not Michael," he said, "nor his equal. Only false pride could lead me down that road."

"Or necessity," Alexia countered, "if the Dream is not to wither and die upon the vine."

Malachite sighed wearily. Oblivion called, yet he could not loose the barbs she had landed. His thoughts turned to the baron, loyal Thomas, driven to distraction by the destruction of the library he was sworn to protect.

"The city may be the Dream manifest," he said, "but it is not the Dream."

She hesitated. "Perhaps you speak the truth, and the Dream is dead... but can you take that chance?"

"Damnation, woman!" The end was so near, but she would not let him be. *She knows me too well!* The scars of three and a half centuries of serving the Dream were obvious to her.

"Do you turn from the Dream so easily, Malachite? I would not have thought it possible." She seemed wounded by his infidelity, distraught—yet in her distress there was a knowing glint of dark eyes. "If not you, who will rid the city of our enemies? Who will begin anew and carry on Michael's Dream?" She hesitated, waiting for the precise instant when her words would strike deepest. "Or do you hide something from me?"

Hide? If he were not so weighed down by anguish, he would have laughed in mockery of her. *I have not been able to hide anything from you from the moment we met.* Yet within the fold of his robes, there was hidden a secret relic: the shattered tile icon, the broken Archangel, the Dracon-Christ remaining whole.

"There is another," Malachite whispered to himself. "He who with Michael conceived the Dream. Of the three founders, there is one who perchance remains."

"Yes," Alexia said, following his meaning. "There were three who set the Dream in motion. Michael was first among them...." *But we have seen what became of Michael*, she did not say. "Antonius was, in some ways, like a son unto him, but Antonius fell by treachery. Caius, the childe, took his place." She waved a hand dismissively. "Caius was not the equal of his sire. The third—he left Constantinople a mere two or three centuries ago...."

"The Dracon," Malachite said. He pulled from his robes the icon, gazed upon the Christ-face.

"But how will you find him?" Alexia asked.

Malachite shook his head. He did not know. But the idea that he could find the Dracon, an elder so close to the blood of Caine himself, seized him with a vengeance. "For the love he held for Michael and for the Dream, I could call him back." But how to find the Dracon? He had left Constantinople of his own free will. He could be anywhere and, with the blood of Tzimisce flowing through his veins, he could be anyone. While Malachite was bound to the deformed visage of his Embrace, the Dracon could sculpt his flesh to match his pleasure. Malachite gazed still at the Christ-face upon the icon, the form that the Dracon had once worn. It mattered little what the actual Christ had looked like; the Dracon had taken an idealized form of passion with which to inspire the artists, whose works in turn inspired the masses.

But how will I find him? Malachite thought. He looked to the boy, eyes closed and perhaps never to open again.

"I know of one, though she is far from here," Alexia said with transparently feigned coyness, "who speaks of mysteries hidden from the eyes of the rest of us. An oracle. What's more, the Dracon is known to her. It may be that she would see some path of salvation for the city, for the Dream… and there is the boy to consider," she added. "Michael proved little enough help for him."

Malachite's ire flared at the rebuke of the Patriarch. Alexia had ushered the Nosferatu to this road as surely as he had brought her to this darkened chamber. She wanted him to seek the oracle. *I should turn from this path to spite her*, he thought—but he could not.

Infuriatingly, despite his suspicions of her motives, she led him where he wanted to go.

"Perhaps you are ready to give up on the boy," Alexia said. "And everything else."

"I am tempted," Malachite snapped, leaving her to guess whether he was tempted to give up or to press on. "You say this oracle is far from here. Where? How would I find her?"

"You would find her with my aid," Alexia said. "There are none save of my clan's blood who could show to you the temple, though you stand before it on the face of Mount Erciyes."

Malachite felt the barbs pull true. *I would like to have seen the moon rise above Mount Erciyes.* They were the last words of the second of the three boys, as reported by Ignatius, above whom no other was more trustworthy. Malachite cradled the remaining boy to his breast. The silenced voice of the three had yet managed to speak.

"And in return?" Malachite asked.

"In return, you will ask of the oracle the questions that I relate to you. They will serve your purpose."

And yours, Malachite thought. He did not need to look to know the tight-lipped smile that creased the ivory mask. Alexia knew he could not refuse her in this. He sensed, far, far above them, the sun shining over Hagia Sophia; but not yet for Malachite was the sleep of oblivion—only the sleep of day.

"We will go," he said, and finally allowed his eyes to close.

Part Three:

Anatolia

Chapter Thirteen

On each side of the barge, six slender oars moved in unison. They dipped silently into the black water, with their long single draw propelled the vessel forward, then rose and returned home to begin again. With every few strokes, they scattered hundreds upon hundreds of droplets, rings of ripples converging, diverging, swept away by the current, abandoned by their progenitors as the barge continued on.

On deck, Malachite looked back over their moonlit wake toward the receding walls of Constantinople. From here, the city looked to be at rest, peaceful.

A corpse can look peaceful, he reminded himself.

By now most of the fires had been extinguished or had burned themselves out. The worst of the looting was done. The Latins collected their stolen riches in immense hoards so that they might divide it among themselves, each according to his station. Such honor among thieves was admirable. Franks and Venetians sat in council, drawn-out affairs and often heated, to decide who among them would profane the imperial throne and call himself master of them all. Already there was the sense that none of the crusaders wished to kneel before his fellow, and so arguments and threats and bribes abounded.

Meanwhile, the common people—those who had survived, those who had not fled, never to return—attempted to resume their normal lives. Fish did not fill the nets by magic and harvest themselves. Many of the boats had been damaged or destroyed during the siege and must be repaired, replaced. Artisans sifted through the ruins of their shops, salvaging what they could. The need for pottery and furniture and tools and cloth did not vanish simply because the emperor had fled the city. There were mouths to feed, as well, including the invaders' army; and the shattered imperial bureaucracy to refashion to the liking of the empire's new rulers. An ambitious merchant or landowner who dealt generously with the Latins might find himself awarded a lucrative office in perpetuity.

For the mortals life will go on, more or less, as it would after any one of the disastrous fires that sweeps through the city every so often, Malachite thought. For the Cainites, however…

The ruling Trinity families, scattered or destroyed.

The New Trinity of Malachite's Nosferatu, the baron's Gangrel, and the Lexor Brujah, sundered, lapsing into open warfare. The Library of the Forgotten, destroyed.

Constantinople overrun by Latins, from the Quarter and abroad.

Centuries of progress, of nurturing Cainite and mortal, all for naught, Malachite thought. For the moment, with the moonlight reflecting against the shiny dark surface of the Golden Horn, he could almost let wash away with a current of weariness his bitter feelings at the shortcomings of his kind: the bickering and cruelty, jealousy and envy, self-interest to the exclusion of all reason.

He could not, however, forget the most damning blow.

Michael, destroyed.

Nor could Malachite completely accept it. Not yet. Last night while the Lady Alexia had made arrangements for their escape from the city, he had climbed one of the abandoned towers of the city wall and looked out over the desolation. Even then, the thought had sprung to mind: *Michael will set this aright.*

...Even after seeing the Patriarch's destruction as if it were his own, sensing something of the elation of ascension, after feeling Mary the Black's teeth at his throat.

She is one that will pay for this! he thought, with a sudden surge of rage. *When my duty to the boy is done, I will hunt her down and she will pay.*

The boy. That was how Malachite had justified this journey to Ignatius: for the sake of the boy. If any could understand this failing of body or spirit, it would be the Cappadocians; if not Alexia, then this oracle of whom she spoke. This reason was a part of the truth, at least—though the smallest part. For what could Ignatius know of Malachite's need to preserve the Dream? *The leper knights know to provide comfort where they are able, to minister to the needs of the downtrodden. They would fill the seas one ladle at a time.* Yet the Dream was more—it was what Malachite had felt in the presence of Michael, peace and perfection beyond words, a rightful place in God's order. The leper knights possessed strong backs and kind hearts, but they had not felt firsthand Michael's aspiration.

Though in the end, order had grown rigid, petrified. Perfection had been tainted with madness.

Not the end! Malachite insisted to himself. He would preserve the Dream of a Cainite Eden, even though Michael himself had bartered it for delusions of personal ascension. *Madness! Folly!*

Malachite seethed in the darkness. Now was the time for anger. The guilt would come later, as when years before he had raged against God for the part given him to play in this cosmic passion play. So much easier it would have been simply to live a mortal life, to die. For now, he could find fault with Michael, curse his madness, yet in the end, how could one naysay the architect of the Dream?

"They will not interfere with us."

Malachite turned, saw that Alexia and Ignatius had approached as he was lost in thought. Alexia mistook his consternation for concern that the Venetian ships silhouetted in the distance might waylay the barge and search it. She had paid what she called "a mountain of gold" in bribes to ensure that the barge would not be harassed by Venetians, nor by anyone else.

"So you say," Malachite said, believing her but also sensing how his seeming skepticism grated on her.

Ignatius might have held that concern—Ignatius, who had refused to stay behind while Malachite struck out across the mountain wilds of Anatolia, who had been the first to take Malachite's hand when he staggered forth from the haven of the Patriarch. While Alexia had spent the intervening night since then spreading bribes and calling in favors, Ignatius had used the time to set affairs in order. He had called together the Order of St. Ladre and told his brothers that he would be accompanying Malachite beyond the city walls, on a journey of unknown duration and peril. Also accorded such honor, it was decided, were Armand, Theodore, Basil, and a half dozen trustworthy ghouls. Zoticus would remain behind, for the time being, head of the order.

Ignatius may be wary of the ships, Malachite thought, *but not so wary as he is of Alexia.*

"Why is it that she wishes to take you to this oracle?" Ignatius had asked. "Not for your welfare, nor the boy's."

Ignatius had been similarly displeased that Malachite had granted Verpus, the Gangrel Turk, permission to accompany them. "He failed to destroy you here in Constantinople, so you take him to the wilds, to his own lands, away from the protection of family and clan, for him to try again?" Ignatius had protested.

"He can do me no harm while you are at my side," Malachite had answered. "And it *is* the land from which he hails. Alexia may know our destination in Cappadocia, but she is not so seasoned a traveler as is Verpus."

They were a company of eight Cainites and the six ghouls—and the mortal woman, Miriam of Damascus. He had forgotten about her until seeing her board earlier. "And what of our bargain?" he had confronted Alexia.

"There has been no time," Alexia had said, all soothing innocence. "I will inform her before the night is through—unless of course you would like to be the one to tell her that her learning at my side is done, and in its place she has an eternity of your charms to look forward to?"

It was not for my benefit that I demanded her as payment, he had thought, bristling. But he would not be baited and so did not respond.

"I thought not," Alexia had said. "This way you will have several weeks to enjoy her company, and, who knows… perhaps she will prove to be of some use."

He had wondered at that, thinking that it would be better if Miriam stayed behind in the city. In the end, though, he had decided that no part of Constantinople—as Miriam had pointed out to him when they had first met—was completely safe. Neither could he deny his interest in observing this brave woman, whose people had been persecuted for centuries. *They have no home*, he had thought, fearing that, in this, he had become like her.

"They will not interfere with us," Alexia said again. She and Ignatius were still standing beside him, watching the silhouetted ships. Then perhaps the Cappadocian sensed a bit of his true mood. "Do you miss the place so already, Malachite? And it not yet out of sight?"

He regarded her stoically. She was not the beast that Alfonzo was, with his casual brutality, but she wielded cruelty with a certain purposefulness, nonetheless. Malachite could not shake the sensation that her words resounded in his mind; he could not forget her tongue forming ancient sounds as his blood had mixed with Michael's ash. *Perhaps better than any other, she knows my loss*, he thought. *She knows what Michael was to me—and she mocks my suffering.*

"There have been centuries that have passed," he said, "without my setting foot beyond the city. But you are right. It is trifling sentiment—of no more consequence than the midnight tears of a bereft lover. Surely it will pass."

Alexia stiffened. For perhaps a second, her eyes narrowed, but then the ivory mask was again intact. "Mourning that which has passed is natural," she said. "But yearning for that which can never be regained—therein lies pure folly." With that, she turned and left the two Nosferatu.

The sharpness of her rebuke was not lost on Malachite. He had not mentioned the name he had learned from Alexia's past—Andreas—but he had come close. *Better to keep that to myself*, he thought. To expose her secret purely for spite would be a waste. *She thinks that her love Andreas will come back to her. That is what she told me, without meaning to do so.* The knowledge could prove helpful, though there was a certain risk, Malachite realized, in trading hidden barbs with a creature centuries older than himself. *Still, she will think twice before mocking me again. Let her dwell on that and wonder how many of her inner secrets might have been revealed to me.* He mouthed silently the name *Andreas*, knowing it for a weapon he could set against her if need be.

Ignatius watched, puzzled, as Alexia went the other way.

"Perhaps she is not accustomed to spending so much time in such handsome company," Malachite said.

"I would that she remained unaccustomed."

"You fear that I trust her, Ignatius; that I am blind to her malice. Do not trouble yourself on that count."

They stood silently then, as Constantinople grew more distant and the Tower of Galata on the opposite shore closer with each passing stroke of the oars. Ignatius's unvoiced questions crowded around Malachite in the darkness. He and the leper knights had been furiously occupied with making hasty arrangements for the journey. They had not had the time—nor Malachite the inclination—to speak of Michael.

I cannot speak of it yet, Malachite thought. *And so I cannot tell him that I consult the oracle so that I might find the Dracon. It is enough that Ignatius believes I do this for the boy.* There was some truth in that, at least: the boy, the city, the Dream. "I would rather have made this journey alone," Malachite said.

Ignatius shook his head. "You helped us come to this city when the Kingdom of Jerusalem fell. I will see you safely wherever it is you feel you must go."

I could never have asked for loyalty such as this, Malachite thought.

All the while, Constantinople fell farther distant.

***

After Ignatius returned to the other Nosferatu on the barge, Malachite felt the need to look away from the diminishing walls. Still they loomed like the expectations of many of those Cainites he had met since returning: that he would be the one to rally the faithful, to drive away the invaders, to return order and meaning to the eternal nights.

But I am not a savior, he thought, *merely a disciple.*

Was not the disciple's duty, however, to take up the cross once the Savior was taken away? *Otherwise, I am no better than Libanias and his wretched, mindless flock. No, I must find the Dracon, if within his breast rests the heart to save the Dream. This must be why Michael sent me away, why he chose to spare me while so many others perished.*

Even now, two nights after witnessing the Patriarch's destruction, past and present were still a confusing muddle for Malachite. Yearning for something, anything, of constancy, he looked down to the black waters of the Golden Horn, flowing much as they always had, as they always would. He sought nothing except a few minutes' respite—yet this small comfort, too, was denied him. The glint of moonlight on the night river sparked within him a memory....

Torchlight shining against black, black skin: an exposed wrist, the back of an ebon hand as it quickly adjusted heavy robes then disappeared again beneath a concealing sleeve.

The street was crowded with mortals, mules and horses, a late-arriving caravan heading along the Mese toward the Forum of Constantine. None of them noticed the black hand, no more than they noticed Malachite. He was young then, counting his unlife in decades, though he had not long before surpassed the span of his mortal life and was flush with a sense of immortality. He had no need of cloak and hood. The power of his blood hid him from the eyes of those he would not have see him, much the way a parent tucks a toy behind his back and confounds an infant. Malachite alone saw the momentary flash of unnaturally dark skin. He alone was curious, determined to unwrap all the secrets that the city and the night had to offer.

Slipping among the merchants and slaves and teamsters, he kept the dark figure in sight. Even heavily bundled, the shape was so slight as to suggest a youth. There was not the stiffness, the slouch, of an old man or woman worn down by years. As the figure passed, animals shied away ever so slightly. Burly mortals pulled tight their cloaks as if against a chill wind.

It is no mortal, Malachite thought, *nor any Cainite that I recognize.*

"True on both counts," said a voice from nearby.

Malachite jerked around, shocked that anyone should have found him out. An instant later he realized that the voice had responded to his unspoken thoughts, and icy fear gripped him.

All around, the Mese was filled with milling pack beasts, mortals of the caravan, laughing, grumbling, cursing. The vital smells of sweat and dung mingled with the sweet aroma of burning oil from a lamp shop beside the lane. Malachite frantically searched the throng for any face that seemed aware of his presence, for eyes that lingered in his direction. The voice had sounded so close, yet now that he tried to remember it, Malachite could not be sure whether the words took shape in his ears or in his mind.

"And now she is gone, our Mary the Black," said the voice.

It was true. Desperately scanning the crowded street, Malachite could make out neither the one who addressed him nor the dark figure he had followed before.

"She has gone in there… into the House of Lamps," the voice said.

Malachite noticed again the small shop, unremarkable aside from the scented oils and the hint of light behind screens and curtains. He moved closer, almost certain now that no spoken words reached his ears. The speaker would have to be nearer than the nearest merchant, close enough to—

He whirled, drawing sword and leveling it at the quietly smiling figure but a few feet behind him.

"Your time with Magnus has left you jumpy," said the Dracon.

Malachite recognized the perfectly sculpted features, inhumanly flawless; and the age-old eyes that seemed to see beyond present company, beyond present time. The sounds of the caravan died away in Malachite's ears. The men and beasts seemed less real, less substantial, than this creature that was among the oldest to walk the Earth—the Dracon, whose eyes seemed to take in Malachite, body and soul. The two Cainites might have been alone on the street, invisible as they were to the mortal world.

The Dracon looked to the raised sword. "Forgive him, Father, for he knows not what he does."

Malachite lowered the blade, ashamed. It was true. He had not known. Or why would he have bothered to draw his pitiful sword in the face of one so aged and wise? He might as well have hurled stones at the moon, or kicked at the ocean. He searched for words of apology, but speech failed him. Instead he touched knee to ground and bowed his head before the divine radiance that was the Dracon. How natural it must have been for the artists who rendered his likeness as the crucified

Christ. To stand before him was to feel the presence and spirit of the eternal.

"I would follow Mary no more," the Dracon said. "She is more human than the best of us, less human than the worst."

Malachite's gaze strayed to the House of Lamps and the shadow play of hidden flames.

"Beware," the Dracon said. "She wields a blade of vitriol and spite, and you will see her again before the end."

"Before the end?" Malachite said. "The end of what?"

But the Dracon was gone. Vanished as suddenly and mysteriously as he had appeared.

The end, Malachite thought. *Of the night? Of the season? Of time itself?*

Again the noise and bustle of mortals closed in around him. They seemed so base and vulgar after even just a brief glimpse of one who existed beyond the ravages of time. Futilely scanning the crowded street, Malachite felt honored that the Dracon had appeared to him, spoken to him—whether he could make sense of the words or no.

He edged toward the House of Lamps nonetheless. The last stragglers at the end of the caravan were making their way past now, and very quickly the wide Mese fell silent, as if the mortals and all of their concerns had never existed. Despite his ability to remain out of sight, Malachite felt exposed and vulnerable. Had not the Dracon seen him easily enough? This strange Mary the Black was not the Dracon, but what was she?

Malachite placed a hand against the outer wall of the shop. A sharp chill ran the length of his arm, made the hair stand on his already cold, lifeless flesh—as if the flames within the building gave no heat, but rather sought it, devoured it ravenously. He saw shadows cast by dark shapes moving before the lamps. Malachite stepped away.

She is more human than the best of us, less human than the worst.... She wields a blade of vitriol and spite, and you will see her again before the end....

Only now, centuries later, crossing the Golden Horn on a barge that carried so many of the dead that it would make Charon the Ferryman proud, did Malachite understand something of the Dracon's words.

Yes, he is the one, Malachite thought. *He is the one who can tell me how to save the Dream and the city I leave behind. All I must do is find him.*

Chapter Fourteen

For the first four nights, Malachite did not approach Miriam. There was too much to do. East of the Golden Horn, there was no lack of refugees abandoning the captured city. The flow of humanity was not so great, though, as he had seen when he had entered the city from the western, landward side several nights earlier. These emigrants were those who possessed wealth or influence enough to buy or bribe their way across the river, or those who had managed to stow away, or who had negotiated the waters on makeshift rafts under cover of darkness. How many of those rafts, Malachite wondered, had floundered, sending women and children to the depths? And how many unscrupulous seamen had accepted payment for transport from a merchant or noble, and then unceremoniously dumped the unfortunate fool overboard and kept the whole of his wealth?

For the most part, the refugees who made it across the river sought cover during the day—the better to avoid roving Latins, largely Venetians on this shore— and traveled at night: a fortuitous circumstance for a band of Cainites. They wore heavy cloaks over mail and sword, most of the company staying near the three heavily laden pack mules. One or two at a time, however, the Cainites would slip away into the darkness, almost a part of it. Unobtrusively, they fed among the mortal travelers, taking no life, raising no alarm.

"Gather your strength now," Malachite told them, "for our journey will take us far from human habitation, and the past nights have demanded much of us."

The first two nights, they found shelter with friends of the leper knights on the outskirts of the settlement of Galata. After that, the Cainites scavenged what cover they could to pass the daylight hours. The path they followed had long been a prosperous trading route, the Silk Road, heading east to Trebizond, Nishapur, Bokhara, Peshawar, and beyond, and with the current unrest there was no shortage of abandoned buildings. The next two nights they found structures with cellars, in which the Cainites passed the day while the ghouls kept watch. The following night, as the settlements grew increasingly sparse and widely spaced, the company made do with a warehouse, after chasing out a small group of squatters.

Once the ghouls had taken up their sentry positions and the leper knights were busy unpacking the mules, Malachite called Ignatius, Alexia, and Verpus over to a corner of the large building. As they gathered, he saw that Miriam was sitting beside the lifeless boy, wiping the dust of the road from his face. She had taken to helping Theodore and Armand care for him, though she had spoken not a word to Malachite, nor he to her.

"We could have traveled for another two hours still," Ignatius said, drawing Malachite's attention back to the Cainites.

Malachite shook his head. "Shelter is difficult to find."

"So it is—for a group this big," said Verpus. "Had we kept to a small group, four or five at most—"

"Then we might have fallen victim to brigands or some other danger," Malachite said. "I entered alone into my own city and met rough treatment," he added with an edge. "I have no taste for stealing into the wilds without adequate means of protection, so I seek to walk the middle of that road, between stealth and security. I hope to avoid the notice of any sizeable force of warriors, while projecting enough strength, if need be, that we might dissuade bandits who value their own skin. In such chaotic times, there will be ruffians aplenty, wanting to take advantage of the weak."

"And to feed on them," Alexia added with the slightest hint of derision. In the morality of any age, she seemed to suggest, one is either the predator or the prey.

"Regardless," Malachite said, "we are not here to revisit past decisions but to chart the course of our future. Tomorrow night we will either continue along the Silk Road, toward Trebizond, or turn south, past Nicaea and toward Konya." He looked to Alexia.

"In the end," she said, "we must journey past Lake Tuz and to the heart of Cappadocia. Which way we take matters little to me."

"Do you not have a route you prefer?" Malachite asked.

"It has been many years since I have traveled to the temple of the oracle."

"Yet we have never been."

"How long ago was it that you traveled there?" Ignatius asked.

Alexia looked away, narrowed her eyes in thought. "The emperor upon the throne in Constantinople at the time of my last visit to Mount Erciyes was… Nikephoros."

Malachite counted back in his mind. Nikephoros III had reigned roughly one hundred thirty years ago. Alexia's knowledge of the region they were to cross might indeed be somewhat dated. Still, he could not deny a small amount of awe at the scope of her personal history.

"Nikephoros I," she added.

Malachite barely kept his jaw from dropping. He tried to count backward through the interminable lists he had learned as a child: Leo V, Michael I, Staurakios... Nikephoros I had sat upon the golden throne almost three centuries before Nikephoros III—before Malachite had been born to his mortal life!

"I see," he said at last. Then: "Verpus, your knowledge of the region is likely more... recent?"

"Somewhat." Verpus watched Alexia warily. To the best of Malachite's knowledge, the Turk had been Embraced fewer than a hundred years ago. Existence among Clan Gangrel was particularly harsh—often short. Likely as not, Verpus had met few Cainites older than a century or two.

"To reach the area that Lady Alexia speaks of," he continued, "we will pass from imperial lands into those controlled by the Seljuks. In both, we would be wise to escape attention. If we go east along the Silk Road, we will undoubtedly encounter the Seljuk customs collectors who tax the caravans. If we go south and pass not too closely to Nicaea, that should be safer. The Laskaris family is powerful there. They will not swear fealty to the Latins and will be watching for a crusader army from Constantinople, by sea and by land. Though a smaller group would be better, even with this number I can lead us past undetected. Then farther south, keeping to the hills, then turn east, past Konya— somewhere east of there, we will cross into Seljuk lands—and into Cappadocia."

"How long?" Malachite asked. "How many weeks?"

Verpus pondered that. "By myself... three or four weeks."

"You are not by yourself," Ignatius reminded him pointedly.

Verpus scowled. "Eight... nine weeks."

Malachite felt the weight of each of those weeks. *How much like a mortal I have become*, he thought. *After hundreds of years, I cannot stand the thought of two months' travel to find an oracle.*

"Why don't we set our bearing more directly?" Ignatius asked. "If Lake Tuz and Mount Erciyes are to the southeast, why not proceed that way?"

"Because," Verpus said with little patience, "to go that way, we would cross the heart of the central plateau, windblown steppes, little refuge from the sun or from the Seljuk horseman who roam there. There is a reason you *Romaioi* have lost all but the coastal regions of Anatolia to the Seljuks."

"To your people," Ignatius said.

"My people," Verpus agreed.

Ignatius turned angrily to Malachite "Why do we follow a Turk into the land of our enemies, the enemies of all Christendom?"

"Yes, I am Seljuk," Verpus snapped, "but I am also the baron's man. I have sworn myself to him."

"Another enemy to whom you can betray us!" said Ignatius.

"Have I done so?" Verpus challenged him. "When the citadel fell, the baron charged us to seek out the enemies of the city and destroy them. I do not count Malachite among that number. No. He is one who might guide Constantinople back to its former glory."

Another who would follow me in restoring the city, Malachite thought. *Alexia thinks I might attempt it. Ignatius, too, would see the New Rome reborn. And Verpus also. Can this be the road that Michael set me upon, the reason he sent me away, so that I might return when all seemed lost?*

"You counted him among your enemies a few nights past," Ignatius said to Verpus, "or was that the treatment afforded a friend: to be savaged and imprisoned?"

"True," Verpus admitted through clenched teeth. "But I have changed my opinion on that matter."

"And we should believe you—you who turned against us when Constantinople lay under siege?" Ignatius's hand was not on his sword, but neither was it far from it. "And why is that?"

"While I was defending the citadel against the crusaders," Verpus said, "your people were freeing Malachite. You overcame a guard, a kinsman of mine, left him on the floor with a stake through his heart. He could see and hear, but not defend himself. You could have destroyed him easily enough, could have concealed for a time your role—but he heard what Malachite said: that if the city was to survive, it would need Baron Thomas's strength."

He speaks of the leper knights freeing me, Malachite thought, *but does he know that they did more than take advantage of the attack on the citadel—that they brought it about by leading the crusaders there? How would that affect his disposition toward us? Or has he seen the baron's madness and the orgy of war it would bring to the city?* Malachite did not dismiss Ignatius's concerns. The fact was, however, that the elder Nosferatu wanted and needed to trust Verpus.

"If he wanted to bring ruin upon us," Malachite said, "he would have led all of the Gangrel back to the chambers beneath Hagia Sophia, back to…" his voice trailed off.

…Back to Michael's haven, where I found him and learned that he succumbed at last to his madness and allowed his own destruction.

"I have offered my counsel," Verpus said. "We should turn south. If that is not your choice, then I will do my best to lead you elsewhere… though I think it folly."

Gherbod Fleming

Malachite looked again to Alexia. She listened impassively, undoubtedly taking note of the strife among them, much the same as Verpus would remember the lay of the land.

"We will go south," Malachite said. He laid a hand on Ignatius's shoulder to soften the blow, but Ignatius did not seem offended.

Verpus nodded. "Even in this, we should keep from the roads. From here on, the fewer people we see, and are seen by, the better."

"We must not strand ourselves beyond sustenance," Ignatius said. "We must feed."

"There are the ghouls," Verpus said with a shrug, "and the mules."

"These men are our brothers," Malachite said, raising a hand to forestall Ignatius's protest. "I would no more feed from them than I would from you. Verpus has passed through these wilds. We will do as he does and hunt as need arises."

Malachite indicated that the council was ended, and Alexia and Verpus drifted away. Ignatius stayed close.

"I trust," Malachite said quietly, "that he has not gone to the trouble of leading us so far only to betray us."

Ignatius was not convinced. "Perhaps he is returning to the Turks and leads us behind him like prizes, horses stolen from the fold."

"Beyond our own blood, Ignatius, we can never be completely certain of what drives other Cainites. Yet we must press forward."

"My fear is that it *is* your blood that drives him—your blood and his desire to taste it."

Malachite chuckled at that. "Verpus is one who hates easily, but not deeply, I think. I do not believe he would have gone to such trouble to settle a score against me. I believe he seeks an alternative to destruction with the baron."

"But if that alternative is to return to the Turks—"

"Quiet, Ignatius. Let us speak of other things." Malachite looked to where Theodore, Armand, and Basil had finished unloading the mules. Thick canvas tarps were spread wide across the warehouse floor, extra protection against the rays of the sun. "How is Basil?"

Ignatius shook his head. "He has not been the same since the battle beneath the Hippodrome, since he grasped the will of the lion. I watch him as closely as I can, but sometimes I think that I no longer know him. At times he looks at me, but it is something far away that he sees. There is an emptiness behind his eyes, a great distance to the man he was."

Malachite nodded. "I have seen that also. I fancied that he thought himself back at the Hippodrome, and when he smiled it was as he ripped apart a gladiator."

"I will keep a close watch," Ignatius said.

"I know you will, my friend."

They returned then to the others, and before Malachite crawled beneath the canvas, he saw that Miriam had already arranged the boy in his resting place. She sat alone in the darkness, away from the Cainites. She, too, would sleep through the day so that she would be rested for travel at night. Malachite started to go to her, but then stopped. He did not know for sure if Alexia had told her yet of the bargain they had struck. How would Miriam take to being bartered like chattel? Perhaps her prayers for him had turned to curses. Malachite pulled the tarp over his face, like a shroud, and awaited the day.

Chapter Fifteen

"Tonight we turn east again," Verpus said.

Malachite felt a sense of relief, confirmation that they were making progress. They were nearly three weeks from Constantinople now, and much of that time they had spent winding their way south through the rugged hill country of western Anatolia. The going was not easy. They tramped through streams in narrow gorges, climbed steep, rocky passes and boulder-strewn rises. In avoiding mortal settlements, they kept to the most rugged terrain, inhospitable, unmarked even by goat paths.

Each night, Verpus set out ahead of them, scouting the way, leaving piles of rocks or sticks to mark the path. At some point before dawn he would double back and lead them to the shelter he had found: a cave, a jagged outcropping of rock at the bottom of a deep ravine. Often the fit was very tight for seven Cainites—Verpus always spent his days apart, and would say nothing of where—and they were forced to pile atop one another like stacked firewood. Utility, not comfort, ruled the arrangements. To Malachite's surprise, not once did Alexia complain about the cramped quarters, nor the indignity of being stuffed into a crevice with six hideous, canker-ridden Nosferatu, from whom no doubt she would have kept her distance, given her preference. Perhaps it was a function of her age. She was older, Malachite suspected, than all the rest of them put together. Whatever the reason of her forbearance, in this matter as well as the hard traveling, she seemed adept at drawing within herself and enduring the physical discomfort, the duration of which must have struck her as inconsequential.

On two different mornings, the group's shelter was incomplete at the bottom of a steep gorge, and they had no choice but to pull the heavy canvas over, against the peril of noonday when the sun would rise directly overhead. Perhaps it was but imagination, yet each night afterward, Malachite swore that during his slumber he had felt the rays of the sun warming his body. Even thinking of the sensation disturbed him—yet at the same time it was strangely alluring, like sight of a harlot to a man vowing abstinence, or the view from a dizzying height and fantasies of plummeting to the bottom.

On these dawns especially, when daylight cover was precarious at best, there arose among the Nosferatu grumblings against Verpus, suspicions that this time his treachery would prove itself. Yet each night they rose, and Verpus was there among them.

They had given the city of Nicaea a wide berth. The defenders of that city evidently remained close to home in preparation against incursions by the Latin crusaders—that, or Verpus led the company so skillfully that they came in sight of not even a single patrol. Southward from there, they had viewed at a distance the occasional village tucked among the hills but had gone near none.

For Malachite, the dearth of mortal contact was an absence that grew as uncomfortable for him as had the absence of daylight during the first years after his Embrace. He had spent the vast majority of four centuries in Constantinople, a city teeming with mortal life and all the filth, grandeur, misery, laughter, and toil that it entailed. To be alone with the hills and the sky, the streams and the stars, with only his handful of companions to break the tedium, was a trial, at times maddeningly so. Especially since the company's every energy was devoted to moving forward, advancing through the hills. Trudging ahead occupied their waking hours, not conversation.

Despite the harsh landscape, the company made good time. The Lady Alexia continued her silence, hovering like an ivory phantom at the edges of the group, watching, absorbing, remembering.

Neither did Miriam complain, though she struggled the most with the hills and rocks and cold of night. For a mortal, she was not young. Over the weeks, Malachite imagined that he saw her wasting away before his eyes. Her hair seemed more gray, her face more deeply wrinkled, her eyes tired. Still she cared for the boy—though there was little enough to do for him except handle him carefully, like a prized piece of pottery, a fragile thing. Perhaps he understood what was happening. Perhaps he was aware that they traveled far from the city, but there was no way to know.

And there was no time that Malachite found himself able to speak with her about this—or anything. He saw to the welfare of his companions, kept track as well as he could of their route, busied himself with conjecture about Alexia and her lost love, about Michael and how the Patriarch's madness had led him to destruction, about the future and what news of the Dracon he himself would take back to Constantinople. Not once did he speak with Miriam. He felt a wall between them, and the longer he did not approach her, the thicker and taller the wall grew. So they traveled in silence.

Three nights past, one of the mules had faltered. It stumbled on a hillside, fell, and could not rise even after its load was taken from it. They drank its blood, and then risked a small fire as the ghouls and Miriam cooked strips of its flesh to carry with them.

The beast's failing had seemed a portent to Malachite, an omen that they might all falter, ghoul and beast, mortal and Cainite. He chided himself that he was no oracle—that was why they had undertaken this perilous journey. Yet the darkness prevailed over his mood.

So Verpus's words were a welcome relief tonight. They would turn east. They had achieved a milestone on their trek.

"In perhaps two weeks' time, we will pass north of Konya," Verpus said, "between that city and Lake Tuz."

"You spoke before of Seljuk horseman east of there," Malachite said.

"Yes. The Seljuks have held Konya before, and Sultan Kay-Khosrow would like nothing better than to possess it again. His warriors press close, and it may be that, with the fall of Constantinople, his time approaches."

Malachite knew Ignatius's thoughts, the lingering suspicion that Verpus would hand them over to the Turks. "Christendom has proved its own worst enemy," Malachite said. "If Konya falls to the Turks, the Latin crusaders will be as much to blame as the sultan."

This night's travel was as difficult as those preceding it, but Malachite found it less burdensome somehow, the climbs less steep. In contrast to these uninhabited wilds, Constantinople seemed ever more and more the paradise upon earth that Michael had sought to make it: basilicas to glorify God, the angels, and the saints; domes of gold atop marble pillars; mosaics of ivory, emerald, and onyx. The Cainites had fouled their own house, yes, but it seemed that many of the worst offenders had fallen in the siege and resultant chaos. There had been irredeemable losses as well:

Michael, Gesu, Fra' Raymond, yet so much of the Dream remained....

Perhaps the faith Ignatius and Verpus place in me is justified, Malachite thought. *Not out of arrogance but from the knowledge that I am God's humble instrument do I say this. Not through my worthiness but through His grace can the Dream be realized.*

From the great distance of these barren hills, the memory of destruction in the city seemed to him less daunting. There was much that could be saved, and if he could reinstate the altruistic values that, in his madness, Michael had forgotten—

The whistling sound distracted Malachite's attention, but it was the forceful blow to his chest that snapped him from his reverie. He staggered from the impact, looked down and saw the fletching of an arrow protruding from his chest. Then came the pain, delayed but with as much force as the arrow itself.

As more arrows rained down on the company, and shouts and curses filled the air, Malachite's first thought was of Miriam's safety. He gritted his teeth and rushed toward the back of the drawn-out column where he knew she would be. The mules bolted past, nearly trampling him in the confines of the narrow defile.

Perfect place for an ambush, he realized, as around him arrows cracked against stone and plunged into the earth with a dull thud.

He called on the blood and vanished from sight, then threw himself against the side of the gorge that seemed the origin of most of the shots, hoping to create a more difficult angle should more arrows come his way by chance. Glancing about, he saw Ignatius and Basil fading away into the shadows, the latter impaled with several arrows. Malachite rushed along. The ghouls were taking cover against the hillside. A few of them had bows of their own. They were peering warily up the slope but had not yet located a target.

He slipped past Theodore, who covered the boy with his own body. Alexia was crouched behind a boulder. Malachite found Miriam next. She had stuffed herself into a depression and was holding a wide, flat stone over her head for a shield.

"Are you hurt?" he asked.

His appearance so close startled her at first. She shook her head, flinched at the sound of each arrow striking stone nearby. Malachite turned and pressed his back against her, defending her from any arrows loosed from the opposite ridge.

"You've been hit," she said.

"It is nothing." He could stand the pain, and that was likely to be the worst of it. The arrow had not severed any necessary muscle or tendon, and there was little in the way of useful organs that it could damage— other than his heart. He had heard tell of Cainites impaled by arrows, the wooden shaft passing through the heart, staking the victim, leaving him immobile, helpless. The odds seemed against it, but with an arrow protruding from his own chest, he was not ready to dismiss the possibility out of hand.

Miriam seemed to take something of his meaning. She was a physician, and by now she knew something about Cainites. If he was still walking and talking, there was little to fear. He would not bleed to death. Infection was not a threat to undead flesh.

After a moment, Malachite realized that the rain of arrows had ceased. He gestured for Miriam to stay put as, virtually invisible again, he stepped cautiously toward the center of the gorge and scanned the ridges for signs of movement. A surprised cry, cut short, came from somewhere above. Then silence.

A few more moments of tense silence passed, then a voice from above: "It is safe, I think. They have fled—those few that could." It was Ignatius.

Malachite kept a wary watch, in case some assailants remained hidden, merely awaiting a shot at unsuspecting prey, but Ignatius seemed to be correct, and no more arrows flew.

A short time later, Ignatius was beside him in the gorge. Armand returned also. From his place in the rear of the column, he had circled around and up just as Ignatius and Basil had from the front.

"Turks?" Malachite asked.

Ignatius shook his head. "No. Simply brigands, from Nicaea, or Ephesus, or Konya perhaps. Who knows? There were ten or so, but they must have hoped surprise would overcome our slight advantage of numbers."

"And so it likely would have if we were a normal caravan, as they must have expected," Malachite said.

"Once we circled around," Armand said, "they never saw us. All it took was waiting for an arrow to fly, and then the bandit soon found his throat slit."

"I suspect they stumbled upon us," Ignatius said. "A properly planned ambush would have taken us from both ridges—better field of targets and more difficult to take them all from behind."

Malachite noticed that Ignatius did not accuse Verpus. The Gangrel was, as usual, scouting ahead. There seemed nothing to implicate him. Yet if the bandits had been Turks, or had their attack been more sophisticated, suggesting that they had been forewarned…

"Basil?" Ignatius called, looking around.

They called up and down the line, but found no accounting of him. Ignatius and Armand hurried off to find him.

Malachite returned to Miriam beside the depression that she had used for cover. "You are all right?" he asked.

"I am unhurt."

They stood silently for a long moment in the darkness, then Malachite turned to leave.

"Had I known it was all that was required for you to speak to me," Miriam said quickly, "I would have arranged sooner for an attack of murderous archers."

Malachite paused, turned back to her. The wall between them suddenly began to crumble; he was unsure now whether it was of his making or hers, yet still he did not know what to say. "I thought to spare you my company," he managed at last.

Miriam cocked her head. "Dragging me across Anatolia is an odd way to spare me your company." She scowled, yet strangely enough the deep wrinkles and her hardened expression were easier for Malachite to take than the silence of the past weeks. "Let me see to that arrow," she said.

"It is nothing."

"Something or nothing, I do not imagine you want to keep it there—or do you think to add more feathers and take flight?"

He let her examine the arrow embedded in his chest. Lethal danger or no, the pain of leaving it would have been too burdensome—not that the pain of removing it was slight. In the end, the angle of the shaft allowed them to break off the fletching and push the rest of the arrow through, punching a hole through flesh and extracting the head from his left side. Malachite gritted his teeth and tried not to cry out. He supposed that Miriam deserved to cause him pain, considering how his kind had used her and uprooted her from her normal life. *But like her*, he thought, *the pain I cause is in trying to help*.

His conscience was eased little. "You know, then," he said, "what transpired between the Lady Alexia and myself."

"She told me," Miriam said, "that her tutelage of me was at an end, and that I was now given over for your amusement. Strange. All this time I had fancied myself a student, not a slave. Yet once she told me it was so, I realized it was true. I was powerless to refuse her, as I suppose now I am powerless to refuse you."

"Little is ever as it seems in dealings with the childer of Caine," he said. "We hold a special place in God's plan, I think, yet bargaining with us is sealing a pact with the Devil."

"Is that so? Then how may I amuse you?"

"Her words," Malachite said. "Never mine."

"Yet a transaction of some sort occurred between the two of you," she said, fixing Malachite in her unflinching gaze, as she had at the hospital. "I hope I fetched a fair price."

Malachite stepped back at the sound of her bitterness. Why, he wondered, did any of this matter to him? One mortal was so trifling when measured against the Dream. Yet Miriam's brave defiance in the face of cursed creatures of the night touched him. *This is why I kept my distance*, he thought. There was a reason he had built a wall—they both had. He only wished that it had held.

"You were an afterthought," he said, lashing out in his own way. He regretted the words instantly, recanted, looking away: "There was nothing she possessed that I wanted. She would not have understood had I not demanded a price of her."

Miriam hesitated, her retort caught in her throat. When she did speak, the bitterness was little ameliorated, though it was directed less at Malachite. "Possessed!" She uttered it like a curse under her breath.

"You learned much from her of sickness and disease," Malachite said. "Of life and death. Wisdom does not come without its price."

"Its price…! My life, my soul? Might she have asked me first?"

"Did she ever drink of your blood?" Malachite asked suddenly. "Did she give you hers?"

Miriam was taken aback, the idea particularly abhorrent to one of her faith.

"Come now," he said harshly. "You cannot be shocked by such thoughts if you traffic with devils."

"Never. I did not drink of hers, nor she of mine."

"Those of her heritage, they create servants bound to them by blood," Malachite said. "When first we met, I thought that it must be so with you, that you would not tell me her name for that reason. Those they truly value, however, those whom they think worthy to join them through eternity, those they teach for many years. And in the teaching, they also study."

"Through eternity…" Miriam whispered.

Does she truly understand? he wondered. "That is what I have kept you from: becoming one like her."

"So that instead I might become one like you?"

Malachite felt the words more harshly than she spoke them. He had long since ceased to be sensitive about his hideous appearance. His groveling was long passed, as was the conviction that Magnus had justly condemned him. Over many years, Michael had shown him the reach of grace and unconditional love, the power of inner worth—yet, still, from her lips, the words stung.

"I could hand you the gift of eternity," he said, and he could see her contemplating the thought. What mortal could not, at the least, entertain the notion? *I would force it on no one*, he thought. *Yet if she saw it for what it was, truly, without illusion, then perhaps…*

"First I would kill you," he told her, "drain the blood and the life from your body, feed upon your very essence. Then, when the divine spark of your soul flickered and darkened, I would feed you in turn with mine own blood, just a few drops. That instant would be the closest you would ever come to your God, for from that moment on, you would be cast out, one of the Damned, for eternity.

"The pain…" he said, as she listened with troubled visage, "the pain would be like nothing you have experienced, nothing you have seen as a physician. Your body would be twisted by the blood, not just dead but disfigured, made a mockery of the human form, and you would feel every instant of this change, such pronounced agony that you would hate me for not letting you die a natural death. And then," he said with a rueful smile, "eternity would be yours."

They stood silently, then, Miriam looking away, Malachite watching her like a hawk.

"This is what you plan for me?" she asked at last.

He shook his head. "I have nothing planned for you. Your future is your own. The Lady Alexia has renounced any claim over you. I renounce any claim over you."

This surprised her. She stood speechless.

"Malachite!" called Armand, making his way past the ghouls, who had retrieved the mules and were securing the loads. "Ignatius sent me back to tell you—

Basil is nowhere to be found. We found his tracks and followed them… he left the bodies of several of the bandits, horribly mangled, but he continued on… away. It may be that he was pursuing more bandits… or—"

"Or running wild," Malachite said, turning from the woman, knowing that she would never make that choice of her own will. He did not blame her, but those who had made that choice needed him now. "It may be," he said to Armand, "that he is now more lion than Basil."

"What are you talking about?" Miriam asked.

Malachite waved away her question. "We must hurry on our way," he said to Armand. "Tell Ignatius to come back. If it is God's will, Basil will find his way back to us."

Armand rushed away.

"You will abandon him?" Miriam asked.

"I will not make plans for his future," Malachite answered. "He is free to do as he will… as God wills."

***

Later when they were moving again, Alexia made her way to Malachite's side. "So you have no designs for Miriam," she said. "Very admirable."

Her smugness grated, yet Malachite tried not to rise to the bait. "I will not Embrace a mortal against her will," he said, leaving unstated the implied contrast with Alexia's ways.

"How noble," she said dryly, then added: "I would be careful in renouncing claims over mortals. We always have one claim or another over them."

Malachite forced himself to keep walking and contain his anger. How much of what he had said to Miriam had she heard? But more importantly, what did the Cappadocian mean? She uttered no insinuation, cast no aspersion, without purpose.

"Her fate is her own to decide," Malachite said, knowing that it was not true, that it could not be for any mortal who became entangled in the machinations of the Cainite world.

Alexia let his assertion pass with but a thin smile. "Wisdom does not come without its price," she said.

He heard his own words spoken back to him through her lips. He heard also words she had spoken on the barge when they had first left the city; they drifted back to haunt him like spirits from beyond the grave: *Perhaps she will prove to be of some use.*

"You know what the oracle will ask of you," Alexia whispered, the accusation echoing like a pebble tossed down an empty well without bottom.

Malachite drew away, quickened his pace and left Alexia. *I have no way of knowing*, he thought, plagued by dark suspicions. He clutched his robes to his chest and leaned into the dry wind that tried to hold him back. *What price wisdom?* he wondered, recoiling at the possibilities—yet knowing that no price was too great to preserve the Dream.

Chapter Sixteen

"Do you see it?" Ignatius asked.

Malachite peered into the night sky that stretched over the expansive Anatolian plain and the long, dry grasses that leaned in the wind, pointing the way east. The moon was half full, the stars bright. "I do not see it, but I know I heard it."

They had all heard it: the screech of a hunting bird piercing the night.

"A falcon should hunt during the day," Miriam said.

That had been their refrain for the past three nights now. *A falcon should hunt during the day.* Yet this falcon had seemed to follow them. Never too closely, never within bow range. It would disappear for hours at a time, but always it reappeared, announcing its presence with its high-pitched call.

"We do not have time to tarry here," Malachite said after a few moments. *Perhaps one night's travel across the open,* he thought. That was what Verpus had said before hurrying off just after sunset. *Pick a spot on the horizon and make for it as quickly as you are able. My path will not be obvious, nor could I be sure that you would see my markers. Keep to the east. I will find you. If all goes well, we will make cover of the far hills by sunrise.*

And they had traveled hard. Malachite felt the raw edges of hunger. He had not fed since having his fill of the slain bandits two weeks previous. The ghoul knights were weary, their steps faltering every so often. Miriam showed signs of exhaustion.

I could give her just a few drops of my blood.... Malachite thought. But he rejected that option. He would not taint her decisions with the lure of strength and vitality that was merely a trade-off for dwindling humanity.

He considered having her ride one of the mules, but those two beasts were fatigued as well, no less so because a few of the younger Nosferatu, unable to abstain from blood as long as Malachite, had needed to feed from them. Occasionally the mules required a well-placed taste of the crop to continue onward.

The falcon, though perplexing, was a welcome diversion—one they could not afford themselves.

"Press on," Malachite said.

Like a cart groaning against the pull of a mudhole, the company lurched forward. Malachite fell back to walk beside Miriam. She wore an expression of grim determination, and above that a bonnet against the biting wind. The headpiece originally had been bright white, but Verpus had insisted she rub it thoroughly in the fine dirt, so the color would not stand out like a beacon in the night. Like the bonnet, Miriam was dirty and wrinkled, as were all the travelers.

"What was his name?" Malachite asked her.

"Whose name? My father's, my first lover's?"

They had taken to this type of conversation over the past weeks—not riddles exactly, but vague questions that, themselves, raised more questions than answers. The quiet talk helped the hours of drudgery pass more easily. Malachite had seen, also, how the isolation of the first weeks of the journey had weighed upon Miriam. For himself, her company was both reprieve and penance. He told himself that he had saved her from an eternity of servitude to Alexia—but for what? He could not escape the shadow of the terrible choice that lay in wait for him. So instead, he lost himself in the minutiae of existing night to night, in conversation, as if he had not already made the unbearable decision about the fate of this woman.

"The monk," he said, "at the hospital. What was his name?" He saw Miriam's face darken. She, too, remembered the man hacked asunder by a crusader's sword.

"Francis. His name was Francis."

"Did you know him before that night?"

"No."

In that moment, it was as if Malachite could hear the screams again, smell the smoke rising about the building. He wanted to ask Miriam what she had found when she went back—had there been anyone to save?—but he could see by her face that memory of that night was painful.

"I should not have brought it up," he said. Perhaps he deserved to tear open the past like a raw, unhealing scab, but Miriam did not. They lapsed into silence.

There was a reason, Malachite realized as they walked, that he dredged up thoughts of the slaughter in Constantinople. Increasingly he found himself surprised at how much of the city he had left behind, how far away, almost foreign, it seemed in the wilds of Anatolia. Leaving had been painful, yet week by week the pain receded. *And I would keep it fresh. The pain points the way of my purpose: to save the Dream*, he thought. *And the purpose justifies what crimes I may commit.* Yet he shied away from that realization, looked beyond himself, to those around him.

What of Ignatius, and Alexia? he wondered. Did they suffer this growing displacement? Or were they wed to the idea of returning to Constantinople where, presumably, Malachite would claim the mantle of leadership?

And Verpus—did he sense any of this? The Turk was the only one of them truly at ease out here, whether among mountains or dry, windswept plain.

"You knew him though," Miriam said.

"Sorry?"

"The monk, Francis. You knew him."

Malachite shook his head. "No."

"He seemed to do your bidding."

"He was of my people... newly initiated to the blood. I had seen him, but I did not so much as know his name."

"Yet he laid down his life for you," Miriam said.

"Not for me alone—for you or for any of those people he could have—"

"And these others," Miriam continued, "they do not follow your orders grudgingly. They would sacrifice themselves for you. To see to your safety is why they are here."

"I would not say that the Lady Alexia—"

"Not her," Miriam protested. "She is not one of your people. You have shown me that she does what she does for her own reasons." She paused, contemplating perhaps her time spent with Alexia. "She is beautiful and terrible."

"While we are only terrible," Malachite said playfully, but he turned serious again quickly. "Do not be so sure that we do not all do things for our own reasons."

"You have said that the oracle may be able to help cure the boy," Miriam said, ignoring his self-deprecation. "What other secret purpose sets you on this path?"

Malachite's blood froze. In that instant, he was certain that she saw him for the hypocrite that he was. *A purpose so great that I will pay any price that the oracle demands*, he wanted to say. But then he saw that she was merely teasing him. Her question held no double meaning. She trusted him.

"Just the boy," Malachite said, relieved, tormented. "Yet the words of an oracle are a double-edged sword," he continued. "They may see your path clear, while at the same time cutting you to the bone." He put his hands to the fragments of the icon tucked within his robe. *What can this mortal understand of Michael and the Dracon?*

But their conversation was cut short by cries from the head of the company.

"Halt there, you!" they heard Ignatius call.

Malachite saw a figure dashing through the darkness toward their small column. He told Miriam to stay where she was, then rushed to Ignatius's side. Both Nosferatu had swords in hand as Verpus came clearly into view.

"You'll have the chance to use that soon enough," he said, brushing aside the tip of Ignatius's blade, "but keep it out of my face."

"Use it soon enough?" Malachite asked. "What do you mean?"

"A raiding party of Seljuks has picked up our trail," Verpus said tersely. "They will be on us shortly. By the way, you veered far to the south. Had I left you to yourselves, you probably would have circled on around and ended up back in Ephesus on the Aegean coast."

"Seljuks. How many?"

"A score or so."

"We can handle that many mortals," Ignatius said.

"If they attacked outright, perhaps," Verpus said. "But they will not. They will harass us for miles and miles, as far and as long as it takes."

"And then the sun will rise," Malachite said.

Verpus nodded. He spoke very quickly. "We must drive them off.... No, destroy them, or they will follow us or send for help. Listen now." He tore bare a patch of grass and with one of the dry stalks began to diagram his instructions in the dirt as the others gathered around. "They will split into two groups, maybe three. Some will come at us from that direction, north. Others..." He sniffed at the air, tested the wind, "from there, west. The women, the boy, the mules, the ghouls—they stay here. The three with bows have them ready, although you will be no match to the *ghazis* in range or accuracy, but put on a good show. The rest of us," he indicated the full-blooded Nosferatu, "will hide in the grass to the west. Can you do that, out here with the light of stars and a half-moon?"

"You would trip over us yourself," Malachite said.

"Very well. They are mounted, skilled riders every one. They will ride in close, as if charging—but before they reach you, they will rear their mounts, reverse direction, and loose their arrows. You with your bows, shoot when they rear, then take cover from their volley.

"The rest of us in the grass, we will take the band from the west by surprise as they pass among us. We must kill them all, for if they escape they will pick up the trail later or bring reinforcements."

"How do you know they will come from that direction?" Ignatius asked.

"The wind—it is strong tonight. It will be with their arrows and against any who should attempt to shoot back," Verpus said. "If the other group—or groups; remember, they might split into three; watch for that—if they continue to attack, we must circle round, cut off their line of retreat. If they flee, then I will follow them. The rest of you must regroup as quickly as possible."

"You follow them?" Malachite asked. "Alone? What kind of folly—?"

"Have you been listening?" Verpus asked, his words flowing more furiously with each passing second, his eyes scanning the distant plain. "If they escape, they will pick up the trail later, likely in the day."

They understood. "We would be defenseless," Malachite said.

"You would be destroyed," Verpus said. "If they break off the attack, I will track them down. The rest of you, gather as quickly as you can and get as far from here as possible. Because you veered so far south, you will not reach the hills before dawn, even without this little diversion. You have spades on the mules?"

"A few," Ignatius said.

"Give yourself enough time to dig a hole—two, three feet deep to be safe. Your grave, for one day at least. Cover yourselves with the canvas. The ghouls and the woman bury you." He turned to the mortals. "Then get away. Far enough that you do not attract attention to the spot if anyone were to happen by, not so far that you cannot rush to defend your masters if someone does take an interest."

The plan was full of dangers, but Malachite had no alternative ready at hand, and by Verpus's growing distraction, he could tell that time was short. Ignatius shot the elder Nosferatu a concerned glance. Malachite signaled him: *Obey.*

A moment later, they were fanning out to the west, keeping low in the tall grass, but moving rapidly nonetheless.

"I smell them," Verpus said. "Down. Hide."

Malachite could smell nothing on the wind, but having seen Verpus take the form of a wolf before, he could believe the Gangrel's senses might be keener.

Where an instant before five Cainites had stood, now there was only grass.

There would be six of us had not Basil run off, Malachite thought, but there was nothing to be done about that.

He crouched and waited, sword in hand, knowing that by the gifts of his blood he would remain unseen by mortal eyes. He had enough time to guess what might be running through Ignatius's mind: that Verpus had divided their part so that they could be destroyed piecemeal, the ghouls and Alexia first. And Miriam. He resisted the sudden urge to rush back to the seven of them grouped by the mules. *If Verpus had wanted to destroy us, he would have had better opportunities without leaving the city*, he told himself.

He felt the approach of the horses before he heard them, thundering hoofbeats that reverberated in the balls of his feet, his knees, his chest. The sound grew out of that. These horses were not so bulky as the war mounts of the crusaders, yet by the feel and the noise above the wind he envisioned a massive herd of them, an army of *ghazis*, Turkish warriors of the faith. He hazarded a glance, parting the grass with his bony fingers—

Fewer than a dozen, he saw. A comforting sight. But they were approaching rapidly. He wanted to look to the north to see how many were charging the others, to see what Miriam was facing. There was no time. As quickly as the thought crossed his mind, the *ghazis* were upon them.

Verpus leapt to the attack first, the Nosferatu an instant later. Then everything was a blur of flailing limbs, flashing blades, momentum beyond control, bodies human and equine tumbling in a spray of earth and uprooted grass. The air was filled with a cacophony of shouts, surprise and pain, screams of horses, death cries.

Somehow Malachite's sword was torn from his grasp as he brought down a rider. He latched onto the Seljuk's arm as they fell, then shoulder, then neck—snapped it with his bare hands.

On his feet, wielding the rider's blade. One rider remained mounted, confused by the dust cloud his comrades had disappeared into. Malachite dove for him. The rider fell dead, run through the chest, before he hit the ground.

There was no seeing through the dust cloud, the miasma of fine alluvial silt that seemed to cover all the plateau.

"They are turning tail," Verpus shouted. "The other group is fleeing. Go, quickly!"

"Gather the horses!" Malachite shouted.

There were eight, but one had a broken leg from its fall. The Nosferatu mounted, leading the two other healthy horses back toward the mules.

"He was right!" one of the ghouls with a bow called out to them. "The Turks charged and wheeled. We loosed our arrows then dove to the ground. I do not think we scored a hit, but they saw what happened to their fellows and withdrew. We took no worse than we gave."

"Not so," said another, pointing to one of the mules that staggered then fell to its knees, an arrow buried deep in its chest.

"We leave the mules, regardless," Malachite said. "Secure their loads to one of the horses. On the others we ride double. The boy will be a third for one, but he weighs little enough."

"If we ride hard, the horses will not last long under that burden," Ignatius said.

"Then we will ride them till they drop," Malachite said. "We must get as far away from here as quickly as we can. Verpus may not be able to catch the others. How many charged you from the north?"

"At least a dozen," said one of the ghouls. "Maybe more. He will never kill them all."

Malachite searched out Miriam among them, saw that she was well, reached out his hand to her. "All the more reason for us to make haste." She took his hand and he hoisted her into the saddle behind him.

In another cloud of dust, they were gone.

***

He did not wait for the others to dig him out. The press of canvas and dusty soil was as oppressive as the tight, dark confines of the sewers beneath Constantinople. The Nosferatu had spent centuries constructing tunnels there so they would not have to crawl through waste like rats. Neither did Malachite have any desire to be a mole. He tore aside the canvas tarp and clawed his way through the loose dirt. Dry, crumbling Anatolia filled his nostrils. He felt its weight against his closed eyes.

Boring through the upper layer, he was greeted by fresh air and the sound of wind in swaying grass. The faintest hues of pink and orange hugged the western horizon, and as he watched the last burning gold of the plain turned cold purple and gray with the onset of night.

Beyond the patch of freshly turned earth, the ghoul knights looked on, and among them Miriam. Reflected in her eyes, Malachite saw his own image, a horrific beast clawing its way from the grave. He was relieved when she looked away, as did the ghouls. They peered into the night sky, searching for the shape of the falcon that cried above.

Chapter Seventeen

"How is it that your people endure their suffering?" Malachite asked. "Generation after generation of persecution and wandering, yet you keep to your faith."

Miriam paused in tearing a strip of dried mule meat between her teeth and looked up at him. These breaks were largely for her benefit—as well as that of the ghouls and the four horses. Of the seven the company had taken from the battle site a week ago, three had faltered after the desperate ride that morning. Their blood had proved useful. The other four now served as pack animals, bearing the loads that before the mules had carried. Of all the travelers, the Cainites least of all needed to pause in the nightly marches.

"We are not made prisoners by our faith," Miriam said. "We are liberated by it. It is not so much a matter of choice, to be kept to or cast aside. It is who we are."

"But your suffering…"

"Hardship is as much a part of life as is joy, but in the end after all else, there is joy."

"That is where we differ, I suppose," Malachite said, "for in the end my race, above all others, is damned. I may have all eternity until that end, but judgment will come." He turned and walked away from her, sensing without looking her confused gawking. How could she, a mortal, understand? The surety of her faith angered him, as did the surety of his own—of what he must do. The glorious, guiding light that had been Michael was removed from the world, and Malachite walked in darkness. He would do whatever was required to restore and preserve the radiant Dream. The moment of dire decision approached, and he felt it like a raised sword over his head. His anger stemmed from guilt: guilt that he would have to sacrifice this woman, and guilt that he was reluctant to do so in service of a greater good.

How can I face that judgment at the end of days if I have not done all I can to see that the Dream persists on the earth? he thought. Yet he wished that this cup would pass from him.

He looked to where Alexia sat alone, away from the others, and wished that he could lay the blame solely on her shoulders. But she did no more than reveal the path, knowing that, having seen it, he could not turn away. She handed him the knife. She did not wield it herself.

The open expanses of the Anatolian plateau had given way to the sandy scrub and craggy stone hillocks of Cappadocia. The limestone outcroppings stood like daggers raised toward the heavens. In this region, there was no lack of caves in which to wait out the day, just as Verpus had said. Verpus, who had never returned from his pursuit of the Seljuk *ghazis*.

"He will bring all the sultan's armies down on our head," Ignatius had supposed.

"Then why did he help us defeat the raiders in the first place?" Malachite had countered. "You may prove right in the end. There may be treachery in his heart, but I do not think it is against us. I think Verpus truly abhors what has befallen Constantinople, and as long as he believes we will stand against the Latin Cainites—Bishop Alfonzo as well as the invaders—he is as good a friend to me as you are."

Perhaps it was Verpus's disappearance as much as the desolate landscape that darkened Malachite's mood. Or the fact that the company drew close to the oracle now—that which he should have anticipated above all else, instead he dreaded.

He walked on, to where Theodore sat beside the boy. Malachite put a hand to his childe's face. *Will the oracle tell me anything that will save you?* he wondered. *Or have I dragged you all this way simply to—*

"Malachite!" called Ignatius, as he ushered Armand in his direction. The young leper knight had taken to scouting ahead since Verpus's disappearance. "Tell him," Ignatius urged the knight. "Tell him what you heard."

"A voice!"

"Really?" Malachite bowed slightly. "Many who hear voices are proclaimed saints. I would be careful, though. They often end badly."

"A voice from deep within a cave," Armand continued.

"Start from the beginning and tell him all of it," Ignatius said.

Armand nodded. "As I was roaming ahead, I saw the falcon that has been following us. It flew into one of the caves on that hill—that one." He pointed to one of the craggy outcroppings not far away. "It has been strange for the bird to follow us so long, I thought I would follow it. A rough trail—if you can call it that; very rough—leads to the mouth of the cave. I climbed up, but before I entered a voice spoke to me from deep within the darkness. 'Bring Malachite to me,' it said. 'No other,' it said, 'save Malachite.'"

The entire company had gathered round now, and as if spellbound they listened to Armand's account. Around them, the wind shifted and began to howl through the cratered rock faces.

"We will inspect this cave," Ignatius said.

But Malachite forestalled him with a gesture.

Alexia was at his side now without ever having seemed to move there. "Have you come so far to the oracle to throw away the journey on folly?" she asked.

"Do you know what awaits in the cave?" Malachite asked.

She hesitated, then: "I do not."

How much of your words are truth, he wondered, *and how much hidden secrets?* He watched her closely as she smoothed and brushed the dust from her gown. Never had Malachite seen the steely Alexia approach so near to fidgeting. He held her in his gaze.

She felt his unwanted attention, did not meet his eyes. "Ages ago there were hermits among these barren hills," she said finally. "Foolish they were, more than most of you Christians. First one took up in a cave, starved himself, and thought he heard the voice of God—before long the hills were crawling with self-appointed holy men, ants on honey. Lunatics, more likely, lacking the skill to farm, or the charm or wealth to attract women, so why not sit in a dank cave? And of course there were those of the blood among them, charlatans who smelled easy prey and an audience waiting for visions and angels to worship.

"Ah, but the human heart is fickle," Alexia scoffed, "and fashions change. The desert fathers died off or moved to the city, where Simon Stylites started the next ascetic rage sitting atop his column, praying and fasting until his legs withered beneath him. Perhaps a few of the deranged holy men stayed behind. Who knows? They are of no consequence, and the temple is near." She gazed intently toward the eastern horizon. "I think perhaps over the next ridge...."

She thinks ill of holy men, Malachite thought, *yet she would carry me on her own back to this oracle.* He felt the eyes of all the company watching him, felt the urgency to reach the temple of the oracle. He shared the urgency—and feared it. He feared achieving his destination. He feared crossing the threshold of terrible choice. He looked to Miriam and could see in her face that she feared only for danger to him in the cave.

Perhaps I am not meant to enter the temple, he thought. *Did not Moses perish, never to cross over into the Promised Land?*

"I will go," he said. A spark of anger flashed in Alexia's eyes. *She wishes to know what the oracle will say to me. That is her only concern.*

"You will find nothing of value there," Alexia said, seething, and she would say no more. She turned and sat apart from the rest of them.

"What of the boy?" Ignatius urged. "If we are near the temple, should we not press on for his sake?"

Malachite could not ignore the earnestness of Ignatius's voice. It grasped at his heart. *I have become more Alexia than Ignatius,* he thought. *I parade my sorrow for the boy because I fear to speak the truth: that the Dream, if I save it, will trample and crush all that I hold dear. Is this what Michael found?* Malachite looked again to the cave.

"I will go."

Perhaps this is where the cup will be taken from me.

Despite Ignatius's protestations, Malachite went to the base of the mound. The rest of the company followed along—all save Alexia, who remained where she was, seemingly concerned only with the stars in the sky.

Malachite climbed the semblance of a trail. It was steep, and the fine dirt shifted beneath his feet, but climb it he did. And when he stood before the mouth of the cave, as Armand had described, a voice from within spoke to him:

"Bring Malachite to me. No other, save Malachite."

"I am Malachite."

There was a silence, drawn out and deep. All the wind that had whistled through the crags fell quiet.

"Enter, then," said the voice.

Malachite hesitated, then stepped into darkness. He was accustomed to darkness, however—had spent much of his unlife in it, and the strength of his blood lent itself to his vision so that little was hidden from him. From its mouth, the cave quickly narrowed. Malachite bent down to proceed.

"You seek the oracle," the voice said.

Malachite stopped. "I do."

"You are a fool." Now that he had entered the cave, the voice sounded not so deep and ominous, rather the words seemed labored, each one forced out. "No visitor has darkened this door for more changings of the moon than I care to remember, and now hordes descend upon me—hordes of fools, and this the most foolish of the lot."

"And why is it that you name me a fool?" Malachite asked sharply, not brooking insult from an unseen stranger.

"Why? Because you stop and ask, instead of continuing on to see with your own eyes."

Malachite continued to hesitate, then moved ahead, chagrined.

"That is better, my boy," said the voice. "You wish to know who I am, what I am. You could ask me, and I might tell you, but how would you know what to believe? Even if I spoke the truth as I know it, the truth changes with every pair of eyes that takes it in, every tongue that casts it out. Better to see for yourself."

Malachite stopped again. Ahead the tunnel split into three. "Fair enough," he said, "if I know which path to follow."

"Ah, and I could tell you. And if you believed me, you might take the right-hand turn; or if you thought me false, far away from that, the left; or if your heart was unsure, split the difference and take the middle—which could be the worst choice of all. No matter which, I would have chosen for you."

Malachite listened but he could not pin down from whence the voice came. It played in the tunnels like dust caught in the wind, one moment spinning wild in a vortex, the next falling lifeless to the ground. "And if there is no difference to split, but darkness lies all around…" He strode forward through the center tunnel. It grew narrower, and short. He crawled ahead on his knees—and then the passage opened.

As he peered into the chamber, a ray of silver light shot across his vision from ceiling to floor. Slowly it grew broader, and he saw sitting within the widening beam an old man cross-legged on the cold stone. His eyes were thin slits; he blinked painfully in the light, which seemed to form a nimbus around his nearly skeletal head, skin drawn tight over his skull.

"And it may be," Malachite said, "that the middle road is the best choice of all."

The old man shrugged. He wore nothing but a threadbare cloth draped across his waist, and the motion of his shoulders looked as if it might cause his dangling arms, little more than bone, to fall from their joints.

The light, Malachite saw, was moonlight. It shone through a shaft that led upward out of the crag. With each passing second, the moon rose higher in the sky and filled more completely the shaft, and the patch of light grew broader, the nimbus more brilliant. The old man was covered in the fine dust of countless years. It lay upon him like moss upon a stone, yet through it his skin shone alabaster in the moonlight.

"In this case," the old man said, "all three paths led to the same place." He shrugged again. "Such is the weakness of metaphor, but will it always be so?"

Malachite stood and stepped closer. "You know who I am and what I seek. Who are you?"

"My name has long since fled with the wind across the steppes. I am of the desert fathers, who are apart from things mortal. I know many things. I know—"

"You know what a single falcon tells you," Malachite guessed.

The desert father's scowl told the truth of it. "You might allow an old man his bluster. Would you take away my cloth as well, and show me to be withered and useless?"

"I think not," Malachite said. "You have wind and bluster here enough for eternity."

"Eternity, eh? At least until the Dark Father claims his due. I have learned many things sitting here for more nights and days than you can count. I shall not shirk the final judgment."

Shirk the final judgment—exactly what I would do by coming here, Malachite thought. "You suggest that I seek to deny my own destiny."

"Do I?" the old man asked, then: "Do you?"

"Yet you name me a fool for seeking the oracle," Malachite said, growing angry. "Your mind is addled by years of solitude."

"Quite likely, quite likely," said the old man. "But the question remains: Do you seek your destiny, or do you seek to have it handed to you?"

Malachite regarded him for a long moment, aggravated by the cryptic words. The moon now was like a disk covering the other end of the shaft in the ceiling. The desert father sat bathed in the full nimbus of silver light. Finally Malachite placed what did not fit.

"You have not moved from that spot in years?" he said.

The old man nodded. "I fear my legs have forgotten how to carry even my slight body."

"You lie," Malachite said. "Or you cannot be of the blood of Caine. The moon shines upon you now—and so would the sun during the day."

"There is worse to fear than the sun," the old man said. "Pursue your dream long enough and, perchance, you might catch it, Malachite. Does the carpenter hold to the nail even after he has driven it home?"

"Perhaps it is simply these ears of a fool, but you speak nonsense."

The old man smiled, revealing teeth and fangs that seemed to cling to little more than bone. "To know destiny seems a blessing, eh? No need for the trappings of life, no need for friends or lovers or fear or doubt."

"Do you mock me?" Malachite demanded. "You, who grovel in a cave while the ages of the world pass you by?"

The old man smiled more broadly. "He who has eyes, let him see."

Malachite shook his head, turned to leave. *Alexia was right, lunatics of no consequence.* "And I have come too far—"

"You spoke of the falcon. Its body lies just over there," said the old man, mirth and mockery gone from his voice.

Malachite paused. He peered into the shadows beyond the beam of moonlight that now was growing narrower as the moon continued across the sky. Indeed, all that remained of the nimbus around the shriveled old man was a halo of lazy silver dust in the air. Looking beyond him, Malachite saw a body lying on the floor—not a falcon, but a man.

The body lay on its back, straight, hands folded on its chest in a pose of death. Stepping closer, Malachite recognized him. "Basil…"

"There the body lies," said the old man, "but the spirit has flown."

Malachite went to Basil, knelt beside him. Other than the grime of several weeks' travel, the knight looked no worse than when Malachite had last seen him, following Ignatius against the bandits in the gorge. The shafts of three arrows still protruded from his body, the fletching snapped off short. No grievous wound explained why he lay as if dead. *And he is not returned to dust*, Malachite thought. *He is not destroyed.*

"How did he come to be here?" Malachite asked.

"The first time, he walked in upon his own two feet," the old man said. "I do not remember that, in the olden days, what visitors I did receive were so ugly—but no matter. Very agitated he was at first, very close to the hunter who rules our blood, but I showed him that the Beast was nothing to fear. If his accounting to me of recent history was correct, then more than five hundred years have passed since I tasted blood. I find that I can think of it now without… but never mind that. You wish to know of your lost friend.

"He is not lost, I say, but found. He called out to the falcon. It came to him, and now they are one…. They will remain one, I think.

"He ranged far and wide, and seemed quite pleased to have found you again. When first we spoke, he said he followed the most worshipful Cainite ever he had met, the Nosferatu called Malachite, who sought the oracle."

"He was young still," Malachite said. "He had not met many Cainites."

The old man chuckled, the sound of bone scraping against rock. "He is safe enough here for as long as he chooses to soar," he said, then added: "You may leave the boy as well, if you wish to set him aside from harm."

Malachite stiffened at mention of the boy. What the old man said about Basil was likely true, and the desert father seemed to have done him no harm—yet thought of leaving the boy, of being forevermore without the sight which had been blinded these past weeks....

The boy is one of the last remnants of the Dream I have, Malachite thought. *How dare this old fool try to usurp that?*

"This one came to you of his own will, and you seem to care for him well enough," Malachite said, backing away from Basil. "But no other will I bring to you and your addled ramblings." Suddenly he could not deny the rage of one whose greatest care is scorned. The cave seemed now not a place of seclusion and peace but of mockery. Revulsion drove him away from the desert father. "The boy is mine!" Malachite shouted. "You will not taint him with your madness!"

And the desert father...

The old man was gone.

Malachite turned and fled, scrabbling through the darkness. Almost before he realized, he was out of the cave, stumbling and sliding down the semblance of a trail.

The others rushed to him: Ignatius, sword ready, scanning the hillside for whatever pursued his master; Miriam, concern in her eyes.

"Let us be away from this place," Malachite said, "at once."

"Yes!" Alexia was not at hand but called from a nearby ridge. She pointed to the east. "It is well past time, and as I thought. There lies Mount Erciyes!"

Chapter Eighteen

"I am Qalhara. Follow me if you wish to stand before the high priestess." The woman stood a full head shorter than Malachite, yet her proud, quiet bearing filled his awareness. She had the gait of a warrior, easy grace and power without bulk, eyes that missed no detail of those in her charge. The rich earth tones of her skin spoke of mortal days along the upper Nile.

She seemed the only *real* thing within this ghostly temple carved deep into the side of the mountain, her eyes the only ones that would meet his. Monks and priestesses traversed the cold halls, faces down-turned in impenetrable contemplation of the vague mysteries of death. Distant chants reached out with invisible fingers only to withdraw into the depths of endless corridors and unseen sanctuaries after a chilling tap on the shoulder. Despite the constant sensation of whispers just beyond hearing, silence reigned. Each footstep rattled like a stark, dry death-cough; a cleared throat was the bellows of an army charging across a plain to its doom.

Outside, the face of the mountain was the face of the monastery, adorned with stairs and battlements, ornate and wind-worn patterns chiseled into stone like arcane marginalia, decipherable only to the learned scholar. Behind the face, the catacombs, of which Malachite had seen but a fraction, delved deep into the Earth—and there was the sense that the Earth would have preferred to keep her dark secrets.

Time, too, drifted and receded here. Malachite had lost track of how many nights had passed since he had entered this place. Three, four?

The wardens of the gate had seemed not at all perplexed to receive visitors in the midst of nowhere. *I am not the first to seek out the oracle*, he thought, and then: *She is an oracle. Of course they were not surprised.*

He had approached the gates with the boy in his arms, Miriam and Alexia behind. They had been ushered inside and then separated. "Do as they say," he had told Miriam, seeing her worried expression before robed figures and indistinct whispers took her away. Then, gone, she was less than memory.

They led him into a small chamber that smelled of lime and muslin. *Death shrouds.* Then three ivory crones had taken the boy and laid him on a bier of stone, caressed him as a mother caresses a worried child, their skeletal fingers passing easily over each other's, like snakes or lovers. Not a word crossed their lips, yet Malachite strained to hear what he was certain passed among them. The next thing he knew, they were gone like a morning fog, and there was only the cold, dead boy.

The sequence of events became increasingly imprecise after that. Cainites walked the line between life and death, yet this high temple of the Cappadocians, the so-called Clan of Death, slanted that line toward the grave. *There is nothing of mortals and humanity here. The race of man could pass from the Earth, and these creatures would feel but a tremor.*

Time somehow simultaneously stretched out and rushed headlong with inexorable momentum. He remembered at some point Alexia was at his side. She spoke in hurried, furtive whispers. "Your sacrifice holds you in good stead," she was saying.

Sacrifice. Malachite searched for the name but could not find it in this place of ephemeral whispers, forgotten memory.

"When you speak to the oracle, High Priestess Constancia, you must ask about the return of Andreas," Alexia said.

Andreas. She uttered the name as if it burned her lips to do so, as if it were the last rattling kernel in her empty, black soul.

"This will be a signpost in your search for the Dracon," she said. "It will aid you. Andreas. You must ask after Andreas." Her sincerity was as thin as the crones' fingers, brittle as glass. Neither could she disguise her own hunger for the words of the oracle.

She lies, Malachite knew. Andreas was her lost love, she had inadvertently shown him. Her barely restrained mania was proof enough that this Andreas had nothing to do with the Dracon. *So this was her true purpose for me all along*, Malachite realized. *I was meant to think that she wanted me to see her past the cult into Michael's chambers, and if I looked further, that she would support me and wield me as the new Patriarch in Michael's stead—but this, this was the reason beneath it all.*

"Andreas," she hissed, gripping him tightly by the shoulders. "Do not forget. You must ask. Andreas!"

Malachite thought to confront her, to call her lie, but his mind was awhirl, and there was no time. Between them intruded the rasping footsteps of the crones—whispers, everything was whispers in this place. Alexia backed away as the three husks of women entered the room.

"We must prepare you for the oracle," said one.

"Do you give yourself over to us?" asked another.

Malachite fought the urge to flee from them, from the temple. This was his purpose—though suddenly the harsh wilds of Anatolia seemed a pleasing alternative. *For this did Michael choose me*, Malachite thought. The Nosferatu did not flee. Instead, he nodded.

The third crone smiled. Into the room filed slaves, all hollow cheeks and bulging ribs, skin pale as chalk dust, one after another, nine all told. Their eyes were closed—held that way, sewn closed with coarse black thread. So too their lips, and their ears. Yet they moved with practiced ease, deliberate in their appointed task. As they pressed in against Malachite, he saw that they bore bone needles and more of the coarse thread that smelled of dried intestine.

Do you give yourself over to us? The words haunted him for three days and three nights. During that time he knew nothing of the outside world, for beneath the hands of the slaves he was borne to the ground. He could have fought them, could have crushed their brittle bones with his strength, yet to yield to them was part of his purpose. He had given himself over to them. He crossed his hands across his chest and watched as they drew thread in and out of his skin, pulled tight his lips. When the thread tore through his sloughing flesh, the slaves began again. When they had sealed his mouth, they took their bone needles to his eyes, by feel sewing the lids to his gaunt cheeks. He heard the punctures of flesh as the slaves forced the needles through his tough, withered ears, drawing them tightly closed like canvas flaps. He heard the last needle driven through, the last knot tied off by adroit blind fingers.

Then nothing....

Nothing but the whispers he could not quite make out, secrets of the Earth, denied him. Time turned in on itself like the serpent Ouroboros swallowing its own tail. At some point Malachite realized that he was bound, his arms wrapped against his body, feet fastened together. Perhaps he could have torn free of the bonds, broken them as easily as he could have removed the thread from his flesh, but this was his passion, his torment, his purpose.

For hours on end, the voices of the crones danced in his mind, as did Alexia's lies and her words of his sacrifice.... There was a name she would have him remember... and another that lingered just beyond reach....

A fever gripped him, or perhaps it was the chill inhumanity of the place he rebelled against. But in the end he had felt the curved edge of a dagger at his face, tugging at thread.

"Those who have ears, let them hear," one of the crones said as she sliced through those stitches.

"Those who have eyes, let them see," said another, with a deft flick of the dagger. Malachite struggled to open his eyes, the motion itself pulling the thread through his eyelids.

Through black bars of thread, he stared up at the third crone, she who silently freed his lips.

The intervening hours had been a blur, but now dark, strong Qalhara was leading him through endless stone corridors. He felt that, should he fall behind, or turn aside from the path she chose, he would be lost forever, a shade condemned to an eternity wandering in search of fading memories. Qalhara was more real than the implacable gate wardens, than the ivory crones, than Alexia.

And how Malachite hated them all.

They allow me that which I want, he thought. *They make me love the knife, plead for it....* They partook freely of his painful choices. He watched the space between Qalhara's shoulder blades as she led him. *That is where I should plunge the knife, and then into Alexia, and then every Cappadocian until this entire mountain crumbles to dust.* Yet he followed.

Whispers tugged at the hem of his robe, enticing him, luring him away. But his path was chosen.

For the Dream.

Qalhara and then Malachite passed through a low arched doorway, which then opened into a larger chamber—a hall of bones. On the walls were mounted a hundred torches in a hundred skulls that laughed in the dancing light and shadow. The impervious stones of the corridors gave way here to a woven tapestry of ivory: ribs and femurs, wrists and clavicles. They formed the floor and walls, an architectural mélange of the dead; they were as many as the whispers of the mountain were relentless; a cold, white ocean of the past, which any seeker of the future must cross.

In the center of the chamber was a large hole, black as pitch, though it was lined with bones, and beyond it stood the black-robed high priestess, terrible in her beauty. Her hair was shorn and her face perfect of line, stained with indigo pigments into a death's-head as finely crafted as any statue or marble column, and as cold.

Rhythmic chanting pressed upon Malachite now, and he saw for the first time that interspersed among the torches were monks, white-skinned bodies and pale tongues that spoke to the past.

"Cross to the high priestess," Qalhara said to Malachite, "but do not pass too close to the Well of Bones."

He was walking on the bones. They were tightly packed, immutable as history. He wondered at the smooth solidity against the soles of his feet: What had happened to his sandals? He thought with vague, fading memory of the rites of purification, a needle of bone passing through his skin... but then that knowledge was gone, pulled down the Well to rest uneasily among promises uttered in deepest night and broken beneath the fire of the sun.

He gave the Well of Bones what space he could. *How close is too close?* He looked back to Qalhara but could not find her—only capering shadows and whispering bones. And now he was facing the priestess who had always been before him, and beneath was the Well.

He stood before her, proud in his hideousness, so little different from the bones over which his feet passed. She shrugged off her robe and was a monument of white skin marked with indigo bones, tight breasts that would never give suck, dark ringlets covering barren sex. Her eyes held no more humanity than her tattooed body, beautiful and gaunt as death itself.

"You bring a token," she said.

Malachite raised his hand to her, found that he clutched a portion of the painted icon between his bulbous knuckles: the ascendant Christ, face of the Dracon.

She touched the icon, touched Malachite's fingers—but he would not let go. He felt the pull of the Well. It terrified him. He could not relinquish what remained to him of the Dream.

She nodded, and then backed away from him. She stepped to the Well, to its very edge, so that Malachite feared she would cast herself in rather than tell him what he had come so far to know. She took in each hand a chalice of blackened gold, chalices Malachite could swear were not within reach but a moment ago.

The whispers began to swell and swirl. Pregnant with meaning, they pulled Malachite toward the rim of the Well. Gradually they knitted themselves together to form hushed words that might have come from the ivory lips of the high priestess: "All that is dead carries the echoes of life."

She raised high her left hand so that fine ash poured into the Well, swirled and roiled as if the whispers now took on the form of a churning mist.

"All that lives hears the call of its death."

She turned up the chalice in her other hand. A thick stream of fragrant vitae flowed into the darkness, piercing the misty veil.

"We, who stand on the threshold of the grave, frozen in the moment between life and death, seek these echoes and callings for guidance. We call to the remains of the dead and the cries of the dying to answer us."

Malachite felt the earth—*the bones*—shift beneath his feet. He staggered, and when he had regained his balance saw a large arched door where before there had not been one. Two black-robed figures led a woman in a plain white shift.

"Miriam," he said, and the whispers took up his call, until the chamber rang with the hollow echoes of her name. For an instant their eyes met. He saw none of the resignation of her brave talk—only dismay, fear. "Pray for me," she said weakly, mouth dry, throat straining.

Terrible choices.

For the Dream.

And they cast her into the Well.

***

Blackness—as if he were falling through the mists without end. The whispers were a tingling scratchiness in the back of his throat, a voice, though not his own.

"You have paid the toll of the dead," said the high priestess. "You and you alone. They find your sacrifice acceptable."

I have not paid the toll, he thought. *Miriam has paid it*. The Beast laughed within him, as if the tribute of blood had been paid to it. But the whispers crowded closer now, circling, almost taking on substance. They feasted not on their own gain, but on the enormity of Malachite's loss: not only Miriam, but part of his own humanity, his own soul.

"For you and you alone," said the high priestess. "What is it that you seek?"

He thought fleetingly of cursing them—the voices, the bone-white Cappadocians—but such would not retrieve Miriam from the bottomless Well. The terrible choice was made. This was his purpose. For the Dream.

"I seek the Dracon," he said. "He who with Michael and Antonius conceived and bore the Dream."

At once the voices grew stronger, guttural mutterings like those of hags at the loom, excitedly passing gossip along a line that curved into an endless spiral. "The Dracon... he says the Dracon... he seeks the Dracon...."

"Your road is long and your wanderings far," said the high priestess. "Listen, and let he who has ears hear."

And then the whispers had their say, voices long dead, blood and ash having soaked back into the Earth from whence they came, rising, swelling to a crescendo, and then spilling forth from the Well of Bones:

"I see horsemen steeped in blood," said the voice of a child, faceless, sexless, timeless. "And I see the wolf at the door." The child fell silent.

"I see the tired and the ravaged," said an old man. "Throngs beyond counting. They flee destruction only to pour out their lives in the sand... hunted... hunted for their blood even among the tents and shacks in which they cower. Your childer await you among them. They bow down before you and the tidings you bring."

My childer? Malachite thought. *Tents and shacks… could this be the camp near Adrianople? But there were only a few mortals there….*

The voices swirled around one another, anxious to be heard, but already they began to recede into the Well. Now a woman spoke: "I see bones crumbling to dust, the Well collapsing in upon itself. I see the doom of the Clan of Death, swallowed by its own—"

"Silence!" bellowed the high priestess with a power that belied the frailty of her shell of flesh and bone. Her words sliced through the other voices with the edge of an icy dagger. "Not for the blood of a thousand mortals should this one hear such things!"

The voices of the dead were not stilled. On they spoke, but now in words incomprehensible to Malachite, the language as old as blood and earth, which once before he had heard.

"I have paid the price!" he protested. "Tell me!"

"Ingrate! Silence!" hissed the high priestess.

She is listening to the voices, he thought. *I have paid the price, yet she heeds the secrets and keeps them from me!*

"Tell me not of your dear price." The high priestess's words dripped scorn. Amidst the tempest of the churning voices, she knew his thoughts as well as his words, his heart as well as his deeds. "Whose ashes and blood did I pour from the two chalices?" she demanded. "Yours? I think not. I'll not hear of your price. Nor shall I cheat you of a single drop of the blood-price that was paid."

Yet the voices, clamoring all the while, were rapidly diminishing. *How would I know if she cheated me, regardless?* Malachite wondered. And what would arguing gain, but to waste precious time as the Well sought to reclaim what was, by rights, its due?

Seeing little other choice, he listened, and the voices again were made clear to him:

"I see flames," spoke again the child, "lapping over the grand court which love cannot abide. I see with his fiery halo the branded of God fleeing back to the wilderness, and after him the seeker who will awaken and find the truth of the Dream." For a moment the child fell silent, though the other myriad voices buzzed on incomprehensibly. Despite the blackness of the Well, which filled his awareness, Malachite felt that he was being observed, judged. Then again the child spoke, with a clicking of tongue: "*Tsk, tsk*. To seek out he who so recently you stood before and rejected…"

The words struck Malachite like a blow. *Recently stood before? Rejected?*

"No fiery halo that time," said the child, "but one of silver."

Silver…? And then the words struck meaning for Malachite. "The lunatic in the cave… the desert father… the Dracon!"

"Many faces will he wear," said the child. "Many faces in many places, but never in your precious city again. He will not come to you. You must go to him. Again."

Malachite could have torn out his own eyes. *I stood before him and hurled insults at him, rejected him! Fool! Imbecile!*

The tide of voices swelled once again and swept the child away. Ever more strongly did the blackness of the Well pull. Death's grip was powerful, its patience infinite.

"Speak quickly," the high priestess told Malachite. "What else do you seek?"

He fumbled for what to say. Would they tell him nothing else, then, of the Dracon? *What if I return to the cave? Will I find him there?* But surely they would have said so; surely that chance was lost to him. He imagined the sound of whispers as they were dragged back down into darkness....

"Quickly," the high priestess urged him.

"The boy," Malachite said. "I seek the way to cure the boy of his affliction."

The buzzing continued, but quieter, more distant. And no single voice rose from the myriad to speak.

"What of the boy?" Malachite demanded, growing desperate.

There was no response.

"The dead will not speak to this," the high priestess intoned. "Berate them and waste your toll, or ask after something else."

Is there no hope, then, for the boy? Malachite wondered. *Why will they not tell me?* But he could hear the whispers falling more distant. A name shot into his mind: *Andreas*. Yet that was one of Alexia's lies. *The return of Andreas....This will be a signpost in your search for the Dracon. It will aid you. Andreas.* Malachite recognized her deceit, yet even in her lies there were ever the seeds of truth. It was possible that she might help him in ways she did not intend.

"I seek the return of Andreas," he said.

The voices fell silent.

A sickening feeling took hold of Malachite, a sharp pain, as if he had thrown himself upon the knife.

"Know this," said the high priestess, her voice coiled with barely restrained anger. "That the Well of Bones reveals its secrets to he who pays the toll, and he alone. You," she said emphatically. "You alone. Yours is not the right nor the privilege to spread these words to any other, lest you bring down upon your head the curses of the dead.

"Know, too, that I see what you ask is not of your heart, but of another's. To attempt to cheat the dead is a dangerous prospect, yet there is a voice among them who would speak to your question. I will allow it to do so—but for a price."

Malachite's heart was churning with conflicting emotions as fiercely as was the Well with overlapping whispers. His ire flared at these Cappadocians: at Alexia for her lies; at the high priestess for holding him to rules they had not seen fit to tell him. He bristled at the dead, prostituting their secrets, extending vagaries about the Dracon and silence regarding the boy. And he spared no contempt for himself, for it was his own purpose and terrible choice that allowed them all to hold sway over him.

"I have paid the toll of the dead," he said.

"True," said the high priestess. "So if you wish to hear no more…"

Damn them all, he thought, *though there is not enough torment in Hell*. But he knew that, in this thing, he was defeated.

"Fear not, suitor of the Dream," she said. "It is nothing beyond your power… a trifling thing, really."

"What then would you have of me?"

The rustling of the whispers began again, though quietly now, and among that and the darkness, Malachite thought he could almost feel the rigid smile of the high priestess.

"The road you follow takes you first near Adrianople," she said.

This much he had guessed from what the voices had said, yet to hear her say it, a great emptiness engulfed him. He would forsake the city he hoped to save. Wherever the road carried him, he would not return to Constantinople. At least not for a long while. All in the name of the Dream.

Adrianople.

"You will wait there," said the high priestess, "until I send word… and in that word I shall reveal the price required of you."

Malachite liked it not at all. "And if I refuse?"

"Such is your right."

"And the voices fall silent," he said.

"And the voices fall silent."

Malachite could not conceal his disgust. Terrible choices, false choices—yet if there was indeed a seed of truth in Alexia's lie, something that might help him find the Dracon…

"I will do as you ask."

"Very well." No surprise from the oracle.

Already the voices of the dead began to twine one around another, though they were fading now, growing fainter with each passing moment. Above the others, a new voice spoke, a man's voice that perhaps once was young, headstrong, confident, but was long since beaten down by death, set in its place. "I remember the name Alexia," said the hesitant voice, "but no longer can I make out her face. She has awaited my return for time beyond measure, for in our shared days on Earth we were lovers, I think…." Neither words nor memory came easy to this shade long dead. Only haltingly did it speak. "I was a slave and her father my master. We vowed, she and I, that if we were denied our love in life, we would share it in death. But only I crossed over—poisoned by my own hand. We were found out by her father. He stayed her hand, and my last mortal sight was her anguished face… watching as I died…." The shade faltered, then fell silent.

"Andreas," Malachite whispered. He could feel the tugging of sympathy for this long-dead man, and even for Alexia, her love turned to cold obsession. But Malachite sought a seed of truth in the lady's lie, a signpost to point the way to the Dracon. "What of your return, Andreas?"

"Yes," said the shade after a long moment in which Malachite thought he might hear no more. The voice sounded farther away now, receding into the bottomless Well. The other voices, too, had died away to little more than a fading hum. "I will return," said the shade of Andreas. "I will be born again."

Malachite strained to hear. The whispers pulled at him, invited him to join them. He felt a hint of breeze, as if the long-dead Andreas sighed, marshalling all his strength to speak. "Yes?" Malachite urged on the voice.

"I... will... be born again."

When? Malachite wanted to know. *Where? What ties do you have to the Dracon?*

"Only my name... in this time..." Whether because of the fading rite of the oracle or the fact that this question was not Malachite's own, the voice struggled to continue. "Not my soul before... Alexia... is dust.... She... never... sees me...."

And then no more. Silence of the grave. Black infinity of the Well of Bones. The voices of the oracle had spoken, and in the void that was the absence of whispers, light, life, Malachite remembered the words of the desert father, of the veiled Dracon himself: *The truth changes with every pair of eyes that takes it in, every tongue that casts it out.*

Whose truth had the voices spoken? And whose had been the choice? Miriam might have asked the same.

Chapter Nineteen

The gates of the temple clanged shut with the finality of true death. He cradled the slight form of the boy, the sightless, lifeless childe, to his body.

The Lady Alexia awaited. He had expected her with every whisper-plagued step he had taken in the temple, but she was here beyond the gates. She stood patient but attentive, an alabaster statue in the dusk. Despite her façade of control, Malachite could sense her tightly coiled anticipation, her desperation born of many centuries.

"You emerge," she said.

Malachite nodded. Though Alexia's need was palpable, she was no more than a distraction to him. He wanted to rush past her, to run to the cave over the ridge where the desert father—the Dracon!—had summoned him. But Malachite knew what he would find. Naught but an empty cave. Dust that gave substance to moonlight, but no silver halo. *I passed by destiny to reach the oracle*, he thought, *so that the voices might set me on a longer road.*

"You are wary," Alexia was saying, her casual manner failing to blanch the yearning from her words.

"I have always been wary," he said. *I have always been wary of you.*

"But now you are wiser as well."

"The oracle can impart knowledge, but not wisdom. All that has changed is that I have made terrible decisions, and an innocent woman has joined the voices of the Well. The Dream becomes that much more weighty a burden." *And you have that to answer for*, he thought. Beyond her, Malachite could see the company approaching, Ignatius and the others.

Alexia saw them as well. "Such is the price of a great purpose," she said, attempting to make common cause, though her heart was not in it. His great purpose was not hers. "You spoke of knowledge...."

How many hundreds of years has she waited to find out about Andreas? he wondered. *Far more than I have existed.* He felt pity for her, and contempt. More importantly, though, he still held on to the hope that her lie contained a seed of truth, that Andreas's return might lead him to the Dracon.

"Would you have me bring down the curses of the dead upon myself?" he asked her.

Alexia feigned disdain. "The Priestess of Bones overstates some dangers...."

"Is every member of your clan Embraced with a forked tongue, then?"

For an instant she drew back from him, pride striving against her yearning, but yearning won out. She smiled, a cold, ingratiating smile. "I forgive you that," she said, "for in truth a few... euphemisms were in order to bring us to this point."

"Euphemisms," Malachite scoffed. "Lies."

"And you told no lies, sanctimonious one?" she asked with arched eyebrows. "Our dear Miriam was free to choose her own fate, as you told her? Blame me for your own obsession if doing so will ease your conscience, but we have other matters to discuss."

Malachite felt the sting of her parry. He forced himself to be careful of the boy in his arms and not to crush the frail body in his rising anger. Distractedly he saw that Ignatius and the others had drawn much closer.

"There is no cause for us to bicker," Alexia said, soothing, placating. "Between us, we can restore the Dream to Constantinople. We can bend the other

Cainites to our will. Just tell me what you learned of Andreas."

This is where she must believe I already know the truth, the emptiness of her words, he thought. *Otherwise she will simply spin more lies.*

"All that you told me of Andreas was a lie," Malachite said. "Neither he nor his possible return has anything to do with the Dracon."

She hesitated, gauging his words, trying to read the lines of his horrid visage. A faint tremor took hold of her. Wrinkles, like cracks in the ivory mask, creased her face. "Tell me…." she whispered, pleading with the pent-up desire of centuries.

She cannot deny it, Malachite thought. *She cannot craft another lie. She brought me here, brought Miriam here, for this sole purpose.*

"I spoke with the shade of Andreas," he said.

And with those words for the first time he saw the ivory mask vanish. Alexia waited pale and unguarded, trembling, all unbridled hope and fear.

"I know that which you most desire to know," Malachite said. "Yet you mock the Dream. You would use it for your own ends."

Alexia's eyes flared. She clenched her hands into fists, gritted her teeth and bared her fangs. "Tell me, you monstrosity! Tell me! You throw away your city, your Dream! Tell me, damnable beast!"

"I do not return to Constantinople," Malachite said. "My road lies elsewhere. I am bound by the silence of the grave, the curses of the dead."

"No!" Her agonized cry echoed from the mountain face, the temple walls. She brandished at him her grasping fingers, nails as long and sharp as daggers. Faced with his resolute silence, she flung herself at him, taken by the raging Beast.

Malachite turned to shield the boy—but other hands intervened, pulling away the crazed Alexia. She lashed out at them, at Ignatius, Armand and the others, as they dragged her from their master, then shoved her aside with the flat of their blades. With the desperate scream of a wild animal, she raked Ignatius across the face.

He staggered back with a dazed expression, sunken eyes open wide as, from the point of her blow, the skin began to grow tight against his face. One by one, the festering boils that marred him swelled and burst, then rapidly dried up. His entire face was shriveling, his feature contorting in pain and dismay, as now his eyes bulged, then withered away to nothing. No moan escaped his splintered lips as he fell to the ground and did not move.

The other Nosferatu watched in horror as the foremost knight of St. Ladre collapsed—then they turned their furious gazes, and their swords, on Alexia. She seemed to have regained her senses, though burning hatred still haunted her.

"Enough!" called Malachite, and the knights paused in their attack. "Enough. It is better that she goes on, not knowing, than that she perish here and now."

For an instant he thought she would throw herself at him again, at the other Nosferatu and any who denied her most precious desire—but another figure stepped between them.

"Enough," said swarthy Qalhara. "You will not sully the gates of the temple." She carried her own bared blade, and doubtless there were other warriors of the Cappadocians ready to come to her aid if needed. "And the Lady Alexia has that for which she must answer to the high priestess."

A brief flash of anger and fear crossed Alexia's face—and then the ivory mask was again in place. She stood tall, regal, dismissive of the hideous creatures that would do her harm. But she would not look toward Malachite. She could not, lest the fury and the Beast take her again.

Malachite signaled that the others should take Ignatius, then turned his back on the Cappadocians. He saw for the first time that Verpus—Verpus, run away or lost—was among the Nosferatu. "The oracle has spoken," Malachite said. "There is nothing else for us here."

***

Climbing down the slope from the temple gates, the boy seemed to weigh more than ever he had before, and though it was Armand and Theodore who bore Ignatius, still the loss burdened Malachite sorely.

"I have seen a Cainite recover from a curse such as this," Verpus said, gesturing toward Ignatius.

Surprise at the Turk's presence must have shown on Malachite's face, because one of the ghouls stepped forward at once to explain: "He returned the night after you entered the temple."

Malachite turned to Verpus, who nodded deferentially. "I pursued the second band of *ghazis*," said the Turk. "Ten of them there were. Six I took down that very night, but the other four rode on after dawn. I tracked them the next night, overtook them, killed two more. The two remaining fled. Three more nights I tracked them, but in the end they did not reach their army to warn anyone of our passing."

Horsemen steeped in blood, Malachite thought, *and the wolf at the door*. He laid a hand on Verpus's shoulder. *Already the words of the dead prove true*. He looked around, trying to gauge the time of night, but his senses still swayed from the eternal whisper of the temple. "How long until morning?"

Verpus regarded him quizzically. "The night is very young still."

Malachite considered that. "I must rest," he said, "though I long to depart this land before more ill can befall us."

They must have sensed something of his ordeal, of his exhaustion. None asked the cause of Alexia's uncontrollable rage, or the whereabouts of the mortal woman.

Miriam. For a moment Malachite felt as if the whispers had escaped the Well of Bones and snaked after him in the night. He could almost hear them, almost make out the words....

In the end, it was Verpus, not one of the Nosferatu, who spoke to him: "You will not return to Constantinople."

He heard, then, Malachite thought. "No, I do not. My road lies elsewhere." *Adrianople for now, and then wherever the search for the Dracon might take me.* Wearily, he regarded the Turk. *He seeks a warlord, someone to stand against the Latins, as Alexia would have had me believe that she did.* "Does that cast me again as your enemy, Verpus? Would you strike me down?"

Verpus looked away, and then after some while shook his head. "You are not my enemy. You are not enemy to the city. I will travel with you while our roads overlap, but I must return to Constantinople."

Malachite understood. He turned to the rest of the Nosferatu. "Any who wish to do so, you may return to Constantinople with my blessing," he said loudly enough for all to hear. "I shall not enter the city. For now, my road lies to the west, toward Adrianople. For how long… I cannot say. Any are welcome to join me on my sojourn, but none are bound."

He could tell from Verpus's bearing that the Gangrel was resigned, if not pleased. *He will return to the city*, Malachite thought, *and wage the war that is already lost. So be it.*

Within a few minutes, the horses were loaded and the company turned its back on Mount Erciyes and the temple of the Cappadocians, though never did Malachite feel that he would be free of the whispers.

***

He had known what he would find. An empty cave, no Basil, no desert father. *No Dracon.* But Malachite needed rest. In the shaft of moonlight, he sat stroking the hair of the boy. In his free hand, the elder Nosferatu held the fragment of the icon that showed the Dracon-Christ. A path of dried blood crossed the face from when Malachite had clutched the tile in his fist, lest the high priestess cast it into the Well. The words of the dead ran over and over through his mind—words for him alone.

Not until a sparkle of moonlight caught his attention did he realize that the boy's eyes were open, staring into his own as they had many times before.

Long-denied relief gripped Malachite—but almost at once turned cold in his heart. "No, my childe! The words of the dead are not for you!"

But too late.

"I see," said the boy, his knowing eyes fluttering closed. "At last I see." And then he crumbled to dust in his sire's arms, leaving Malachite alone to reap the curses of the dead.

World of Darkness Novels by Gherbod Fleming

The Trilogy of the Blood Curse:
Vol. 1: The Devil's Advocate
Vol. 2: The Winnowing
Vol. 3: Dark Prophecy

In the Clan Novel Series:
Clan Novel: Gangrel
Clan Novel: Ventrue
Clan Novel: Assamite
Clan Novel: Brujah
Clan Novel: Nosferatu

In the Predator & Prey Series:
Predator & Prey: Judge
Predator & Prey: Werewolf
Predator & Prey: Jury
Predator & Prey: Executioner

In the Tribe Novel Series:
Shadow Lords (in Tribe Novel #1)
Black Furies (in Tribe Novel #2)

Dark Ages: Assamite

ISBN 1-58846-818-6
WW11206

STEFAN PETRUCHA

Dark Ages Vampire

Enjoy the following preview of **Dark Ages: Assamite™**, the second Dark Ages Clan Novel, available in September, 2002.

Near Adrianople, May 4, 1204

The woman who called herself Amala watched amazed, as with an uncanny obedience, Sihr Haddad's black Arab charger responded to an unspoken command and halted inches from the massive blockade. Her own dark brown yearling, though well-trained, stopped only when she tugged on the reins.

An *advantage*, she thought, *of having your mount bonded to you by the blood*. She was used to ghouls, humans made to serve vampires with a periodic taste of their master's blood, and to lesser human thralls kept in control through a vampire's will, but the Bedouins were known to feed their blood to their horses—and now she was beginning to understand why.

But even that strange bond couldn't overcome the impossible. Though both steeds could manage steppes, slopes, sandy dunes, wide frozen rivers and all manner of severe weather, here, on the northern road that led to Adrianople, they had met their match. To the left was a ravine, one hundred feet down to a rushing river, to the right, a rocky hillside at an angle too steep for a goat, let alone a horse.

A crossbow bolt whizzed by her head. A second caught her in the shoulder.

Two armored men, positioned atop the wall of timber and branches that blocked the road moved to reload. One paused to shout in Greek, "Back to your barbaric holes, you damned Bulgars!"

Amala cursed herself for a *fidai*, a novice, and winced a bit from the pain. She saw Sihr was about to draw his blade, but gave him a sharp glance and gestured that they should retreat. The tall, black-skinned man was obviously surprised, but he turned and rode away obediently, his worn burgundy robe twirling in the air behind him. Two more bolts whistled into the ground nearby. Amala pivoted her yearling to followed Sihr.

Once safely around a bend, she pulled the offending bolt from her shoulder. It had failed to pierce any bone, and the wound was already closing thanks to Amala's potent blood. She leapt from her mount and landed silently on the dirt and rock. Sihr let out an audible, contemptuous, "Tch."

"If you must make sounds," she said in a low, level voice, "at least speak."

Sihr was abashed, as if he'd been asked to dance naked during Ramadan.

"I should not question you," he blurted in a voice so deep it made her chest shake a little. "It is not permitted."

"Yet you constantly do," she answered, glaring as she tossed the bloody bolt away. "With shifts, rustles and facial tics. You're like an old woman, too tired to bother standing when her bladder is full of piss and needs to be emptied."

Goading the powerful sorcerer was dangerous, but better to discover the limits of his self-control now. As it was, an angry spark glowed briefly in his eyes, then faded.

"I realize having spent so much time alone, communication must be difficult, but it is essential. This is not Alamut. I am neither Haqim himself, not the Caliph, Amr, or Vizier, or even an elder in our clan. As long as you obey my commands, there will be no penalty for speaking your mind," she said.

For Amala's part, to traffic only with a horse and the pitiless stars would have been preferable to journeying with this inscrutable, brooding figure, but there were reasons the clan elders had paired them.

Though also an Assamite, Sihr had spent centuries alone in desert wildernesses, following a moral path—or *tariq*—that necessitated a nomad's existence. As a lone predator answerable only to his honor, he had honed his sorcery in communion with Allah only knew what. According to his tale, he'd heeded mystic visions and sought to reconnect to the Assamite leadership several months ago. But many of those leaders, who dwelled in the hidden mountain stronghold of Alamut, did not trust him.

To live by instinct as vampiric Bedouin like Sihr did was suspiciously close to domination by the Beast. So Amala, though much younger and of the warrior caste, was put in charge of this mission and in direct command of the sorcerer. Obeying her would be a test of his loyalty and discipline.

"Why did we not attack?" he said at last, as if speaking each word were an unpleasant task.

"In the darkness, the fools mistake us for Bulgars," she answered. "Let them be mistaken until we learn how many there are. If one survived, they could alert others to our presence. Besides, they're not the issue so much as the wall."

Seeing her dark companion's expression had not changed, she added, "Something else?"

Suddenly concise and determined, as if his hesitation to speak had been a ruse, Sihr nodded sharply toward the pile of debris that blocked their way.

"A mile ago we spotted that. I told you there was no sorcery I possessed that could clear it and suggested we double back. You refused, but didn't explain why. Now we've lost time. In a few hours, it will be dawn. We'll have to skip prayer for want of shelter from the sun," Sihr said.

A small smile played across her face.

"Good," she said, nodding. "Now, perhaps I can teach you something."

Sihr raised a single black eyebrow in response. It was the only part of his body, or of the horse for that matter, that moved.

Amala turned her head right, and left, scanning the blockage's full surface and trying to count the guards that lay hidden in the darkness atop it. Sihr watched her closely.

"It will take two nights to clear," he warned. "And we still haven't dealt with the guards."

"I'll answer your question of a mile back, then. Doubling back would costs us a week. Going ahead without the horses, something I doubt you would approve, would do the same," she said. "Already we've had word of the Latins passing through as town after town surrenders to them. In Constantinople the mortals will crown that merchant's whore Boniface as their emperor soon. The Frankish clans of Cainites will possibly act in tandem in choosing a new prince. Events move quickly and if our mission is to have any meaning, *we* should be part of them."

Allowing herself a small smile, she silently positioned herself as close to the wall as possible without resorting to any powers of her blood. She knew the ways to fade into near-invisibility or become as quiet as the tomb, blessings of Haqim upon his warrior caste, but she wanted Sihr to watch and hear. The Blood is a weapon—it is the wielder's skill that matters most. Satisfied she had her companion's attention, Amala folded her tall, slender body, covered with leather leggings and a vest for warmth and protection, into a cross-legged position. Despite the Damascene scimitar dangling from her belt, not a pebble was disturbed. Even the veil she wore as a Muslim woman, which covered the lower half of her face, did not so much as flutter.

To help her focus, she whispered a passage from the Qur'an: "No vision can grasp Him. But His grasp is over all vision: He is above all comprehension, yet is acquainted with all things."

Then she fell silent, meditating on the tangle of dead substances that blocked the road. As a cold wind blew thick clouds across the sky, the dead wood, trunks, sticks and stones that had been piled to render the mountainous road useless, danced in faded color between light and dark. Each piece was insignificant, but taken together they were as formidable as the high protective walls of Adrianople, the city that was to be the touchstone of this mission into infidel lands.

Amala stared.

Suddenly, she stood and sprinted down the road towards a spot on the irregular blockade's right side.

"Back for some more?" the guard shouted. Two more bolts zipped through the cool air. Both missed by yards. She'd been expecting them.

Sihr turned his mount back toward the wall just in time to see Amala spin, leap two feet in the air and execute a sharp kick. Her snapping heel found the center of a great log hanging catty-corner in the pile, its far end vanishing into the browns, grays and blacks of the labyrinthine mass.

There was a loud crack. The great timber split down the center. The two guards, precariously balanced at the top, recklessly moved to reload. As the first was ready to fire again, the pile lazily shifted. With a rush of falling, splintering wood, the wall gave way.

The guards clung to each other. For a moment it looked as if they might catch their balance in the shifting pile, but Sihr pushed his arms out at the air and, in response, the two fell as if shoved. In seconds, the two screaming guards and most of the wall's fragments tumbled into the ravine.

Sihr and his charger trotted up, leading Amala's horse by the reins.

"They were alone?" he asked.

"Yes," Amala said, looking up at him. "Thank you for your help."

Sihr nodded and said, "They probably would have fallen on their own shortly."

Together, they cleared what remained in minutes. Sihr was silent for the duration of their brief work, but when their horses heads were turned once more toward Adrianople, he spoke again.

"Your patience humbles me," he admitted.

"Tch. "Now it was Amala's turn to use the deprecating sound. "Impatience is my greatest flaw. But I know that one person, in abject submission, doing the right thing at the right time, *Insha'allah*, can move mountains."

Sihr nodded. But did he believe her?

After they located a suitable cave, some distance from the road, they made camp for the day. At the proper time, they started the dawn *salat* with the first of two *rakas*, or prayer cycles. Bowing southeast toward Mecca, they chanted:

Alaahu-Akbar
Subhanaka Allahumma Wa Bi-Hamdika
Wa Yabaraka-Ismuka Was
Ta'Ala Jadduk Wa-La Illaha Ghairuk

Pacing the prayers with due solemnity, they finished just in time. The mountains' ridged back had turned ruby, as if life's blood were pooling to the surface of the world. The glow was also a reminder of the Final Death that exposure to the sun would entail.

During the day, though the shadowy cave shielded them with darkness, Amala, with great physical effort, woke herself twice, for the noon and afternoon prayers. She was pleased to find Sihr awake and ready. It was rare to find a Cainite willing to suffer so for the ritual. Amala thought that in their faith, at least, they had found a strong commonality.

Still, for much of the next evening's journey, Sihr returned to his stoic silence, riding tall and stiff, the appearance of his lanky, weathered body made fuller by his shifting robes. She wondered if she would ever understand him, or if he could ever be understood.

Some time after the road leveled from rough hilly forests of thick, old growth, into more verdant plains rife with poplar trees, Amala watched with some concern as Sihr halted his horse and pricked up his ears.

"Shouting," he said. "Rushing feet, less than half a mile due west."

"I hear it," she responded. Her face twisted in light surprise as she made out a few words, "Is that *Arabic?*"

***

Far off the road, in the shadowed patches of wood, a running man, Arabic, white-bearded, with many wrinkles in his dark skin, cradled a sack as though it were his very heart and narrowly ducked a crossbow bolt.

"*Elif air ab tizak!*" he shrieked at his three armored pursuers.

Though on foot, he moved fast as a wolf, ducking between the narrow spaces between trunks, sliding along fallen leaves, picking up a momentum that would leave any man, much less one of his apparent age, tumbling. Unfortunately, the dark figures pursuing him, only slightly slowed by their chain mail, were equally unnatural. While the largest paused to reload his crossbow, the other two fanned out in an effort to surround their quarry.

"There he is!"

"I have him!"

"*Where*, you jabbering idiots?" the larger said, reloading. Then, with a terse, "Ah!" he let fly another bolt. The lucky shot perforated the old Arab's right elbow, immobilizing the joint. His arm suddenly rigid, the precious sack it cradled tumbled to the ground. A few leatherbound books and scientific instruments spilled out. Though clearly expensive and well cared for, these things were not his greatest concern. Rather than flee without the precious item that yet remained covered, he threw himself down on it, prepared to die in its defense.

As the crusaders tromped nearer, using his good hand, the Arab yanked at the bolt in his elbow. With a sucking sound, it loosened. He was able to slide it half out before the tip stuck on bone. Normally, he could heal the wound quickly enough, but he had not fed in quite a while. Worse, there was not much time. No war-hardened fighter, he hoped only that he might take a few of the Shayatin with him.

A heavy boot slammed down on his back, shredding the humble peasant robes he wore, but stopping short of breaking skin.

Their pace leisurely now that the chase was over, the two others sheathed their broadswords and wrested the sack from his good arm. As they did, they said odd things like, "That's a good fellow!" as if such words might be of comfort.

He hoped for a moment they would fight over the prize, but a grunt from the man whose foot held him in place made them hand the sack over. As the Latin invader moved to open it, the Arab put up a frantic effort to squirm free, the Beast in him welling as he struggled.

Stay in control or the prize is forfeit! he thought.

"Don't! You mustn't!" he finally managed to say in clear Latin.

"Stop struggling," the crusader said, digging his heel deeper into the old man's back. "You'll see your precious Allah soon enough, and you can tell Him your worries. Still, it's lucky we found you and not the Greeks. After all, *we're* true Christians."

His companions smiled in agreement, showing white, pointed teeth. The Arab closed his eyes and waited for an opening. After rummaging about in the sack, the crusader, puzzled and annoyed, withdrew what looked like a crumbling scroll. The Arab gasped at the sight.

"All the gold of Constantinople litters the wilderness, but you stopped running for this old paper, Saracen?" The crusader turned the sack upside down and emptied it onto the dirt. As each clump of aged scroll hit the ground, the pinned Arab grunted and growled.

Not yet! Not yet! There may be some pieces still left!

Finally, he decided to speak, in the hopes that if they knew what they held, they might not destroy it completely.

"That may well be the last extant copy of Aristotle's *Comedia*. I rescued it from the fires at Constantinople, nearly dying in the process. I would have seen it protected, guarded, copied by practiced hands for posterity," he shrieked.

"Muslim hands, you mean."

"Civilized hands," the Arab said.

He was considering telling them how much gold it was worth when the crusader who held him fast moved his other foot down toward the pile, as if to rub the scrolls into dust. It was the opening he'd been waiting for.

Now! something in him screamed.

With his captor's weight slightly shifted, the Arab thrust his good arm toward a hole in the man's leggings and smeared the naked skin with a dark liquid that flowed like black water from the center of his palm.

The crusader was confused at first, disquieted by the warm, wet sensation. He stumbled backwards, his feet ripping and tearing the precious scrolls as he went. As he fell to his knees, grabbing his throat, his two fellows once more drew their weapons.

"Poison!"

"Must be one of those Assamite devils!"

"Yes," the Arab said, hissing as he stood. "An Assamite devil. That's what I am exactly."

Rattled by the moans of their leader, one of the crusaders took a fearful step back, as if preparing to run. Trying to press the faux advantage he held, the Arab yanked the bolt fully free from his elbow, tossed it on the ground and forced his body into what he hoped looked like a battle stance. Promising his baser instincts a fine meal in exchange for a few more precious moments of control, he inched forward, snarling, hissing theatrically, trying to position himself between the Latins and what remained of the scrolls. But the second crusader didn't scare quite so easily. His eyes narrowed and he raised the tip of his sword toward the Arab's face.

"Hold on. Do you *really* think this scrawny scholar is one of those Saracen killers? A Childer of Hay-keem?" he sneered, purposely mispronouncing the name. "I mean if he *really* was, shouldn't we all be dead by now?"

At that moment, though the night had been relatively clear, a cool fog started rolling in, obscuring the darkened view even further. Delighted, the Arab waved his hands about mysteriously as though he had conjured the sudden change in weather.

"You would have been, had I not been so concerned with saving that book!" he intoned melodramatically.

Unimpressed, the crusader spat, "Now, you don't expect me to believe you control the weather, now, do you?"

"No, I expect you to die!" With a dreadful scream, the Arab lunged, palm out. The crusader stabbed with his sword, but the Arab shifted out of the way, then tried to smear his body's venom on the man's face. The crusader stepped to the side and quickly knocked the slight Arab down.

The Arab's chilling scream was enough for the frightened one, though. He whirled and ran into the denser patches of fog. After two quick steps, he collapsed to the ground in a fluid motion, his severed head rolling off to the side. Seeing the fate of his companion, but clueless as to its cause, the remaining attacker rapidly turned his own head this way and that, sword first, searching the misty darkness. Seeing nothing, and remembering the Arab with his strange poisons, he turned back to him, and prepared to strike.

Another blow from the unseen source freed this last crusader's head from his body as well. His body shriveled as it fell, first into a leathery textures, then into simple dust, leaving behind only worn chain-mail and a tunic with a faded cross.

"*Salaam aleikum*," Amala said, wiping the blood from her scimitar as she faded into view.

Wordless, the old Arab sprang upon the remaining decapitated corpse and fed. As the heady Cainite vitae quenched the Beast, and most of his anger, the Arab recalled his manners and turned back toward his savior.

"And peace be with you, as well, in the name of Ar-Rahman," the Arab replied. "And my apologies for… for… this," he added, indicating the blood on his face.

Amala shook her head. "There is no shame in feeding on them. These Latin dogs are clearly unworthy. Their blood is our right. I am Amala, child of Haqim."

"Oh," the Arab smiled, wiping his lips. "I don't apologize for that, Amala, but for my rudeness in feeding ahead of you who killed them."

Feeling her own hunger surge at the site of fresh blood, Amala quickly leaned by the body and collected its remaining juices in a small ceremonial bowl.

The Arab watched, recognizing the ritual of an Assamite warrior.

"I saw them off the road, took them for kine and thought to pick through their holdings," he explained. "You never know what the mortals will be carrying these days. Oh my…"

Reminded of the scrolls, he turned toward what remained of them. A sharp wind tugged the vestiges along the ground, where they mingled with the fog, twigs and black night.

"*Masha'allah*," Amala said, and meant it to be of comfort.

"Yes, His will, no doubt. On better nights, I walk the Tariq el-Umma, pledged to protect both Cainite and mortal, but I'm embarrassed to say, I'd have sacrificed any number of lives for those words."

"Including your own?" Sihr said. His ebon charger cantered towards them, with Amala's yearling in tow.

"That is Sihr Haddad," Amala said. "You can thank him for the fog."

"A blood sorcerer, then. To answer your question then, friend, yes," the old Arab answered. Eyes narrowing, he peered curiously into the darkness past the lanky newcomer, to see if there were more visitors that as yet remained unseen.

"Such thoughts form the edifices of the soul," he endeavored to explain, "paving the roads we walk, providing shelter and home."

"Like a city?" Sihr asked, dismounting.

"Yes, like a city," the old Arab answered wistfully.

The sorcerer pulled a dagger from his side, opened a small cut in his palm and cupped the wound against the horse's mouth.

"I have no use for such fools' temples," he said, not bothering to look at the vizier.

"Fools?" the Arab said, aghast. "I know your names, but who are you to say such things? How many of you are there? Do you journey from the north? Not from Constantinople, surely…?"

"How many of *you*?" Amala said politely. Having finished half of the bowl, though her hunger begged for more, she fought to keep it at bay, as part of her discipline. She offered the bowl to Sihr, who took it and drank quickly.

"Of me, there is only what you see. One of a school of viziers from Constantinople, where we lived peacefully among the Greeks for years, in Michael's 'glorious' shadow. Until, of course, someone foolishly pointed out to the Latins that there was yet a piece of earth they'd left unsullied." The vizier furrowed his brow. "If you're not fleeing, why are you here?"

Finished, Sihr handed the bowl back. Despite her control of a mere moment ago, Amala couldn't resist licking the dredges. Suddenly aware of her weakness, she let the warm liquid rest in her mouth as a test of her endurance. A sudden, bestial surge sent a powerful tingling through her limbs. She shivered visibly to contain it, but finally gave in and swallowed.

"Now I know some of your history, but not your name," Amala said.

"Fajr," he said simply. "And I thank you for your efforts on my behalf."

"Fajr?" Sihr repeated. Amala was surprised to see the grin on the Bedouin's usually expressionless face.

"Yes. Fajr," Fajr said. It meant "dawn."

"You were following the road from Adrianople. How fairs that city?" Amala asked.

"Still Greek, barely. Still fearful of Bulgar attacks. I headed north before I reached the city to avoid a large refugee camp. Cainites and their followers, all fleeing Constantinople gather there, it is said, at the behest of Michael's ally, the Nosferatu Malachite. I hear he is, most wisely, not present himself. There is no law, only despair, nightmare and the Beast's rule. For some, I suppose, this is better than remaining in the shell of Constantinople."

"Will you take us to this refugee camp, Fajr?" Amala asked.

He shook his head violently. "No. Didn't you hear? It is the Blazing Fire and Boiling Water! That which breaks to pieces, or any other description of Hell you prefer! What in Allah's name do you think would possess me to go there?"

"Are you still of the Mountain?" she asked.

After some hesitation, he answered, "Yes."

"The Vizier at Alamut gave me something," Amala said. She reached into a pouch at her waist and slipped out a small parchment. Fajr, fearing he already knew what it said, took it and read it quickly. Just as quickly, he handed it back.

"It would be a boon have someone with us who has lived in this land for so long, but I do not want a halfhearted vizier. You're free to part our company," Amala said, rising to leave.

Fajr stopped her at once. "Do not embarrass me so. I will honor my commitment to my blood. In this quest I am your humble servant, " he said.

"Good," was all Amala said in response.

"Since we are all thus joined, uh… what might our quest be?" Fajr asked.

"We are here, among others of our clan, to ensure the Latins have no immediate plans to move forward into Islamic territory," Amala said. She turned to the sorcerer and added, "Sihr, help Fajr gather his belongings."

Practicing his humility, the sorcerer obeyed. He even, to Amala's surprise, offered to share his mount with the newcomer. Fajr, for his part, adjusted the dials on his astrolabe, checked it against the position of the stars, then directed them slightly further off the road, promising he would take them on the most direct route.

For the rest of that night and the following night they rode, Sihr had reason to regret his gracious offer. Their once relatively silent travels were now marked by an unending series of questions from Fajr. Sihr noted with equal disdain that whenever they rested, the vizier spent a great deal of time scribbling down notes in handwriting he was at pains to make as small as possible, his store of paper being small. His annoyance with the vizier, however, forced him to speak more often to Amala.

"There is something about him I do not care for," Sihr confided to her in a moment when they were alone. "He has the wasteful mind of a city-dweller, collecting bits of information, as if they were things, indiscriminately. How can such a mind ever travel lightly in the world?"

"It can't, I suppose," Amala said. "But in a complicated society, it is difficult to tell what will prove useful."

"That," Sihr explained, "Is why I chose the desert."

The sorcerer's distrust grew, until, on the third dusk, his worst suspicions were confirmed. He opened his eyes to see Fajr's hand inching towards the leather backpack that contained Sihr's scant worldly goods.

The sorcerer rubbed his fingers together in a fluid motion. At once, his dagger slipped, of its own accord, out of the scabbard beneath his robe. Untouched by human hand, it sliced into the air, stabbing down to imbed itself in the dirt, in the small space between two of Fajr's fingers.

Fajr gasped, then snapped his gaze towards Sihr, to see the sorcerer glaring at him.

"Please, friend Sihr, you have to understand my curiosity," Fajr offered abjectly. "It's not something I can really control. There are things I just *need* to know. I mean no harm, and what I learn is often quite useful and…"

The sorcerer stared at the sheepishly grinning vizier with pitiless eyes. He let him go on with his banter, until his voice finally trailed off, as if melted into air by Sihr's dark eyes.

"Would it have been worth the loss of your finger?" Sihr asked.

"That depends," Fajr answered truthfully, shrugging, "On what was inside your sack."

Sihr's eyes narrowed in rage. His arm moved as if to complete the slice.

"Sihr!" Amala shouted, now awake as well.

She nodded toward the dagger. Begrudgingly, the tall sorcerer withdrew it by hand, never once losing eye contact with Fajr.

"Thank-you," Fajr said, turning to Amala. "He does not understand, he does not realize how totally harmless…"

Amala cut him off. "If you try to take or examine anything of his or mine again, I will not hold him back. In fact, I will join him."

Sihr smiled at that, and Fajr made no further incursions into property that was not his. But the Bedouin's resentment only grew.

Later that night, a strange stench reached them, and grew steadily stronger as they progressed. When the high walls of Adrianople peeked through the spaces between poplars, Sihr insisted it was the smell of the city, but Amala and Fajr knew it was something far worse. Amala had them stop a half mile away from where Fajr indicated the refugees could be found. Leaving the horses and much of their supplies in a small grove, they marched the remaining distance on foot.

Their ears soon filled with barely human howls—fevered prayer, mixed with dying screams and a cackling laughter that verged on tears. There were no defenses to speak of. A mere fifty yards from the perimeter, Amala scaled a tall oak and took in the sorry view.

To call it a camp seemed wrong, since the word implied order. This place was less planned than the helter-skelter wall that had blocked the mountain road. Horses and livestock wandered freely, a few mortal prisoners, hands and ankles tied, stumbled about, hoping to find an edge to the camp from which to flee. Members of the clans that had once thrived in Constantinople were all present, but even these distinctions were muddied by ubiquitous despair. The mass of canvases and cloths insulted into shelters by badly cut branches looked more like refuse. It was a wonder any had survived the daylight, and from the few steaming corpses that lay beneath fallen shelters, it was clear that some had not.

The carnage did not surprise Amala. *With foes such as this*, she wondered, *why hasn't Islam already conquered the world?*

For a thousand years,
the vampire Lucita has
lived under the shadow
of her tyrannical sire, Monçada.

Now, the monster who defined her
existence is gone, destroyed
in no small part thanks to her efforts.

All she wishes is to
at last find a place for herself
in these Final Nights.
But to the rest of
Clan Lasombra,
she is a rogue and a killer,
a rebel who has assassinated
one of their greatest elders.

The hunt is on.

CLAN LASOMBRA TRILOGY
SHARDS
BOOK ONE

AVAILABLE NOW

White Wolf is a registered trademark of White Wolf Publishing, Inc. Clan Lasombra Trilogy and Shards are trademarks of White Wolf Publishing, Inc. All rights reserved.

EXALTED

Trilogy of the Second Age™
by Richard Dansky

Journey to the Second Age of Man, a time before the World of Darkness, in this first fiction release for Exalted. Meet Eliezer Wren, a simple priest who makes the mistake of stealing the Prince of Shadows' plunder and ends up on the run from the Prince's unliving hunters. With him comes Yushuv, a boy who comes face-to-face with his own destiny, and with the Unconquered Sun.

BOOK ONE	BOOK TWO	BOOK THREE
Chosen of the Sun™	Beloved of the Dead™	Children of the Dragon™
ISBN 1-58846-800-3	ISBN 1-58846-801-1	ISBN 1-58846-802-X
WW10080	WW10081	WW10082

©2002 White Wolf is a registered trademark of White Wolf Publishing, Inc. All trademarks are owned by White Wolf Publishing Inc. All rights reserved.